Scissors, Paper, Stone

Scissors, Paper, Stone

ELIZABETH DAY

BLOOMSBURY

LONDON · BERLIN · NEW YORK · SYDNEY

First published in Great Britain 2011

Bloomsbury Publishing, London, Berlin and New York
36 Soho Square, London W1D 3QY

A CIP catalogue record for this book is available from the British Library

ISBN 978 1 4088 0761 3

10 9 8 7 6 5 4 3 2 1

Typeset by Hewer Text UK Ltd, Edinburgh
Printed in Great Britain by Clays Ltd, St Ives plc

www.bloomsbury.com/elizabethday

To Kamal

And to my parents,
for being nothing like Anne and Charles

Prologue

A T FIRST HE DOES not realise he is bleeding. He wakes in a state of numbness, with no memory of where he is. It takes him several minutes to notice the glutinous dark-red liquid but, even then, he cannot work out where it is coming from. It trickles past his nose with a slow insistence and gathers in a small pool at the tip of his finger. It smells of uncooked meat.

He can make no sense of his position. He appears to be lying on hard grey flagstones, his face parallel with the serrated metal surface of a manhole cover. His left cheek is pressed painfully against the pavement and he cannot open one eye. The other eye, sticky and blurred, is focusing on a blackened blob of chewing gum, trodden into the ground a few inches from his nose.

He rolls his eye around frantically in its socket, straining to see as much as possible. Out of one corner, he can make out the bridge of his nose. An arm is spread out underneath his head, disjointed and bent out of shape. He wonders briefly whose arm it is and then he works out with a jolt that it must be his and a sickness rises up inside him.

He finds that he cannot move. It is not that he feels any pain, simply that any physical exertion is impossible. Something is loose and rattling in his mouth. He presses at it with the tip of his swollen tongue and thinks it must be a tooth.

A voice that he does not recognise, male and throaty, is speaking. After a few seconds, he notices that the words make sense.

'All right mate, all right, just keep still. The ambulance will be here soon.'

That is when he realises he must be bleeding. Instantly, he feels a desperate surge of white-hot panic. His one eye starts to weep, silently, and the tears drip down from the corner of his eyelid to the tip of his nose and on to the pavement, where they mix in with the blood, thinning it to a watery consistency. He tries to speak but no sound emerges. His mind is filling with infinite questions, each one expanding to fill the space like a sea anenome unfurling underwater.

What is happening?

Where am I?

What am I doing here?

He feels himself at the brink of something, as if he is about to fall a very long distance. He is overwhelmingly tired and his eyelid starts to droop, obscuring his field of vision even more. From the squinted sliver of sight that remains, he sees the rounded edge of a black leather boot. The boot is battered and laced and has a thick rubber sole and it is coming towards him and now it is treading into the redness that seems to be covering a larger area of pavement than before. As the boot moves away, he notices that it leaves an imprint on the ground, a stencilled trail of wet blood.

He can make out snippets of a conversation that is taking place above his head.

'Yeah, he was knocked off his bike, poor sod.'

'Christ. Was he wearing a helmet?'

'Don't think so. Driver didn't even stop.'

'Where's the ambulance?'

'On its way.'

His eyelid is pressing down, and despite telling himself that he must stay awake, that it is important to remain alert, he is power-less to stop it. Soon, he is enveloped by a throbbing darkness, a beating tide of black that crashes against the bones of his skull. He hears the sirens and, just before he allows himself to fall into nothingness, he has one startlingly clear vision of his daughter. She is twelve years old and lying in bed with the flu and he has made her buttered toast and she is too hot so she has drawn back the bedsheets.

The last thing he sees before his mind collapses is the precise curve of the pale flesh of her kneecap and he is saturated by love.

*   *   *

It was a curious thing, but when she was told that her husband was almost dead, her first thought was not for him but for the beef casserole. She had been in the process of boiling up a stock when the doorbell rang, tearing up parsley stalks and rummaging blindly in the cupboard for an elusive box of bay leaves. She answered the door while still wearing her apron and her hands were slightly damp as she unlocked the safety chain. A speck of indeterminate green foliage had attached itself to the cuff of her floral printed blouse. She was attempting to swat it away when she became aware of the uniformed officers on her doorstep.

There were two of them – a white man and a pretty Asian woman, standing shoulder to shoulder underneath the porch awning as though their primary purpose was to advertise the police force's ethnically diverse recruiting practice. Anne braced herself to receive a fistful of glossy leaflets and a promotional plastic keyring, but then she noticed that neither of them was smiling.

'Mrs Redfern?' the man said, and the silver numbers on his epaulettes glinted in the mid-morning light.

'Yes.'

'It's about your husband.' He had flabby pink cheeks and small, round eyes and a kindness that hung loosely around his lips. He looked as though he should be outdoors, building dry-stone walls and eating thick ham sandwiches. Anne felt a twinge of sympathy for him, for how difficult he was finding it to enunciate the words. There was a short pause that Anne realised she was expected to fill.

'Yes?'

'I'm afraid there's been an accident.'

She felt a coolness seep into her bones but she stood straight-backed in the doorway and did not move. The policeman looked relieved that she was not breaking down. The pretty Asian woman reached out to touch her arm. Anne became aware of the pressure of her hand and although she usually disliked the tactile presumption of strangers, she found it oddly comforting.

The man was talking, telling her something about Charles being knocked off his bicycle and being taken to hospital and the fact that he was unconscious: still alive, but only just.

Only just. She found herself thinking how strange it was that two small words could encapsulate so much.

Then the woman was talking about cups of tea and lifts to the hospital and is-there-anyone-you-could-call and Anne found that she was not thinking of Charles, of what state he might be in or of how worried she should be, but that instead her mind was filled with the perfectly clear image of four unpeeled carrots that she had left draining in a colander in the sink.

She told the police officers that she would drive herself to hospital.

'Are you sure?' the man asked, eyebrows pushed together in furrowed concern.

She nodded and added a smile for good measure.

'Perhaps you'd like us to come inside and sit with you for a bit?' said the woman, her eyes darting beyond Anne's shoulder into the hallway.

'No, honestly, I'll be fine,' Anne said firmly. 'Thank you,' and she started to close the door before they could say anything else. The casserole. She had to finish the casserole.

As she walked back through to the kitchen, she passed the ugly dark wooden hat-stand at the foot of the staircase. Charles had brought it home with him one evening several years ago, with no explanation. When she asked where it was from, he replied coldly that a colleague had wanted to get rid of it. She had known, by the tone of his voice, not to push the point any further.

The hat-stand struck Anne as a particularly useless piece of clutter, but it had taken up permanent residence in the hallway, casting grotesque shadows over the tiles like a stunted tree, its branches gnarled and misshapen into arthritic wooden fingers.

She had grown used to it and normally never gave it a second glance. But this time she noticed that Charles's cycling helmet was still hanging on one of the lower hooks. She winced. A sudden vision of his bloodied skull, squashed and bruised like overripe

4

red fruit, rose unbidden in her mind. She pushed the thought back under and returned to the chopping board.

For twenty minutes, Anne peeled carrots and diced potatoes and roughly sliced the marbled red beef that was springy and cool to the touch. When she lifted away the polythene bag in which the butcher had wrapped the meat, it left a trickle of bloodied water on the metallic indentations of the sink. Anne shuddered when she noticed, wiping it away briskly with a cloth.

She slid all the ingredients into a big saucepan, angling the chopping board at its lip and pushing the vegetables into the simmering stock with the back of the knife. She left it to boil and then she took off her apron and went upstairs and brushed her hair, tucking it neatly behind her ears. She unbuttoned the floral blouse and changed into a loose-fitting V-neck scented with the ferric freshness of fabric conditioner.

She was conscious of the fact that she was behaving oddly and she wondered for a moment whether she might be suffering from shock. But Anne did not feel shocked. She felt – what exactly? She felt cocooned, un-tethered from actuality. She felt vaguely anxious, but there was an underlying sense that nothing was quite happening as it should. It was not so much unreal as hyper-real, as if she had just been made aware of each tiny dot of colour that made up every solid object she looked at. It felt like the pins and needles sensation she got in the tips of her fingers after she warmed her cold hands against a hot radiator, only then becoming aware of the completeness of her physical presence.

The smell of the casserole wafted up from the kitchen, steamed and earthy. Anne walked downstairs, taking her time, placing each foot carefully in front of the other. She was conscious of the need for extreme caution because, whatever happened when she got to the hospital, she would need somehow to deal with it and she wanted to stretch out this small scrap of leftover time as long as she could. This, now, here: this was still the time before, the space that existed prior to knowledge. She had no idea yet what would be required of her or how badly Charles was hurt.

She could not work out how much she cared. She found that, given everything that had happened during their years together, she was not unduly upset by the thought of his death but then, almost simultaneously, she felt a bottomless nausea when she allowed herself the rapid shiver of contemplation of her life without him.

But she did not have to face him until she got there.

So she would finish making the casserole and then she would get into her car and drive to the hospital and from then on, her life would be different in some way that she could not yet fathom.

But not just yet.

The saucepan bubbled, the lid clattering gently against its sides.

*   *   *

Her mother's name flashes up on her mobile.

'Mum?'

'Can you talk?'

'Yes.'

She knows immediately that something is wrong.

'It's Charles . . . I mean, it's Dad. Daddy.'

All at once, she is sick with anticipation. A desperate calm settles itself around her heart. For a second, she thinks her father is dead. The certainty of it filters through her skin, leaving a trail of goose-bumps along one arm. A coolness tightens around her shoulders.

'Oh God, no. No.'

She hears her voice begin to shudder. A gasping, dry sob rises in the back of her throat.

'It's all right,' her mother is saying on the other end of the line. 'Listen to me. He's OK. He's alive.'

She hears the words but does not, at first, understand them. She lets them slot into place, slowly reforming the sentence in her mind.

Not dead.

Alive.

Still living; still part of her.

And then, she no longer knows what to feel.

PART I

Anne

WHEN ANNE WAS A child and her parents returned late at night from a party, she liked to pretend to be asleep. It was partly because she knew the babysitter had let her stay up longer than she should but it was also because she enjoyed the feeling of play-acting, of feigning something, of playing a trick on adults.

She would hear their footsteps on the stairs, the heavy and deliberate murmur of drunken whispers and half-giggles, and she would flick the switch of her bedside lamp and shut her eyes tightly, drawing the blankets up around her. Her parents would approach her bedroom and halt for a moment outside, shushing each other with exaggerated seriousness, before pushing open the door and poking their heads round. Her mother's voice would say her name softly, each movement punctuated by the tinny jangle of earrings and bracelets.

Her mother would tiptoe over to the side of the mattress and lower her head to kiss her daughter gently on the cheek, and Anne, her senses heightened by the darkness, would feel the dryness of face powder and the creamy texture of her lipstick and inhale the thrilling adult tang of smoke and drink. Still, she would not open her eyes. Her parents must have known that she was awake but they played along. It became a harmless childhood lie.

She thinks of this now as she looks at her husband, lying on his hospital bed, attached to various tubes and drips. It looks like a pretence, this enforced sleep. His chest rises and falls. His eyes are closed. His mouth is turned down at the corners and over the last few days stubble has appeared on the pale folds of his face, like bracken stealing across a hillside. The sleep doesn't seem at all convincing. It looks as if he's trying too hard. Occasionally, his left eyelid will flicker slightly, a tiny electronic pulse emitted from some unidentified synapse.

She knows the facts. She has been told by the doctors that he is in a coma and she has nodded and been serious and given the reliable impression of a woman in her mid-fifties who understands what is expected of her. She has taken care of things, informed people, she has been calm and logical on the phone when issuing necessary instructions. She has been to the police station to pick up his bicycle, eerily unmarked by the accident, its metal frame sleek and grey and cool to the touch. She has packed bags and tidied and filled in forms and arranged for his transfer to a private hospital covered by his insurance. She has frozen the beef casserole. She has carried on, knowing that this is what everyone wants her to do.

But there is a secret part of her that thinks it is a colossal joke and that this isn't actually happening at all. Her husband is lying in front of her, pretending to be asleep and he is once again the centre of attention, just as he always managed to be when he was awake. She knows he is pretending; he is misleading her into believing in something that does not exist. Well, she thinks to herself, I'm not going to be fooled this time.

And then, looking at his prone body, she becomes all at once aware of her own absurdity. She is shocked at her casual dismissal of her husband's condition. She tries to think fondly of him, to remember some affectionate exchange they might have had in recent days. But instead all she can remember is the last conversation they had, just before Charles walked out of the door, dressed in his high-visibility cycling jacket, the zip undone so that the sides of it flapped in the breeze as he went.

He had not told her where he was going, and when she had asked, he did not lift his head to acknowledge that he had heard her. Instead, he carried on sipping his mug of breakfast tea in a succession of noisy slurps.

'Charles?'

He raised his eyes to meet hers with familiar indifference.

'Yes?'

'I just wondered where you were going,' Anne said a second time, hearing the meekness in her voice, the whining undertone, and hating it.

He put down his mug of tea with a quiet force. The mug gave a thunking sound as it made contact with the table and some of the liquid splattered on to the pale pine. Anne stared at the thin rivulets of brown, trying not to make eye contact with him.

'Why would that possibly concern you?' he said, his voice perfectly level. That would probably have been the end of it, but Anne had taken a dishcloth and started to wipe away the spilled tea and something in Charles had seemed to crack. No one else would have noticed it, but for Anne the change was immediately visible: a darkening of his pupils, a deliberate relaxing of the shoulders like a boxer priming himself for the ring, the ever-so-slight whistling sound of breath through his nostrils.

After a moment he spoke, his voice carefully modulated, as if holding itself back.

'Do you know what I think of you?' he asked, and although the question seemed out of place amid the mundane to-ing and fro-ing of the morning, Anne knew that he would have a reason for it.

She kept silent, balling up her hands into tight fists so that she could feel her fingernails digging into her palms. She concentrated on the discomfort of it, on the effort of marking her skin to prove she existed. When she relaxed her hands, there would be a row of sharply delineated crescents pock-marked across the tender pink flesh.

Charles was staring at her, his eyes stained with contempt, his head tilted in a quizzical pose. 'Well?' he asked, slowly, as if speaking to a stupid child.

Anne felt each muscle tense and prick against her flesh. She knew she had to answer or there would be no end to it. 'No,' she said and she could feel her voice disappear almost as soon as it hit the air, evaporating into wisps of nothing. She stood still, braced and alert for what would come next, the damp cloth cupped in her hand.

Charles coughed gently, a balled-up hand in front of his mouth. He looked at her and his eyes seemed dulled, like the dustiness on a window-pane when it caught the light. When he spoke, his tone was unchanged, innocuous, smooth like wax. 'You disgust me,' he said, so softly it was almost a whisper, and she wondered, once again, if she were in fact going mad. 'Just looking at you, at your dishcloths and your dirty aprons, at your pathetic face. Just listening to you, your incessant whining, your pleading, snivelling voice asking me pointless questions.' He paused to take a sip of tea and for a moment Anne thought he might have finished, but just as she was about to turn away, he put the mug down with exaggerated caution and continued. 'You.' He jabbed a finger at her. 'You. You, with your tired eyes and your wrinkles and your housewifely flab spilling over at the sides and your thin lips and –' He broke off and shook his head, as if disbelieving. 'You used to be so beautiful.'

Anne went to the sink and busied herself with the taps so that she did not have to look at him. She felt herself about to cry and wondered why he still possessed the capacity to wound her so deeply. She had become accustomed to his bouts of callousness, to the random outbursts of his bristling, restrained fury. Surely she should be inured to it by now, should be able to sweep his cruelties aside? Why did she not simply walk out of the kitchen? Why did she not walk out of the house, out of this man's life for good? Why did she stand here, bound to him, receiving each verbal blow as though she deserved it?

There was something that kept her here, a silken thread that tied her to him, that twisted around her wrists, her ankles, her chest, so tightly she could not move.

She found herself thinking about her youth, her dried-up beauty and the effortless slenderness that Charles had prized so highly. Once, in the very early days when they had been in bed together, he had lifted her skinny arm up to the light so that the delicate webbed skin between her fingers glowed like oyster shell held against the sun.

'Almost translucent,' he had said, before dropping her arm softly back on to the sheets and turning away from her. And she remembers now how happy she had felt with that small, dispassionate compliment. Had she really asked for so little?

But that had been years ago: a different woman in a different time. When she looked round from the sink, her vision blurred with the imprecise fuzziness of tears, she saw that Charles had gone.

The nurse comes in to check on the drip and smiles at her with a brisk nod of the head, just as they do in hospital dramas. It adds to her notion of play-acting. Of course, she thinks, the nurse is in on it too. He has somehow paid off the entire hospital to go along with this joke of his. How typical, she thinks, that he would go to such lengths to make her feel so beholden to him. She feels a familiar surge in the pit of her stomach, a pang somewhere between hunger and pain that she recognises as the beginnings of a small but lethal rage.

She has got used to these sudden, inexplicable bouts of anger and now barely notices them until they have subsided. She seems to be able to swing from extreme sadness and self-pity one minute to uncontained fury the next. Recently, at the wedding of a friend's daughter, she was given a sparkler from a packet and told to light it and hold it aloft as the happy couple left for their honeymoon.

'It's instead of confetti,' said the mother of the bride, an officious woman who prided herself on her organisational skills.

'Oh,' said Anne, realising she was meant to be impressed. 'How . . . inventive.'

The sparkler burned quickly, throwing out bright shards of flame like dandelion spores. The guests whooped and waved until it all seemed a curious facsimile of joy, and then the mother of the bride started ushering people into taxis and Anne was left with the sparkler in her hand, a limp, ashen strip that smelled lightly of sulphur. It struck her then, after too much champagne, that this is what happened to her inside when she felt that heated explosion of intense disappointment. It burned bright, and then it burned out, and no one ever knew.

She had wanted to talk to someone about this, about the feeling that her life was gradually draining itself of purpose, revolving around the same dull axes, but she could no longer share such intimacies with Charles and her limited scattering of dull suburban friends would have been shocked by her honesty. Until Charles's accident, she had felt oppressed by the cyclical nature of her days, as though she were stuck on a roundabout in an anonymous provincial town like the outer fringes of Swindon or a place called Blandford Forum that she had been to once with Charles; a town that had sounded vaguely Roman and exotic but that turned out to be full of grubby teashops and Argos outlets.

The worst of it was that it had all been entirely her doing. She had loved Charles, loved him completely, and probably still did in spite of no longer wanting to. But instead of giving her the contentedness she had once craved, her life with Charles has left Anne with a perpetual restlessness. She finds fault with everything. She picks at the stitches of each day with a relentlessness that leaves the seams frayed and the material torn out of shape. She does not understand happiness any more, cannot remember where to look for it, as if it is something she has mislaid – a coin that has slipped down the back of a sofa. She cannot remember the last time she laughed. She feels her core has been chipped away like marble. She no longer likes herself very much and can feel herself being ground down by her own defensiveness. She wishes she could be different, but it somehow seems too much effort to try.

She hadn't always been like this. When her mother died last year after a prolonged descent into blindness and infirmity, Anne had sorted through the overstuffed little retirement flat and come across an enormous cache of family letters. Sifting through the postcards of long-ago mountainsides and the browning edges of airmail envelopes, she had discovered a series of letters written while she was at boarding school. Each of them was so funny, covered with illustrations and jokes and witty imprecations not to forget to make her favourite flapjacks for the holidays. She had been stunned to meet this youthful version of herself: so effortlessly full of character, so unaffectedly joyful, so naively sure of who she was. There were so many exclamation marks. She never thought in exclamations any more.

The asthmatic, mechanical, barely-there sound of her husband's breathing interrupts her thoughts. He is still a handsome man, she thinks, looking at the clear, pronounced angle of his jawbone jutting out from beneath his earlobe as if welded in place. The skin around his eyes has been marked by a series of fine, engraved wrinkles in the last few years, but the crow's feet suit him; give him an approachable air of bonhomie and sunkissed good health. His eyes look like crinkles of paper, twisted at the ends like packets of picnic salt. His lids are closed now, occasionally twitching as if a small bird's heart is thumping delicately just below the surface of his face. But when they were open, his eyes were the bruised blue of faded hydrangea petals: flat, pale, remote.

The door opens and a nurse – the nice one with the dimpled smile – peers round the door. 'Cup of tea, Anne?'

She nods her head, just as she is supposed to.

Anne; Charles

CHARLES REDFERN WAS WHAT her mother called 'a catch'. She spotted him on the first day of lectures, sitting at the back in a tangle of splayed-out limbs and slumped shoulders. He raised his head briefly when she walked into the auditorium and she just had time to make out the arch of his eyebrows, peaking like precisely pitched tents, before his attention turned back to the well-thumbed paperback in his hands.

She couldn't read the title. She found out later, much later, that it had been James Joyce's *Ulysses*, a book that Charles had never read in its entirety, always giving up about a third of the way through the second chapter. But he liked to carry it around with him in those first few weeks of university in order to cultivate an impression of enigmatic intelligence; an aloofness that he thought made him both attractive and indefinable.

He was right, of course. Almost every girl had a crush on Charles Redfern by the end of freshers' week. There would be a gentle buzz of whispered giggles when he walked down the corridor. Girls pressed their noses to the glass when he jogged past their windows on the way to an early morning training session by the river for the college rowing team. He was reported to have a girlfriend at secretarial college whom someone had once met at a hunt ball and who was believed to be astonishingly glamorous with unparalleled taste in clothes.

His was the type of beauty that lost all its originality in description. He was broad-shouldered and tall and possessed of a disarming smile that crept slowly over one side of his face when he was about to laugh. His hair was the gold of hard-boiled caramel. Once, a friend back home had asked her to describe his profile and she thought immediately of him lying next to her in the hazy light of early morning.

'He's like a Greek god,' she said, totally serious.

'What kind of answer's that?' shrieked her friend. 'A Greek god? You've got it bad.'

'Honestly. I think he's the most handsome man I've ever met.'

'And he's your boyfriend? Well, I think you're awfully lucky.'

The friendship hadn't lasted much longer after that. There was something about Charles that made her both defensive and perpetually insecure – she feared never living up to his physical superiority, never being interesting or charming enough to keep his attention, as if his eyes would always drop, after a few seconds, back to a paperback he would never read all the way through.

But – miraculously, it seemed – he claimed to be smitten with her. He started seeking her out after that first lecture, turning up at odd intervals in the porter's lodge of her college, a scuffed leather satchel slung across his shoulder. He would be there when she went for coffee on campus, sitting at a corner table with a group of boys in rugby shirts laughing raucously and throwing the occasional, level glance in her direction. He was there, standing in between the bookshelves of the university library, his unmistakable silhouette casting its shadow over the dusty spines. He was there at a cocktail party thrown by the German Society, an event she had gone to under duress from Frieda, her friend at the time. Frieda was a self-consciously dramatic Modern Languages student who believed that men her own age were all hopelessly immature and sought out the companionship of graduate students or professors wherever she could.

'Come along,' said Frieda, in that curiously mocking way she had. 'You never know who you might meet.'

So she had gone because Frieda was too forceful to refuse. As a bribe, Frieda had lent her a greeny-blue shift dress, beautifully tailored from a length of raw silk inherited from her Parisian grandmother. It was the sort of material that was rough to the touch, yet glistened as smooth as an oil slick in the evening light. She was delighted with it.

'It suits you,' said Frieda. 'I am too flat-chested to carry it off.'

'Nonsense,' she said, unsure whether to be offended or complimented. 'Oh, I love it. Thanks so much for lending it to me.'

'Pleasure. I'm glad it's getting some use.' Frieda stopped at the mirror above the basin in the corner of her room where she had been applying her make-up. She let the mascara wand hang in her hand in mid-air. 'My grandmother went mad, you know. She ended up in a lunatic asylum, thinking she was Marie Antoinette.'

'Oh,' Anne said, because she wasn't sure what else was expected. Frieda's conversations were full of such brutal truths, buried strangely in the middle of a perfectly normal exchange. They would surprise her with their very matter-of-factness, their sudden bleakness bringing her up short and making her feel somehow frivolous, as if she had stubbed her toe against a half-concealed boulder.

Half an hour later, they set off, arm-in-arm, not quite intimate enough to be true friends and yet not antipathetic enough towards each other to bother much about this fact. She found that university was full of such thrown-together alliances. She planned to stay for an hour at most at the cocktail party, then walk back to her room and finish an essay that was bothering her.

As soon as they walked through the door, Frieda became engrossed in conversation with a lugubrious-looking professor who bounced up and down on his tiptoes every time he got excited. She, meanwhile, hung about on the fringes, feeling rather trivial. For some reason, as she had walked through the college gardens, she had been seized with the desire to pluck a bright purple bloom from the flowerbed and put it in her hair. Frieda had looked at her disapprovingly and she saw now that Frieda had been right: it was a studiedly whimsical gesture that all at once seemed out of place here, in this dark room, filled with earnest undergraduates in elbow-patched jackets and wire-rimmed spectacles. Along one wall, a long table was half-heartedly filled with two trays of damp mushroom vol-au-vents and bowls of Twiglets. Someone had tried to make a hedgehog shape with cocktail sticks of cubed cheese and pineapple, but the sticks appeared to be too heavily weighted, so that the display looked wilted. The desultory strains of an ana-chronistic harpsichord were emanating from a slim record player in the corner.

Anne hated clubs and groups and societies as a rule – had spent most of the first half of term avoiding enthusiastic recruiters for hockey teams or film appreciation discussions – and now here she was, feeling uncomfortable and cross with herself simply because she had been too weak to say no.

She was smiling listlessly, working herself into a gradual state of agitation, and then she turned round and Charles Redfern was suddenly in front of her, holding a bulbous champagne glass filled to the brim with a violently crimson liquid.

'I want to take you out for a drink,' he said, as simple as that.

'You don't even know me.'

'I do. I know your name is Anne Eliott. I know you are a first-year History student at Newnham College, Cambridge. I know that you are approximately 5ft 6 and that you have –' he broke off, leaned forwards and squinted intently at her face, 'dark brown eyes flecked with green.'

'They're not flecked with green.'

'Yes, they are. You should look at them some time.'

She couldn't think of anything to say to that. He smiled, still looking straight at her, and she noticed that the smile didn't quite reach his eyes but stopped at the bridge of his nose. Although she never usually blushed, she could sense an unfamiliar warmth creeping up from her clavicles to her face.

'It's much easier to say yes now. Otherwise, I'll have to keep pursuing you and you'll have to keep pretending to ignore me.'

'How do you know I'm pretending?'

'I don't know . . . something about the tilt of your head. When you're concentrating on a lecture, I've noticed that you sit very upright. And when you're chatting to friends or whatever, your hair sort of bobs from side to side. But when you're pretending not to notice me, it's neither one nor the other. You stand very still and you stare very intently at something you're meant to be concen-trating on, but there's a slight . . . well, I suppose it's a tremble, for want of a better word.'

'A tremble?'

'Yes. Like when you pretend to be asleep, but other people can tell that you're not. Like that.'

She couldn't say anything much for several seconds and he just kept on looking at her, gravely and with such intensity she couldn't help but think it meant something. He seemed irrevocably in control of the situation, silently directing its progress according to some plan he had already formulated and would not be diverted from. His calm, focused insistence was intimidating but also oddly flattering. She was disarmed by his attention.

Then, just as she was preparing to say, yes, take me for a drink, I'd like that, he smiled at her, lifted his right hand so that it was just level with her cheek and quickly, so quickly she wondered afterwards if it had actually happened, brushed a tendril of her hair behind her ear, letting his fingertip graze against the nape of her neck. She breathed in, sharply. Then he turned and walked away.

So then, inevitably, she was smitten too. A week later, she ran into him again in the library, sitting at one of the long wooden desks in the reading room, rolling a cigarette.

'Hello, Charles.'

He looked up and a grin spread slowly across his face.

'Anne Eliott,' he said, licking the cigarette paper. 'When are you going to come for that drink with me?'

They cycled to a pub in Grantchester on a windy, grey day with the flat, grassy meadows spreading out beneath them like wet brushstrokes. Swans dotted the riverbanks, patches of white set with angular elegance against the murky brown water. Charles led the way, with Anne following breathlessly behind. She looked at his back, the dip and rise of his shoulders as he cycled over the ruts and bumps of the path. She saw the way his hair was just long enough to be ruffled by the breeze. She noticed that he kept checking she was keeping up, head turning just far enough to catch her eye. It felt entirely as it should.

Later, after her half shandy, he kissed her briefly on the lips and said she tasted of sherbert. Later still, he took her back to Newnham and pushed her gently against the red brick wall, taking her face in his hands and, without speaking, kissing her lips, her cheeks, her eyelids. Then, because male visitors were not allowed to stay the night, he left and she went up to her room, tingling with the quiet fizz of joy.

When she took him home two months later her parents were predictably charmed.

'Darling, he's wonderful,' her mother said in a theatrical whisper, almost as soon as her father had shown him upstairs to his room. 'What a catch!'

At supper, Charles complimented Mrs Eliott on the perfect pinkness of the roast lamb, and her mother, suffused with pleasure, let the gravy boat slip in her hand so that it almost spilled its contents all over the embroidered linen tablecloth. He engaged Mr Eliott in a lengthy and considered conversation about the American civil rights movement without ever proffering an opinion that might have been deemed overly controversial or uncomfortably radical. He seemed a perfect cut-out of everything her boyfriend should be.

'He's a damned sound chap, Annie,' her father said in the drawing room the next morning, folding away his newspaper and leaning forwards to stab at the fire with a long brass poker.

'Archie!' said her mother, whose unnecessary horror at her husband's language had become a sort of fond family joke.

'I'm only saying, darling. I like him. Like his drive. You could do a lot worse, you know.'

'I'm sure Annie knows her own mind.' Her mother lifted her dark-grey eyes from her sewing. 'Don't you, darling?'

She smiled. Yes, she did. She knew her mind. But, as she was about to find out, she couldn't have claimed to know his.

Charlotte

CHARLOTTE WAS LATE AGAIN and although her lateness had an inevitability about it, this was never the comfort that it should have been. You'd imagine, she thought as she wove perilously in and out of the dense London traffic in her small blue car, that knowing I was going to be late would make me prepare more thoroughly in advance so that I would end up being on time. But she never quite managed the crucial leap between thought and action. Her lateness was now one of her defining features, an aspect of her personality that was gently tolerated and jovially referred to with affectionate exasperation by almost everyone who knew her. She had friends who would deliberately factor in a delay of half an hour when Charlotte arranged to meet them. But her mother was different: she could never be late for her.

She was dreading seeing her, a cold, dank dread that lay fetid and heavy across her chest. Recently, she found that she could not even pretend to relax in her mother's presence: every time she saw her, the whole situation felt so stilted and unreal that their conversations had become defined more by the gaps between what was said than by the words themselves.

It had all stemmed from the time a few months ago when her mother turned up unannounced on the doorstep in the early morning. It was Charlotte's thirtieth birthday, a date that she had been determined to ignore, and she recalled opening the door of her flat and being unable to disguise her horror. She had literally taken a step back, as if recoiling from her mother's presence, attempting to get away from her.

'Anything wrong?' her mother said.

'No!' Charlotte replied, the forced jollity jarring in her ears.

'Well. Good. Thought I'd surprise you. Happy birthday.' And, still standing on the threshold, she had passed her a square, neatly wrapped package, the action appearing unnatural and false.

'Thanks.' Charlotte did not invite her in. She was still in her pyjamas, and her boyfriend, Gabriel, was splayed across the bed in a tumble of duvet and sheet. She became aware that she wanted to get rid of her mother as quickly as possible, for some reason she could not grasp. She hastily tore off the wrapping paper to reveal a shiny dark blue box with a small gold clip at one end. When Charlotte opened it, she saw a familiar silver ring, topped with a small, oval ruby set in diamonds.

'Mum . . .'

'I want you to have it.'

'But, Mum,' Charlotte felt sick. Her heart started thumping. 'What are you doing?'

Her mother cleared her throat. 'It doesn't fit me any more.' She smiled oddly. 'Besides, who else would I give it to?'

'It's your engagement ring.'

'Yes.' And her mother had turned and let herself out of the front door without another word. There had been no time for Charlotte to say she didn't want it.

She braked too suddenly at a set of traffic lights and her handbag fell off the front passenger seat, scattering a motley assortment of hair clips and old postage stamps into the footwell. A necklace with a broken clasp that she had been carrying in her bag for weeks had started to unravel and several tiny purple beads were rolling on to the fuzzy grey carpet. 'Bugger,' she said out loud, although there was no one else to hear her. She scrabbled around to put everything back inside and then the lights changed and the looming double-decker bus behind her started beeping its horn. 'All right, All right.'

Thinking about her mother generally had this sort of effect on her. It wound her up, made her tense and simultaneously guilty for no real reason. She felt somehow responsible for her mother's happiness and yet resentful that the burden weighed so heavily on her. She hated that she still cared enough to try to be the dutiful, supportive daughter. After all, Charlotte thought, her mother had never once said that she loved her. It wasn't her way. Instead, she seemed perpetually disappointed: by Charlotte, by herself, by life and its accumulated disenchantments.

Her parents had never been ones for hugging or good-natured arguments around the dinner table or the rambunctious rough-and-tumble that characterised those large, semi-aristocratic families she was always reading about in period novels. There had, instead, been an unspoken friction, a constant and wordless atmosphere of slights perceived and grudges held.

Supper-times had been the worst. They would sit round the pine kitchen table, straight-backed and solicitous, with wariness in their eyes. Her father would speak first, his comments punctuated by the metronome click of his jaw as he chewed. What he said was never as bad as the way he said it. He would start off with a bland observation, usually aimed at her mother.

'Another new top, I see.'

There would be a pause, pregnant with the electric possibility of disaster. Her mother would make a great show of looking down to see what she was wearing before assuming an unnatural informality.

'Oh this? Yes, I bought it the other day . . .' She trailed off, aware of his uncomfortable stare.

'How . . . extravagant,' he said, administering each word as if it were a drop of acid pressed from a chemist's pipette.

'Not really,' her mother rallied quietly. 'It was in the sale.'

'Oh, I see.' He gave a dry chuckle and wiped the corners of his mouth with the edge of a table-napkin. 'You're saving me money. Well, I suppose I should be grateful.'

Sometimes that would be the end of it. Sometimes her father would keep pushing and pushing until her mother would leave the table, sliding her chair back so abruptly that it would shriek discordantly against the tiled floor. On those occasions, Charlotte would be forced to stay at the table in silence until he had finished eating.

After the dinner plates had been cleared away, there would be no television because every single programme apart from the news appeared to annoy her father, darkening his moods until it seemed all the air had been squeezed to the corner of the rooms and pushed through the cracks in the walls. He would never shout, but the repressed fury of his controlled breathing was somehow worse than anything else.

The tension would be so unbearable, the need to apologise for whatever she was watching so constant in her mind, that the whole thing ended up being horribly unrelaxing. The only time she found she could watch television with impunity was just after she got home from school and just before her father returned from work, a golden period of two hours where she could sit herself on a beanbag in the front room with a slice of Battenberg cake and with the luxurious prospect of an uninterrupted session of *Grange Hill* and *Blue Peter* stretching out in front of her. Her ears were finely tuned into the precise sound of her father's car engine. When she heard the first growling rumbles of his BMW, she would leap up, switch off the television and sprint upstairs, closing the door to her bedroom and opening her school exercise books so that she would not have to talk to him.

Sometimes, he would knock on her door on his way upstairs.

'Charlotte?' He waited until she replied before he pushed the door open, but even then he refused to walk over the thin metallic strip that separated the dark red hallway carpet from the light, beige tones of her bedroom floor. It always felt awkward, his standing there as if on sentry duty, casting his wordless eye over what she was doing.

'Busy day?' he asked.

'Sort of,' Charlotte said and then couldn't think of anything else to add. She smiled at him as neutrally as she could. He stood looking at her in silence for a few seconds, loosening his tie with one hand.

'Good,' he said. He shifted on his feet, as if he were about to step forward and move closer to her. She saw this and instantly she felt her shoulders jolt backwards, a movement so slight it might not have happened, but he noticed and immediately he turned from her and walked out, making long strides towards the bathroom. After a few minutes, she heard the sound of running water.

She did not know if her family was normal or not. She had few friends to confide in. She was a very lonely child, scared of other children and terrified of new experiences. She had no siblings and was unsure how to relate to people her own age. There was nothing she hated more than her mother saying she must go to a party 'because so-and-so's daughter will be there and she's the same age as you'. Or those horrifying dinners where her parents would sit on one table with the adults and all the children would be expected to gather round a shaky fold-out picnic table with novelty napkins and coloured paper crowns. 'It's more fun for them that way, isn't it?' the hostess would say, with a facile smile on her face, when actually everyone knew the only reason for their annexation was that the adults couldn't be bothered to look after them.

It wasn't ever more fun, thought Charlotte. As a rule, she found that most children regarded her with a naked distrust that soon turned into a virulent mutual loathing. The worst thing was getting stuck with a group of girls who were already, through a series of esoteric family connections, the firmest of friends. They would either gang up on her and whisper about her behind cupped hands, or she would try to be friendly to one of them and immediately be accused by another girl of 'trying to take her away from me'. She never seemed to wear the right clothes or to have done the right things. Once, when she admitted she had never watched *Chitty Chitty Bang Bang*, a girl called Kitty with frizzy blonde hair and shiny lips said she was 'odd', which had seemed the cruellest possible insult at the time.

Instead, she revelled in isolation. At home, she would spend hours reading in the shed at the back of the garden, sandwiched between old deckchairs and the greasy oiliness of lawnmower spare parts. The shed was her favourite retreat. Sometimes, when things in the house got almost too much to bear, she would come to the shed and imagine that she had run away. She would sit for hours in between two coal sacks wondering if anyone had noticed that she was no longer there and then, when the floor got too hard and the night-time draughts started to seep through the cracks in the wood, she would be forced back inside and neither of her parents would remark on her absence. And it was this – the fact that they had not been worried about her – that used to upset her more than any unhappiness she might have felt in the first place.

'Get out of the fucking way!' she screamed as a moped screeched to a halt in front of her. She swerved just in time and saw the familiar outline of the London Bridge Hospital down a road to her left. She indicated, then remembered that the left light wasn't working and she had yet to get it fixed. Her father had always told her she should do hand signals out of the window if this ever happened, but she was too embarrassed, so she took her chances when she saw a gap in the traffic.

The thought of him made her shiver.

Once inside the hospital car park, where a space was hardly ever available despite the outrageously high charges, she felt the familiar sense of unease settle like a shroud. She hated hospitals: the smell of disinfectant and surgical gloves, the squeaky linoleum, the endless corridors without windows, the collapsed grandmothers shuffling to the loo in their slippers, the enforced cheerfulness of the nurses that made everything seem so much more terrifying.

'Deep breath,' she said to herself. 'You're not the one who's ill, after all.' She picked up her battered handbag, put it over the crook in her arm and walked inside. The automatic glass doors whirred open into the reception area. Along one wall was an ersatz gift shop which sold newspapers (the *Daily Express* always went first, she had noticed) and sad-looking teddy bears with sickly purple bows tied round their necks. The lift pinged when she pressed the call button and she was soon on the fifth floor. She walked to the end of the hallway, pausing to squeeze a blob of alcohol on her hands from the anti-MRSA dispenser on the wall, and pushed the door on her right, sliding it slowly open.

'Hello, Mum.'

Her mother was standing by the window, looking outwards to the indistinct greyness of the sky. She turned suddenly when

Charlotte walked in. 'Oh, hello,' she replied absent-mindedly, as if she had not been expecting her.

'How is he?'

'Much the same,' her mother said, her eyes obscured by the pair of pastel-framed bifocals she wore for reading. 'The doctor says we should try to talk to him.'

Charlotte looked at the crumpled figure of her father, shrunken and pale against the hospital sheets. She felt unhappiness wash over her. The light in the room seemed to bleach at the edges, draining the room of colour so that everything became shaded in a matt greyness.

It was time to start acting the role that was expected of her. She pushed her shoulders back and smiled too brightly.

At the foot of the bed hung a thin wire basket in which was slotted a cheap blue ring binder containing his hospital notes. Above his head, on an easy-wipe noticeboard, a nurse had written hurriedly in red felt-tip: 'Charles Redfern. 55 yrs'.

'Hello, Dad.'

Anne

A NNE LOVED HER DAUGHTER so much it felt like a glass splinter lodged deep in her heart. Yet she found herself incapable of expressing it and this, more than anything else, seemed to drive them apart.

She was unaccountably cross that Charlotte was late. She had promised faithfully to be at the hospital at 6.30 p.m., but it was now 7.15 p.m. In that time, Anne had worked herself up into a state of highly pitched emotion that was a complicated knot of fury, fear and the suspicion that Charlotte simply didn't care enough about her to turn up. The anger had crept up on Anne so imperceptibly that she had been unable to stop it leaking out in small but significant gestures; a succession of cold stares and raised eyebrows.

She knew that Charlotte picked up on it immediately, that her daughter sensed the tension in the atmosphere as soon as she walked in the room.

'How was the traffic?' Anne asked, trying to pepper her voice with lightness, but sensing in spite of herself the dried-up husks of her words.

'Oh, pretty rubbish, you know. Rush hour. That kind of thing,' Charlotte said abstractedly.

'It's terrible the traffic in London these days,' Anne said, because nothing else came to mind. She gave a dry little cough. 'What time did you leave work?'

Although Charlotte's face remained perfectly immobile, Anne could see that the tendons in her neck were taut with some indeterminate strain. When she replied, her voice was prickly.

'Normal time. Six-ish.' She put her handbag down on the floor, shrugging herself out of her jacket. She sighed, audibly enough that Anne could not help but hear it. 'You know, I didn't mean to be late. It's not deliberate.'

Anne said nothing. She hated it when Charlotte became irritable. She had wanted her to notice her obvious discontent but only because she had craved an affectionate, apologetic response. And now it was too late to backtrack.

'Well,' Anne heard herself say. 'You're here now.'

The air between them crackled.

Charlotte shook her head, so slightly that no one else but Anne would have seen it. But she noticed every tiny movement Charlotte made. It was her substitute for spoken intimacy. If nothing else, she could watch her. She could know her like a collector knows his butterflies: beautiful samples, pinned up in glass cases, wings outstretched so that every marking was clear. And by knowing her this way, by checking every nuance of her light and shade, by detailing each twitch and tremble, every gentle susurration of an unintended sigh, Anne could move as close to her as she dared. She gazed at Charlotte from a safe distance.

She was worried that she loved her daughter too greatly, that to reveal the extent of it would be to overwhelm the precarious balance of their relationship. She felt her emotions were calcified by guilt at not having been a good enough mother, a deep, unspoken, dug-away sort of shame that burrowed away inside like a creature with vicious teeth and claws. To let Charlotte see how much she cared, to be honest about her imperfect love, would be somehow to reveal this failing. Anne was scared at the thought of it.

They both knew where this guilt came from and Charles, when he had been awake, he had known too, but they never spoke of it. Instead, there was a triangulation of silence, a delicate construction of half-accepted ignorance that was as brittle as spun sugar.

Charlotte drew up a hospital chair to sit beside her father's bed. She was close enough that, if she had wanted to, she could have touched him, but Anne saw that she stayed a little apart, in her own separate space. She did not take his hand.

Charlotte's hair hung loose around her face, strands of wavy dark brown that were neither entirely straight nor tightly sprung enough to be curly. It annoyed her, Anne knew, that her hair could never be relied upon. She would use these dreadful hair straighteners each morning that seemed almost to frazzle her hair to a cinder. Sometimes Anne would notice she had burned herself on the top of her forehead, a small reddish imprint that no one else would see. In spite of the straighteners, Charlotte's hair would always be crinkled by the end of the day. Anne preferred it like this, untampered, but she knew that her daughter hated its uncontrollable nature.

Her daughter was a pretty girl, not that she had ever told her this. But Anne knew it, objectively, because other people remarked on it when they saw her photo or when they first met her. She had an oval face and smooth skin with a faint splattering of freckles across the bridge of her nose. Her eyes were large and light blue and quizzical-looking. She had dainty earlobes, carefully defined and covered with soft downy hair that Anne stopped herself from reaching out to touch. Today, she was wearing earrings that looked like pieces of birch bark: silvery brown crescents that shivered when she spoke.

She was speaking to her father in a low, careful voice. The doctors had insisted that talking to Charles could have a positive effect on his recovery but Anne could not shake the unnaturalness of it; the slight embarrassment of a one-way conversation consisting almost entirely of the sort of mundane trivialities that Charles had always hated being subjected to. Listening to her daughter's hesitations and forced jollities, Anne realised that Charlotte felt it too. It had never been particularly easy to talk to Charles. Now, it seemed almost impossible.

She tuned into what Charlotte was saying and realised she was talking about the holiday she had just been on with her boyfriend, a man Anne neither liked nor trusted.

'. . . so then we went to this beautiful hilltop village and it took ages to walk up to the top because it was unbelievably steep.' Charlotte broke off and poured a glass of water from the plastic jug on the bedside cabinet. She furrowed her brow, thinking of the best way to continue and then, before she started to speak again,

Anne saw her quite deliberately force a smile on to her face. She wondered why she did this and then she realised that Charlotte's words now sounded warmer as she spoke them, the curve of her lips shaping each sentence with a brightness that had not been there before.

'When we finally got there, we were both so exhausted and sweaty that the first thing we did was find a nice outside table at this café on the square to drink a *citron pressé* and just look for a bit at the view. It really is the most lovely part of France – un-touristy, for some reason, I suppose because it's not that close to the coast, but . . .'

'Where was this?' Anne asked a little too loudly.

Charlotte looked up, surprised and slightly flustered by the interruption. 'Oh, it's a region called the Tarn.' She stopped and Anne waited for her to continue, just long enough that the silence started to feel scratchy. 'I'd never heard of it, although it turns out that Claudia – you remember Claudia don't you? – well, her parents have a house fifteen minutes from where we were staying, but I only found out when we got back, otherwise we would have dropped in.'

'What's Claudia doing with herself these days?'

'She's, um, she's in banking. Something to do with hedge funds. I don't really understand it.'

'She was always such a nice girl. Very polite. I remember she wrote the most charming thank-you letters when she came to stay.'

'Yes,' Charlotte said, and Anne could see instantly from the vague wrinkle between her eyebrows that she thought she was being unfavourably compared.

'Well, anyway, I'm sure your job is much more interesting.'

'Mm-mm.'

And so the conversation juddered on, halting and uncomfortable and never entirely real, as if they were both reading from a bad script and neither of them knew what to do about it. And there was Charles, lying gloriously in the middle of it all like a stone figurine sculpted for the top of a medieval king's tomb; static yet simultaneously alive, able to hear yet not listening, her husband,

Charlotte's father and yet, at the same time, neither of these things. Not really. Not now.

Later, as they stood outside the hospital doors saying their awkward goodbyes, Anne leaned forward and gave her daughter a half-peck on the cheek. She inhaled the fig-scented perfume that Charlotte always wore, taking a deep breath in and then holding it for a moment, like something precious and breakable, in the pit of her stomach.

'Anyway,' said Charlotte, pulling away, pushing up the shoulder strap of her leather bag that kept slipping down her arm. Her smile was pained, almost embarrassed. 'See you.'

Charlotte turned and strode towards the car park, her silver birch earrings swinging as she walked. Anne watched her climb into the driving seat and for a brief moment their eyes met through the windscreen and both of them seemed surprised by this unexpected moment of recognition. Charlotte smiled and raised a hand. Anne nodded, more curtly than she'd intended.

Anne drove along the main roads to get back to Kew, past the fried chicken shops and the sari emporiums and the queues of tourists outside the London Dungeon and Southwark Cathedral, through the endless traffic lights that turned to red just as she approached them. It would have been quicker to go the back way but she felt the need for bright streetlamps and noise and urban chaos. It felt reassuring to see it all going on as usual, everyday life continuing undaunted beyond the hospital's distillation of loss and hurt and illness.

Her mobile phone rang, the screen flashing up with a ghoulish light. It was Janet. 'Oh no,' Anne said out loud, fumbling to connect the hands-free set with one hand on the steering wheel. 'Janet?'

'Hello, Anne. Just calling to see how things went at the hospital today?'

It was typical of Janet to call at just the wrong moment, proffering just the wrong sort of concern – the kind that required exhaustive explanation and a decent show of emotion. Speaking to her always left one with a residual feeling of baseless unease, a sense of not having quite met up to the exacting standards of her goodness. She was so unremittingly nice it was impossible not to be irritated by her and yet simultaneously ashamed of this irritation. It made for draining conversations.

They had met years ago at the local Salvation Army Christmas carol concert, an event that Anne had found herself attending with dreary regularity in an attempt to paint herself as an upstanding and contented member of the community, a family-oriented mother and wife, a fund-raiser for assorted charities and a dedicated watcher of *Antiques Roadshow*. For a while, she had believed that pretending her life had some sort of meaning would actually give it some, as if the acting was half the effort.

Charles had never come along with her – he called himself an atheist and made a great show of shirking any sort of religious pomp – and this had been a relief, in a way. It allowed Anne to create an alternative persona: one of wholesome cake-baking goodness and jumble sales. She found a safety in this pretence, singing along heartily to rousing carols and contributing generously to the collection plate. She liked Christmas and discovered that seasonal festivity was the perfect opportunity for anonymity without isolation. Strangers smiled at her and caught her eye, but it was easy to elude conversation, to slip out just as the mulled wine was being poured.

That was until she met Janet. Janet had suddenly appeared one year, wreathed in jollity and home-knitted scarves, bearing Tupperware boxes filled with mince pies. She made a bee-line for Anne as soon as she spotted her trying to leave.

'Sure I can't tempt you?' Janet asked, a beaming smile on her face. Anne looked at her and noticed the filmy eyes, perpetually on the brink of some extreme enthusiasm and the garish, orange-red lipstick beginning to bleed into tiny lines around her trembling mouth. She felt sorry for her, a small, unfamiliar twinge of empathy, a sense that Janet too was struggling to fit in, was desperate to find her own place in all of this communal bonhomie.

'I was just on my way home, actually.'

'Oh go on!' Janet tinkled cheerily. 'One mince pie won't do any harm. I made them this morning. Grab one while you can.'

So Anne had taken a mince pie and the pastry had crumbled all over her coat and Janet had been so pathetically grateful that Anne stayed far longer than she wanted, trapped by the force field of Janet's self-conscious jollity.

The friendship had stopped and started over the years, like a wheezy old car that struggled to accelerate up hills. But each time it threatened to extinguish itself completely, Janet had come up with some novel ruse to keep it going – free tickets to Chelsea Flower Show, a cake recipe she'd been dying to try out on someone, the chance to go to a lecture on Darwin's evolutionary theory at the Natural History Museum, a new cheese shop that had just opened round the corner and was meant to stock the most fabulous Pecorino. And each time, Anne had capitulated – partly because it was easier that way and partly because, in spite of herself, she found Janet's company strangely soothing. She never had to make any conversational effort in her presence and found it easy to let Janet's cheerful monologues wash over her, smiling and nodding her head when it was required. She was, Anne supposed, her only real friend.

Once, but only once, Janet had stared at her across a café table and said, out of nowhere, 'You never really listen to me, do you?' Anne had protested unconvincingly and was mortified to see tears well up in Janet's eyes. She couldn't think of anything else to say, so she had lapsed into silence. After a while, the tears receded and Janet flapped her hands in front of her face. 'Sorry. Ridiculous. Don't know what's wrong with me today.' And that had been that.

This Friday, they had been due to go to Paris for the weekend – 'A girls' trip,' Janet had said when they booked their Eurostar tickets – but now it all had to be cancelled. Janet was being purposely cheery about it, as if living up to her own notions of what a 'trooper' she was. She had insisted on dealing with all the paperwork, in enquiring about refunds and phoning up the hotel to let them know they would no longer be requiring two single rooms with en-suite showers. And then she had told Anne all about what she'd done, seeking approval with a single-mindedness that recalled a dog gripping a stick between its teeth. Anne knew that what Janet most wanted was someone to reassure her how selfless she was, how wonderful she'd been in a crisis, to say, 'I don't know what I'd do without you,' and yet it was precisely because she was so needy, so oppressively grateful for any morsel of attention, that Anne found herself feeling perversely disinclined to play the game.

She knew this was mean and she was half-horrified by her own capability for small cruelties, but she couldn't help herself. To an extent, her friendship with Janet enabled her to vent the frustrations accumulated in the rest of her life: it was the only situation she remained entirely in control of. For some reason, that was important.

'You sound tired,' Janet was saying now on the phone. 'Was it a terribly draining day?'

'No, no,' said Anne. 'It was fine.' A mini-van stopped suddenly in front of her without warning. 'Oh, bloody hell.'

'Anne? Are you all right?'

'Yes. Just a van driver who doesn't know his highway code.'

Janet tittered on the end of the line. 'So is there any update from the doctors?'

'Much the same. They never really want to say anything in case they get sued. In any case, they've got to wait for the brain swelling to go down before they can be sure.'

'Sure of what?'

'Of whether there's any permanent ... well, you know, brain damage.'

There was a self-consciously dramatic intake of breath on the other end of the line.

'They said that if he'd been wearing his bicycle helmet he might have walked away unscathed. I kept telling him to wear it,' Anne said, rather pointlessly, she thought.

'Are they any closer to finding out what happened?'

'No. The police say there were no witnesses, which frankly I find hard to believe, but they never care much about cyclists, do they? The doctors think his bike was clipped by a passing car and he was thrown off. He was lucky to have landed on the road. If he had fallen into the path of a moving car, then it could have quite possibly been fatal. As it is . . . well, he's in this coma.'

'Goodness, Anne. How horrific.'

'I suppose it's just something we'll have to deal with,' Anne said, her impatience breaking through. 'He might wake up tomorrow and be absolutely fine.' She found she was unable to muster the requisite good cheer that this thought should have provoked.

'I think you're being a tower of strength, I really do.'

Anne stayed silent for a beat too long.

'And you needn't worry about Paris. Because we cancelled more than forty-eight hours in advance, the hotel has very kindly reimbursed our deposit, although it took quite a bit of doing, I tell you. My schoolgirl French isn't what it used to be.'

Another tinkle of forced laughter.

'Anyway, Anne, I should let you get on if you're driving. Did you see Charlotte at the hospital?'

'Yes, she came after work. Turned up late, obviously.'

'Oh . . . well. That was nice of her to make the effort.'

'Mmm,' said Anne, non-committally. 'I think she had a nice holiday in France with the man, although she never really tells me anything.'

'Well, it's a tricky one, isn't it, Anne?' Janet cleared her throat, preparing to take a leap into dangerous territory. 'Perhaps she feels you might not approve.'

'I don't approve of him. He's married, for goodness sake.'

'I thought he was separated?'

'Separated, maybe, but certainly not divorced from what I can make out.'

'Well, Anne, these things do take time, after all.'

'How would you know?'

There was a small, offended pause.

'Sorry, Janet. I'm rather at the end of my tether at the moment.'

'Of course,' she said, the words sounding strangulated. 'Well, look after yourself, Anne, and I'll call tomorrow.'

'Thank you. Bye.'

'Bye.'

Janet hung up and Anne sat still for several minutes, hands on the steering wheel in a precise ten to two position, glaring at the traffic jam in front of her. Then, after a few minutes, she turned on the radio and rotated the volume dial until it was almost too loud to bear.

Anne; Charles

S O CHARLES AND ANNE became an item, inevitably, irreversibly and without much questioning on either side. Anne had never slept with anyone before, had never even had a boyfriend, and was always mildly astonished if a man expressed that sort of sexual interest in her. It hadn't really crossed her mind that her friendships with boys could be misinterpreted and this made for several uncomfortable exchanges when news of her alliance with Charles trickled down through the college hierarchies.

'But I thought you liked me,' said a second-year undergraduate called Fred, with meek desperation. Anne could not conceal her bafflement.

'Fred, we're friends,' she said, shaking her head at the sudden impossibility of it all. 'Can't we just be good friends?'

She couldn't understand why her relations with men were suddenly constrained, punctuated by pockets of conversational difficulty and unease. Charles laughed at her when she told him.

'Can you really not see the effect you have on men?'

'But I've only ever been nice to them,' she protested, feebly.

'That's the problem,' he said. 'You shouldn't be too nice. It's easy to misinterpret.'

For the first few weeks, being with Charles had been a glorious bubble of shared experience – of kissing and hand-holding and staring meaningfully at each other across a restaurant table; of buying roses and eating sticky buns for tea-time; of sitting next to each other in lectures and giggling under their breath at some inexplicable mutual joke. The sex, when it came, had been perfectly nice. It had not been the cataclysmic cymbal-clash that Anne had secretly anticipated for years. Nor had it been a painful, brutal semi-disaster of fumbling and not-quite-knowing. It had been a fleshy clasping of two bodies, a swift exchange of fluids, a brief glimpse of half-shut eyes and then, for a few seconds afterwards, a sense of tenderness, of having achieved a closeness that seemed secret from the rest of the world. He enjoyed it more than she did, if enjoy was the word. He seemed to view it as some sort of necessity or duty: a task to be performed to his best ability, without much concern for the pleasure it could bring the other person.

But, at last, Anne felt she had gained access to a tantalising adult existence that had only ever been hinted at. She assumed that other people had sex just like they did, the same physical bargain struck swiftly under the blankets. She never questioned Charles, given that he seemed so much more experienced than her. He knew what to do. She let him get on with it.

As if to compensate for the lack of physical passion, she became gently obsessed instead with the trace and curve of his body: the downy plump cushion of his earlobe, the unexpectedly ticklish patch behind his knee, the twisted purple of veins running down his forearm. She liked to kiss him awake in the mornings, starting at the tip of his forehead and running down past the fragile skein of his eyelids, meeting his lips at the last moment, the exhalation of his breath metallic against her tongue.

'Morning,' he would say, blue eyes lazily opening.

Frieda was unconvinced and sulky about the burgeoning relationship. 'You spend all your time together,' she said at dinner in hall one evening. 'I never see you any more.'

Anne found she had no answer to this and no desire to give one. It was true that she increasingly spent as much of the day with Charles as possible, returning to Newnham only when she had to, swaying into bed with a sort of tired happiness. She could not understand Frieda's angst or the constant background hum of her friend's strained anxiety. Nothing in Anne's life had ever caused her to question good fortune: it was simply there to be taken for granted and not to be worried about or overly analysed. Later, she would look back at her earlier self and be astonished by how guileless she had been, how improbably arrogant to assume that contentedness was a gift that everyone was given. She had been sheltered all of her life. By her parents, her privilege, her cleverness and her beauty.

Because although she liked to believe she never thought about it, Anne knew instinctively she was beautiful. She knew it, and yet she had no idea how to deploy it, how to use it to get what she most desired or how to subtly craft it into a knowing sort of charm. At nineteen, Anne was a girl-woman. Her sophistication was a pretence; her maturity unfinished. She was an innocent with the looks of an older woman, ill-equipped to recognise her own fatal power. She found herself on the edges of situations that she did not fully understand – with Fred, with countless other men who felt she led them on with her teasing, unwitting flirtation. Yet she was not courageous enough to admit the shortfall of her knowledge. And once she was able to, she found that she was too trapped to do anything about it.

At the start of her relationship with Charles, she ignored any faint intimations of disquietude, pushing them to the far corners of her mind and telling herself not to be so ridiculous. She spent the days in a library haze, surrounded by the open pages of books, making half-hearted notes underneath the strip-lighting of the History faculty. At nights, she would occasionally sneak him into her room to stay over, squashed into the rickety single bed, his feet barely covered by the sheets.

Once, she had woken up as the sun was creeping in through the curtain crack to find that he was no longer beside her. She put on her dressing gown and tiptoed across the uncarpeted floor-boards, opening the door a crack in case the porter discovered she was entertaining an illicit male guest. She peered up and down the corridor but Charles wasn't there. Then she heard the gentle rumble of his laughter. It was coming from Frieda's room. She knocked and heard a sudden scrabbling and the sounds of Frieda shushing briskly. The door opened.

'Anne,' said Frieda, her face impassive. She was wearing a silk nightgown over a grey cashmere cardigan pulled tight around her breasts. Her hair, slick and dark, fell straight to her shoulders. Her angular face seemed to be faintly powdered and there was a smudged bruise of red lipstick on her mouth, despite it being just past seven in the morning. 'Come in.' Anne had immediately felt out of place in her dressing gown and thick blue pyjamas and her uncombed tangle of hair.

Charles was sitting on the end of Frieda's bed, fully clothed and cradling a green mug of coffee. There was a deep-blue Indian throw slung artfully over the sheets, with intricate patterns sewn on it in thick red thread. 'Hello there,' he said, a familiar sheepish grin on his face. The sun lit up the back of his head so that he appeared silhouetted against the window. 'Frieda offered me some of her Turkish coffee and I couldn't resist.'

'Do you want some?' Frieda asked, eyebrows raised.

'Um, no thanks,' said Anne, sitting down beside Charles on a small corner of the bed. He did not move to make room for her, she noticed, nor did he touch her as he usually did. 'I might try and get back to sleep, actually.'

Frieda laughed. 'It's amazing to me how you manage to sleep for so long, Anne. I love this part of the day: the freshness of the air. It feels more, more . . . alive, somehow.' She swept up her long hair and pinned it back in front of the small mirror on the back of the door. 'I can't imagine dying in the mornings.'

Anne rolled her eyes imperceptibly. Frieda was always so unnecessarily dramatic, so unrelentingly dark and solemn. She thought it was something to do with her exotic upbringing – her father was a diplomat and Frieda had grown up in various far-flung countries, never settling in one place for long. She had once, in a rare moment of confession, admitted to Anne that this made it difficult for her to keep friends.

'I know exactly what you mean,' said Charles. Anne looked at him with undisguised surprise. He hated mornings, she thought. He could quite happily spend the whole day in bed, reading newspapers and eating toast. But she didn't say anything.

There was a strange little silence. The room felt shrunken and airless, infiltrated with a creeping sense of awkwardness. Anne looked at Charles sideways. He was staring straight ahead, his eyes resting on the nape of Frieda's exposed neck, sipping his coffee quite calmly.

'Well, then. I might go back to bed,' she said in a final desperate attempt to stem the flow of silence that oozed between them. She got up and reached an arm down towards him.

'Charles?'

He looked up at her. 'Yes?'

'Are you coming?'

He smiled at her, a touch of condescension in his eyes. 'Actually, I might stay here and finish this,' he said, lifting up his mug. 'If that's all right with you,' he added, and she felt he was making fun of her.

'Of course.' She tied the flannel belt tight around her waist and walked out, closing the door behind her to the soft murmur of their voices.

A bit later, when she was fitfully dozing back in her own bed, Charles came in and snuggled up beside her. He put his arm along her waist, his fingers gently stroking her hipbone. 'Hello,' he whispered, holding her tighter, and Anne smiled to herself and thought she'd been overly sensitive about the whole thing. She'd probably still been half-asleep. She took a deep breath. Nothing to worry about, after all.

'Hello.'

So then everything was all right again, at least for a while.

Charlotte

C HARLOTTE WAS AT THE office when her mother rang.
'Charlotte?'

'Yes,' she replied, trying to keep her voice low so that none of her colleagues would hear it was a personal call. 'What is it?'

'Nothing important, just thought I'd catch you if you weren't too busy.'

Charlotte clenched her jaw. Unthinkingly, she started scratching the tender patch of flesh just behind her earlobes. Her mother's insistence on calling her at work was a source of constant irritation. She had told her several times not to do it because it was an open-plan building and she was conscious that everyone could hear her murmured replies to Anne's familiar litany of daily complaints – workmen who hadn't turned up, weeding that had yet to be tackled, a brand of washing powder that the supermarket had discontinued for no reason, and so on. At least when Anne called on the mobile, Charlotte could recognise the number and choose to ignore it. At work, there was no escape.

'I am in the middle of something, actually,' said Charlotte, almost whispering. From across the room, Sasha, the perpetually nosy office secretary, strained to look over the felt-board partition like a meerkat scanning the landscape for food. Charlotte turned the swivel chair away from her.

'Oh. Well, I don't want to bother you.' But the way that Anne said it managed to convey exactly the opposite – she employed a wheedling, semi-offended tone that always made Charlotte feel terribly guilty. It was at times like these that Charlotte wished she had a brother or a sister to share the exhausting obligations of being Anne's child.

She blew her cheeks out silently so that her mother would not hear the resigned exhalation of her breath. She checked herself. Why was she being so unsupportive? Clearly, Anne needed someone to talk to, Charlotte told herself. Charles's accident had taken them all unawares but Anne had seemed especially dazed by it. She found herself thinking of that strange morning, some months ago, when Anne had presented Charlotte with her engagement ring. She had never worn it. The mere thought of that unblinking ruby made her shudder. But clearly there had been something going on with Charles; something not altogether pleasant. She sat up briskly and resolved to be kinder, more patient, more willing to listen.

Charlotte clicked on her mouse and minimised the typed document she had been working on so that it shrank to a thin sliver of grey at the bottom of the screen. Sasha had dropped back behind the partition, her eavesdropping attempts clearly frustrated. Charlotte felt a small pang of triumph.

'No, no, it's fine, Mum,' she said, deciding that the least she could do was to give Anne five minutes of her time. 'It's not too urgent.'

'Are you all right?'

Charlotte tried to keep her exasperation in check. This was a familiar tactic of her mother's, and the more she denied that anything was wrong, the more Anne became convinced she had uncovered some dark awfulness that Charlotte was not admitting to anyone else.

'Yes, I'm fine.'

'You're sounding very flat.'

'I'm at work, Mum.'

'Are you sure that's all it is?'

'Yep.'

There was a pause.

'You know, if you don't want to talk to me you only need to say so . . .' Anne let the sentence trail off.

Charlotte held her breath.

'It's absolutely not that,' she said, with as much cheerfulness as she could manage. 'How are you?'

'Oh, I'm all right. Bearing up. The hospital visits are rather wearing, I must say. I think it's the driving there and back that takes it out of me and, of course, Janet and I had to cancel our Paris trip so that's something else to deal with on top of everything.'

Charlotte twisted the phone cord in one hand, mentally zoning out. Her stomach rumbled and she began thinking about what to have for lunch – there was a café she had recently noticed nearby and she wanted to try it out. It was a traditional London greasy spoon, of the sort that she thought had ceased to exist with the advent of coffee-shop chains and oversized bookstores with 'break-out' armchair areas. She started imagining a jacket potato with melted cheese and cheap mugs of strong tea and then she realised her mother was still talking.

'. . . no idea about the prognosis. I always told him to wear that blasted cycling helmet. Always. But he was so stubborn. He'd never listen to me. Or to anyone, for that matter. Not an easy person, your father.' She let the comment filter though and then added: 'But then you know that already.'

They lapsed into a short silence. Anne's conversations normally led this way – no matter what she began talking about, the subject matter would slide inexorably towards Charles. Charlotte was fed-up of hearing about her father's shortcomings, partly because she was only too aware of them herself, but also because she thought that if her mother genuinely felt this strongly then she should have walked out years ago. It was as if the constant examination of Charles's faults fed into Anne's sense of self, enabling her to ignore her own. The familiar nit-picking seemed to have become integral to Anne's own identity, as though she would cease to exist without being able to define herself in opposition to something. And while she clearly sought Charlotte's sympathy for all that she had to put up with, the truth was that Anne was fuelled by her own unhappiness. She relied on it. Charlotte was pretty sure her mother wasn't the easiest person to live with either.

She had never voiced these thoughts to Anne, but they skulked beneath everything Charlotte said; a shadowy, irresistible undertow that pulled her words out of shape and twisted her sentences so that nothing that came out of her mouth seemed able to convey how she genuinely felt. She tried to quell the frustration she felt tighten in her chest.

'Mum,' she said, as pleasantly as she could, 'he's lying comatose in a hospital bed.'

'I know that,' said Anne sharply. 'I'm just saying, it's been an exhausting few days.'

'Yes, I know. But he didn't have the accident just to annoy you.'

There was a lethal quiet on the end of the line.

'Right, well,' Anne said crisply, 'there was a reason I was ringing you.'

'OK.'

'I'm clearing out the house and I notice there are still boxes of your stuff in your old room.'

Charlotte thought of her childhood bedroom, the single bed in the corner with the pink-and-blue duvet patterned with dancing figurines, the small cabinet piled high with books and the motley assortment of patched-up teddy-bears. She could smell it: the instantly recognisable aroma of lavender pillows and sharpened pencils and toast being made in the kitchen below. She felt her throat constrict with an inexplicable sadness.

'Is there anything you want to hold on to?' Anne asked. 'If not, then I can take a load to the Red Cross, but there might be some things in there that you'd like.'

Charlotte dragged her mind back to the conversation. She knew she should be aghast that her mother was clearing out the house when her father was in a coma, teetering between life and death, but she wasn't, not really. Anne had a curious capacity for detachment and Charlotte knew, from years of experience, that there was little point in trying to penetrate the carapace of her coolness. It was her way of coping. Charlotte held her breath. She sensed that Anne was issuing her with a challenge, was seeking to push her to the brink of something, to goad her into a reaction. She did not want to give into it.

'No, don't throw anything out. I'll come round and sort it out.'

'When?'

'As soon as I can manage it.'

'Well, it would be nice to know in advance.'

'I'll let you know,' Charlotte replied brusquely. 'Listen, I've got to go.'

'Yes, yes, I've taken up enough of your time.'

Don't rise to it, Charlotte thought. Just don't do it.

'Bye, Mum. Nice to chat.'

'Bye, Charlotte. Do let me know when you're coming round, won't you?'

Anne hung up. Charlotte stayed motionless with the receiver pressed to her ear and listened to the reassuring crackle of the dialling tone for several minutes.

The rest of the day turned out to be an accumulation of petty irritations. She found that she could not shake the discomfort of her conversation with her mother or the thought that the family home was being disembowelled of memories, that Anne was somehow preparing herself for Charles's permanent absence. She tried to talk herself out of such a fanciful notion, but once it had taken hold, she found that it coloured her mood so that every subsequent thought that passed through her mind disquieted her.

On the way back, she snapped at someone on the Tube for accidentally standing on her foot. She felt at once too hot and too cold, and when she walked down the stairs at East Putney station, she found that she could barely summon up enough energy to get to the bottom.

Charlotte was already dreading the evening: she was going to a private view with Gabriel and she could feel herself slipping helplessly into fractiousness.

She was determined not to have a row. As she got ready, she made a series of increasingly ludicrous bargains with herself: she would restrict herself to two drinks; she would let anything hurtful that was said skim over the surface of her consciousness; she would be mature and thoughtful and wise and she would tackle any issues that arose in the sobriety of the following morning. Above all, she thought to herself as she dabbed at her lips with a gloss that tasted like burnt caramel, she would rise above it – the whispered criticisms, the implied insults, the cold shoulders and the knowing half-stares from Gabriel's disapproving friends – because she, Charlotte Redfern, knew that he loved her above all else.

'Nothing else matters,' he told her, sensing her unease as they climbed into the back of a black cab. 'Stuff happens. People have to get used to it. Besides, it's nothing to do with them.' He took her hand in his and drew her over to his side of the seat. She noticed that he smelled faintly of toothpaste. 'I love you above all else. You know that, don't you?'

'Yes,' she said, and she meant it.

As the cab juddered its way across Hyde Park Corner to the art gallery where one of his friends was curating the exhibition, she wondered about the truth of this. She thought she knew – at least in the sense that he told her so and she believed it, although it had taken her a long time to trust him. She had known Gabriel for two years as a friend before anything had physically happened between them, and much of that time had been taken up with circular discussions about how she could ever trust him. He had been married before – unhappily, of course – and came with a chequered personal history that involved a string of ill-conceived flirtations. There had been a couple of brief affairs with trivial blonde girls, although he assured her that they hadn't 'meant anything'; that they had been symptoms of his discontent rather than being worth something in their own right. Yet his capacity for infidelity made her instantly wary of him. At the same time, she was forced to acknowledge that she was falling in love with him, and could not reconcile the two concepts. Objectively, he was entirely the sort of man she least wanted to be with. But everything he said and did overturned her supposedly infallible preconceptions. He was unlike anyone else, so disarmingly honest about his own failings and so consistent in his devotion to her, that it was difficult to resist him and impossible to protect herself from all that he promised to be.

It had been a spontaneous reaction: a feeling, as soon as they met and shook hands and sat down in the shimmering heat of a July evening, of knowing all that there was to know about each other. Part of Charlotte hadn't wanted to believe it at first because she didn't trust her own judgement that it was happening. For so long, so many years, she had wanted to feel exactly this shared recognition and to call it love. Throughout her twenties, she had projected all she most desired on to a series of not-quite-right men. The relationships had lasted two years at the most because, no matter how hard she tried, nothing ever quite seemed to live out its initial promise.

She had come to believe that love was a matter of compromise and that everyone made a similar bargain – they just didn't talk about it. At the weddings of her friends, she found herself both jealous of the occasion and astonished that anyone could actually go through with it. With every new church reading she had listened to about tree roots growing together, with each choked speech delivered by the misty-eyed father of the bride, with every first dance she had smiled and nodded through, with every scrap of confetti she had scattered on dampened tarmac, Charlotte became more and more convinced of the pointlessness of it all.

Her cynicism became its own worn-down cliché. When, last summer, her friend Susie had asked her to be a bridesmaid, she found herself dreading the prospect but said yes in spite of herself. Charlotte had been out to lunch with her mother when Susie called and, curiously, Anne had proved something of an ally.

'Another wedding?' Anne said as Charlotte slipped her mobile back into her handbag.

'Yep,' she replied, spearing an asparagus stem with her fork. 'And another bridesmaid's dress. Lemon-coloured taffeta if I know Susie.'

Anne smiled dryly. 'It's a phase. Everyone seems to get married at the same time in their twenties, but it will pass.' She took a sip from her glass of wine and looked at Charlotte sideways. 'There's no rush, you know.'

'I don't know if I ever want to get married,' said Charlotte, not convinced that she meant it. 'No one can live up to the overblown romance of a wedding.'

She expected her mother to disagree and half-wanted her to tell her not to be so pessimistic but instead Anne stayed silent, twisting the stem of the wine glass in her fingers, her eyes focused on an indistinct point just beyond the bread basket.

'I don't think soulmates really exist, do they?' Charlotte continued. 'Marriage is a transaction of mutual imperfection.'

'Oh Charlotte, where on earth did you read that?'

'Nowhere. I just made it up.'

Anne sighed and raised her eyebrows, the way she always did when she disagreed with something but could not be bothered to say why.

'So there's no such thing as true love, then?'

Charlotte pushed her knife and fork together on the plate before answering. She sensed a hidden danger beneath the surface of the conversation but was not quite sure why. 'I don't think so,' she said, cautiously. 'I think it's mostly a question of finding a man that you like, who will be good to you, who is trustworthy and with whom you can develop a quiet sort of mutual affection. Love fizzles out. You might as well resign yourself to that from the beginning.'

Anne looked at her and her face was distant and closed-off, like a stranger's. 'Well,' she said, finally. 'I suppose it's good that you have more realistic expectations than I did.' Anne drained her wine. 'Shall we get the bill?' she added, brightly.

But then Charlotte had met Gabriel. She remembered having a feeling of something like fatefulness even before she'd seen him. She just knew, somehow, that he would be important in her life. It was a work thing, at first – Gabriel was the head of a small but fashionable literary agency and Charlotte was doing the publicity for a books prize that they were part-sponsoring – but it had evolved from one post-work drink into a long evening of conversation and mutual teasing. Both of them were meant to be going on to parties. Both of them cancelled. Charlotte was immediately taken with his air of confidence and charm, the way he strode rather than walked, the way he wore an extremely well-cut navy suit over his thin cashmere green V-neck and knitted tie, as if he wasn't quite sure whether to dress like an academic or an advertising executive. She found herself wanting to reach out and touch the velveteen tuft of hair that stuck out at the nape of his neck like a feathery chicken's tail.

As he talked, he had a nervous habit of pushing his tortoiseshell glasses up the bridge of his nose more often than he needed to. His eyes were green-brown and his lips were slightly too full, like a girl's, but the combined effect somehow worked. He was the kind of person you would look at as he passed you in the street – tall and broad and filled with a dynamic energy that made you feel invigorated just to be near him.

Charlotte had been with someone at the time, a boyfriend of several months' standing – a thoroughly decent man whom she loved but didn't feel remotely passionate about. Gabriel offered the possibility of otherness. Nothing physical occurred between them, but there was always an unspoken sense of shared infatuation that made her uncomfortable.

In spite of herself, Charlotte was drawn to him – to the idea that, finally, this might be it – and yet she was simultaneously horrified at herself for her perceived betrayal, reminded of the question posed by her secondary school English teacher about Edith Wharton's *The Age of Innocence*: what was the difference between physical and emotional infidelity? And which of them, ultimately, was the more potent?

After that first meeting, Gabriel and Charlotte would see each other every few weeks, a snatched couple of hours spent in a small pub with a dark wooden interior around the back of Sloane Square Tube station. The walls were covered with a murky green-and-yellow flock wallpaper, its garishness faded by years of nicotine. Framed prints of country hunting scenes hung from the picture rail. In one corner, an old wheelbarrow had improbably been hoisted up and attached to the ceiling as rustic decor.

The pub became a sort of joke between them. It was in the middle of a wealthy residential street of neat little cottages with well-trimmed box hedges and seemed an absurd location for an old man's drinking den. It was the sort of place that, even though they both knew it was there, would take them by surprise every time they turned the corner. The pub seemed to have sprouted up from the ground just for them, illuminated like a surreal bauble for a few hours while they drank inside. There were never any other customers apart from a mustachioed Chelsea Pensioner in full uniform who sat on a high stool at the bar, drinking from his own pewter beer tankard.

'What do you think his name is?' Gabriel had asked her one night when they were carefully not sitting too close to each other, yet just close enough to feel the crackle of tension between them.

'Mmm, I think maybe . . . Richard, no, Geoffrey.'

'Geoffrey. Yes, that's a good one. I imagine he used to have a wife who complained when he forgot to shave and that's why he now takes such pride in his moustache.'

'I'm not sure he was ever married.'

'A confirmed bachelor, perhaps?'

'Or the love of his life fell for his best friend instead of him and he comes here, each evening, to forget.'

They would make up endless nonsense stories like this, to fill the space in between talking about what they both secretly wanted to confess. Once, Gabriel had taken her hand in his beneath the table and it had felt so illicit, so thrilling and so entirely how it should be that she almost couldn't breathe.

Gradually, Charlotte began to believe that he meant what he said; that he loved her in a way he had never loved before. He seemed to want her exactly as she was. She realised then that, for the first time, she was utterly, unthinkingly in love with someone and that she couldn't rationalise it or shape it to fit round her. She simply had to take the leap. Yet this terrified her because she had no faith in herself, no real belief that she was worthy enough. She found that she did not feel Gabriel's love with any inner conviction, but rather drew her conclusions logically from snippets of available evidence.

There was, deep within the folds of her own consciousness, a dark, jagged cave where Charlotte stored all her most awful thoughts. She kept it hidden away, scared of her own twisted imaginings, and, in a strange sort of way, this gave her a sense of power. If she kept it concealed, Charlotte realised that no one else could ever truly know her. And this meant that she was in control. She felt intensely vulnerable under Gabriel's scrutiny but she still had secrets from him. There was a blackness nestling within her, a poisonous seepage of self-inflicted pain that she would never expose to the light.

*   *   *

The art gallery was a single white room, dotted with rectangular plinths that rose up from the white floor like sawn-off tree trunks. To access it, you had to walk down a rickety metal fire-escape staircase and it was difficult to negotiate in heels. Just as she reached the last step, Charlotte tripped up and had to grasp hold of Gabriel's arm to steady herself, so that they ended up spilling drunkenly into the room, almost teetering off balance, and everyone appeared to stop talking at precisely the same moment. Charlotte instantly felt out of her depth. They were late – Charlotte's fault, naturally – and now she could imagine all his glamorous female friends looking at her high heels with the disapprobation mature women reserved for trivial young things like her who wore unsuitable, cheap shoes.

'Gabe!' came a screeching voice from across the room. 'Over here.'

They looked over. It was Florence, a pained-looking woman in her late thirties with a powdered face and a deep wrinkle between her plucked eyebrows. She was, as she never seemed to tire of reminding Charlotte, one of Gabriel's oldest and closest female friends. They had met when both were starting out as trainees at one of London's biggest PR firms in the early nineties and, for a brief while, had shared a flat together. It was a period of time that both of them repeatedly referred to with winks and wistful shakes of the head that signified some boring private joke.

Charlotte had once spent an entire evening with both of them during which the sight of an ashtray on a hotel mantelpiece had triggered a long-ago memory of Gabriel accidentally setting alight a curtain. The two of them were in hysterical fits of giggles even though nothing about the story was particularly funny. Charlotte had found herself laughing uneasily along with the joke, aware that Florence was deliberately pressing home her advantage: this is something I know about Gabriel that you don't, she seemed to be saying, because you will never rival me in this man's affections.

It was Charlotte's contention that Florence was secretly in love with Gabriel – a belief that he dismissed as 'absurd' any time she raised it. 'Besides,' he would say. 'Who would want to sleep with Florence? It would be like shagging a man.'

Charlotte looked at her now. She was a woman who had spent her whole life maintaining a fiction of her own appearance; a woman who cultivated extreme skinniness because it would make other women jealous rather than because it suited her. Her body was straight up and down, usually clothed in black dresses accessorised with a mad bohemian twist – belts made from Caribbean calabash gourds or necklaces woven together with bright Peruvian threads – and neat flat-soled ballet pumps tipped with velvet. Tonight, she had done something odd with her hair so that it was swept back off her high forehead and tucked behind her ears, kept in place with copious hairspray so that the blonde strands looked brittle to the touch. Two veins stood out thickly from the fleshy scrag of her neck.

'Hi, darling,' she said, kissing Gabriel on the lips. 'So what do you think of the photographs? Pretty grim, no?'

'We've only just arrived,' he replied, scanning the walls quickly, 'but they don't look too bad. I like that one.' Gabriel pointed at an overblown black-and-white study of a series of corrugated-iron shacks.

'Hmmm. Very misery chic.' Florence, who had intertwined her arm with Gabriel's during this brief exchange, smiled brightly at Charlotte as if she'd only just spotted her. 'Hi, Charlotte. How are you?'

'Good, thanks, good. Although I did almost fall on my face on the way in,' she said, giggling and simultaneously kicking herself for trying to break the ice by making herself look foolish.

'I noticed.' Florence turned away from her and towards Gabriel. 'How's tricks, Gabe? Any more news on the divorce?'

Gabriel looked taken aback. 'Oh, you know, just hammering things out.'

'Yeah, I spoke to Maya the other day and she said it was taking a while.'

'I didn't know you two were in touch,' Gabriel said, and Charlotte could see the place where his jaw twitched when he was tense.

'Listen, I'm not just going to drop her because you have. She needs support, Gabe. She hasn't found anyone new,' Florence looked at Charlotte pointedly. 'Unlike you.'

The whole evening was played out in a similar vein of extreme discomfort. The photos were dull. The company was acerbic. Every single one of Gabriel's friends, apart from the curator, who was uncomplicatedly friendly because he was drunk, had looked at Charlotte with a guardedness that was inescapable. She felt awkward and unlikeable and far too young. She had worn thick tights and the gallery was so hot that she felt herself sweating underneath the lights, her hair frizzing up and her cheeks acquiring a slippery surface sheen. She drank too many glasses of free champagne. She felt as if her forehead were tattooed with the label 'Other Woman' and sensed the unspoken accusation that she was a walking cliché: a younger model, a mid-life crisis mistress. She wanted to shake everyone by the shoulders and scream at them that it wasn't like this; it was different; something else; something more; something they could never understand.

It was a familiar resurgence: the sensation of not being good enough. Suddenly, without knowing where the image came from, Charlotte saw her father lying comatose in his hospital bed, pale and impotent, like a skinned rabbit. She shivered and then pushed the thought of him away. She did not want to think about him now.

'You're being too sensitive,' Gabriel murmured in her ear. 'Besides, it's hard for my friends to get used to it. Maybe they're a bit uncomfortable but it's nothing to do with not liking you.'

'Why do they all blame me when I've got nothing to do with it?'

'What do you mean?'

'Well, you left your wife. That's one thing. Then you got together with me. That's a whole other event. The two are not connected. You're the one that did the leaving and yet I'm the one who's seen as some brazen harpy who stole you away from your idyllic Boden catalogue family life. Jesus.' She stopped a passing canapé tray and popped a smoked salmon blini in her mouth.

'Charlotte, I'm not going to do this here.'

'Do what?' she said, through an unchewed mouthful.

'I'm not going to have this argument here in the middle of my friends.' He glanced behind her shoulder. Charlotte turned round to follow his sightline and saw Florence looking at them meaning-fully, arms crossed.

'Oh for fuck's sake,' she found herself saying without really meaning to. 'Go hang out with her and reminisce over the good old days if that's what makes you happy. I'm leaving.' She handed him her empty champagne glass, stalked to the cloakroom with as much dignity as she could muster and got her coat. She knew she wasn't really angry but rather putting on a show of what anger should look like. She thought she had a right to be angry, that she should capitalise on this, and yet, beneath it all, she just felt sad.

Her mind wandered back to the phone conversation with her mother, to the thought of her childhood bedroom denuded of all that was once hers, to the realisation that nothing she could ever do would make any of it better and she hated herself for her powerlessness, for acting how she thought she should be acting rather than behaving in the way she actually felt.

And all the while, Charlotte was fervently hoping Gabriel would follow her, wrap his arms around her and tell her he was sorry. But he never came and she left without looking back.

Anne; Charlotte

THEY SETTLED INTO AN unspoken routine at the hospital so
that the days slid into weeks and the weeks became something
approaching permanence. They discovered that it was easy – easier
than it should have been – for life to swallow up the extraordinary
and weave it into normality. Shock became a sort of weariness.
Terror became a numb suspension of time. The anxiety that had
gripped them in the immediate aftermath of his accident transmuted into a dull, nagging sensation of having to do something.
Hospital visits were no longer something to be feared, but rather
an event to be got through, ticked off as part of the day's routine.

Anne, who had never held down a permanent job, found that
it was almost a relief to have something with which to fill her
time other than the endless caffè lattes with Janet or the daytime
soaps she pretended not to watch. There was a release, too, in not
having to think of what to cook for supper. When Charles had
been awake, the constant grind of coming up with a new combination of meat and vegetables had loomed over every single day,
assuming grotesquely inflated proportions so that almost as soon
as she woke up she would start tormenting herself with visions of
lamb chops and green beans. Now, with Charles in hospital, she
picked up whatever she felt like from a Tesco Express on the way
home. She delighted in the oddness of her dietary whims. Once,
she had eaten a packet of marinated tofu and two Braeburn apples
and felt utterly content.

She visited Charles every day, so that the receptionists started
to recognise her and wave her through without asking for the

customary ID. It was a nice, private hospital with a river view over the Thames and room service menus offering glasses of Chardonnay (unoaked). The overall impression was one of an efficient business hotel, on the edge of a motorway between cities.

There was a television suspended on the wall in Charles's room that had all sorts of satellite channels that Anne did not have at home. Since he had been ill, she had become a connoisseur of trash. There was an American programme she particularly liked that was a reality search for a new fashion model. It seemed to be endlessly repeated and Anne always liked to watch the 'makeover' episode where seemingly plain-faced girls with dull eyes were transformed, by dint of hair dye and teeth whitening, into glamorous visions of fabricated beauty.

She got an illicit thrill from the certain knowledge that Charles would have hated the programme, would have sat scowling in the room, making his disapprobation painfully obvious with every heavily exhaled breath. The only television he watched was the *News at Ten* or *Panorama*, although he'd gone off the latter when the BBC cut it down to half an hour. Anything else would prompt him to launch into a critical analysis of why Anne felt she had to rot her brain by watching 'rubbish'. She had become used to recording her favourite programmes and looking at them late at night, after he had gone to bed, with the volume turned so low she had to strain to hear what the characters were saying.

Anne liked the hospital for its sense of quiet order and the wordless comfort offered by the nurses' sympathetic glances. Part of her felt she did not deserve their arm pats and smiles. Over the years, she had successfully convinced herself that Charles had become a fact rather than a person, something to be borne, to be lived with and endured rather than loved and looked after. It wasn't that she was callous. It was rather that she had had all her tenderness battered out of her. She found a sense of peace by Charles's bedside that she had not known for years. And, of course, it brought her physically closer to Charlotte.

Most of the time, they did not speak much. Charlotte would head straight for the bedside in a flurry of movement and embark on a cautious monologue of the day's events. Anne would sit in the chair by the window, pretending to look out at the river but secretly stealing glances at her daughter, noting the precise inclination of her head and listening to the easy inflections of her voice. She would try to see, without drawing attention to it, if Charlotte's eczema had flared up. Recently she had noticed a tell-tale series of vivid red dots sprayed across the crease of her daughter's elbow.

Today, Charlotte was wearing long sleeves and Anne could not see whether it had cleared up or not. She looked upset when she walked in, her eyes puffy at the corners, her face pale. Head down, she avoided eye contact.

'Hi, Mum. Sorry I'm late.'

'Don't worry. I'm sure he won't notice.' It was an attempt at levity but almost as soon as the words had left her mouth, Anne had regretted them. She heard herself sounding so bitter, so shrivelled inside and it wasn't how she wanted to be at all. Charlotte hadn't replied, instead setting her mouth in a stubborn line.

'How are things?' said Anne, desperate to make amends.

Charlotte rolled her eyes, quickly but perceptibly. 'They're fine.'

'Busy at work?'

'Yes.'

There was a strained pause. 'And . . . what about . . . Gabriel?' Anne said, barely managing to utter his name. Charlotte looked straight at her.

'He's great, thanks.' She stopped and then seemed to reconsider. 'You know, it's really obvious you don't approve of him, Mum, so you don't need to bother pretending.'

Charlotte's chin started to wobble and she turned away.

Anne was momentarily speechless. It was true that she didn't approve of Gabriel, that she didn't believe he had the character or, from what she had heard, the capacity for fidelity that she desired so desperately for her daughter. But she thought she had disguised her dislike effectively, admitting it only to Janet or, obliquely, to Charles.

'I don't disapprove of him, Charlotte,' she said, frostily. 'I don't know what gave you that idea. I've barely met the man.'

'You met him that time you came round for dinner.'

'Yes, and he spent most of the evening holding forth.'

'What's that supposed to mean?'

Anne took a sharp intake of breath. She didn't want to say something she regretted. At the same time, she found she was suddenly furious, backed into a corner against her own daughter by some interloper who wasn't even divorced from his wife yet. 'He seems to be a very self-confident individual.'

Charlotte shook her head vigorously. 'He knows himself,' she said, her voice oddly choked. 'Is that such a bad thing? At least he's not a professional victim.'

'Excuse me?'

'Oh forget it, Mum, I'm just not in the mood.'

Anne felt the hot pricking of tears, a tightening at the bridge of her nose that signified she was about to cry. She breathed in for a few seconds, digging the nail of her thumb into the palm of her hand to stop herself. Once she had regained her equilibrium, she stood up and shuffled to the door, pausing as she stepped into the corridor. 'Well, I'm sorry you feel that way,' she said, quietly. Then, faux-brightly, 'I'm going to get a coffee. Do you want one?'

Charlotte was sitting by her father's bedside, gently tugging at the edge of the sheets. She didn't even look up. 'No thanks.' The door closed. 'I wouldn't want to put you out,' she added, a beat too late for her mother to hear.

Then, as soon as she'd left the room, Charlotte started to feel the familiar waves of guilt. She shouldn't let her irritate her so. She should rise above it and remember that her mother was a lonely and embittered woman, a woman whose potential had never been realised, who had found herself trapped in marriage and motherhood without discovering fulfilment in either, a woman constantly looking for something else, something more, without the means of achieving it. Charlotte knew that her mother looked at her daughter's life with a curious mixture of wonderment and envy, regretful that she had never had the same opportunities. And it was true that Charles had made her life miserable – the affairs, the bullying, the snide comments delivered like a pinch to the flesh.

But there had always been a part of Charlotte that felt her mother deserved it. She was so constantly on the lookout for the negative in any given situation, so anxious and worried about the consequences of any decision, so determined to assume the mantel of perpetual martyr. Whereas Charles was possessed of a bluff charm, an insouciance that was attractive to those who found themselves within its orbit. He flirted with life. She shrank from it.

Above all else, thought Charlotte grimly, she did not want to end up like her mother. She wondered, not for the first time, whether part of Gabriel's attraction was Anne's disapprobation. She remembered the shock on her mother's face when she had told her he was Jewish – shock and then a hasty cover-up, a rapid rearrangement of the censorious mouth in order not to be thought 'intolerant'.

'Jewish?' Anne had said. 'How interesting.'

'Don't worry, Mum, he's not practising.'

'Why should I be worried?'

'In case you lose your nice middle-class daughter to a hirsute Hassidic gentleman who spends his summers sticking bits of paper into the Wailing Wall.'

'The thought hadn't even crossed my mind,' Anne said stiffly.

Gabriel. Even the smells and sounds of the hospital – the disinfectant, the squeak of a nurse's shoes on linoleum – failed to distract her from thoughts of him. She replayed their argument of the preceding evening as if picking a scab. She had woken up this morning, hungover and tired, fervently hoping that he would have texted her or tried to call while she was asleep. But she knew, even before she looked at her phone, that he wouldn't have done so. She felt sick in the pit of her stomach, a shivering sensation of uncertainty that plagued her for the rest of the day. She started questioning, as she always did in the wake of an argument, whether she really wanted to be with someone whose personal situation was so demanding. It would be easier to be with one of those uninspiring but simple men of her own age, with supportive families and straightforward aspirations, with uncomplicated jobs and a circle of friends she would find easy to charm.

On the drive to the hospital she had actually started mentally going through a list of her single male friends, checking each one off as unsuitable, until she realised she didn't want anyone else or that no one else would want her and this had made her feel even more depressed. By seven that evening, Gabriel still hadn't been in touch and she couldn't stop her mind festering on the whole situation, alternately angry and upset but still determined in spite of herself not to call him first.

'You're obsessed with power,' Gabriel had once said to her while they were lying in bed one lazy weekend morning.

'No, I'm not.'

'You are,' he said, half-teasing. 'You think that if you show a single tiny crack in your armour, I'll exploit it to my advantage and then you won't be in control any more.'

'That's ridiculous,' she had laughed, rolling over to kiss him on the tip of his nose.

'I'm serious. But the thing is, Charlotte . . .'

'What's the thing?' She started to tickle the flatness of his stomach.

'The thing is,' he said, clasping her hand in his to stop her, 'that being in love isn't about control. It's about the lack of it.'

And he had been right, of course, although she hadn't admitted it to him. Her exposed fragility terrified her – the thought that he could hurt Charlotte the way he had hurt Maya, his wife; the thought that he could manipulate her emotions, make her love him and then, one day, simply decide he'd had enough; the thought that although he professed to love her so profoundly, she knew that he had a whole set of secret compartments in his life where he kept his unspoken thoughts and desires; that he was quite capable of concealment if it kept the surface smooth.

Gabriel had admitted to her once that he felt no guilt over his flings with other women. If anything, he said, part of him blamed Maya for not being good enough, for not living up to the expectations he had of her. So Charlotte had instantly become frightened that she would not live up to him either and every time they had a disagreement or a shouting match, she was left overwhelmed by a ripped-up feeling of total insecurity. She would not call first, she told herself nonsensically, because she did not want him to have the power to make her feel like this. Besides, she wasn't allowed to use her mobile in the hospital. Let him wait. Let him worry for once. Let him try and get hold of her and realise she wasn't at his beck and call.

Charlotte looked at her father's impassive face, set with waxy permanence against the starchy pillow. The ventilator made a scratchy whirring sound like an air conditioning unit sucking up flies and dust. She remembered the last time she had seen him before the accident. He had emailed her at work, out of the blue, asking if she was around for dinner. It was something he never normally did and she had found herself feeling a curious mixture of dread and flattery. What on earth would they talk about all evening? Conversations with her father tended to be discourses on important topics of the day and she always felt battered into submission by his superior intelligence, by the breadth of his knowledge.

Just recently, Charlotte had begun to wonder with increasing frequency whether she had any opinions. As soon as she found she had a thought about something, she could just as easily pick holes in it. When someone challenged her, she would find herself agreeing with them and switching sides, not simply because she wanted to keep the peace but also because she genuinely believed that what they said was more convincing than anything she could come up with.

In discussions with her father, this would manifest itself in a sort of half-hearted attempt at an intelligent comment (on abortion laws, on tuition fees, on the various benefits of communism versus capitalism) and then a lapse into silence as Charles expounded his views. She was, she realised, too scared to disagree with him. It was like those sneaked childhood television sessions all over again – an encompassing sense of his brooding anger; the anxious worry that there would be an unexplained explosion of temper and that it would have to be managed or ducked or borne without expression so that she would not irritate him further.

Once, he had asked her, aged twelve, whether she believed euthanasia should be legalised. They were eating a Sunday lunch of roast chicken that, because her mother refused to cook with salt, was universally bland and watery. The meat looked greyly anaemic; the broccoli was flaccid and damp. She looked up from her plate, wide-eyed and unsure. 'I think so,' she said, almost immediately regretting having spoken.

'Why's that?' Charles had looked at her intently, his long fingers forming a steeple under his chin.

'Well, if you end up being paralysed and you've been used to being active all your life or you love horse riding, then it might be too awful to stay alive,' she paused. Charles was still looking at her expectantly. 'I suppose ... you might want to die rather than be trapped ... and ...' She couldn't think of anything else. Her mother sipped silently on a tumbler of water, deliberately not making eye contact.

Charles put down his knife and fork, balancing them carefully on the sides of his plate.

'But how would you know that they wanted to die?'

Charlotte gulped. 'They would tell you.'

'But what if they were so paralysed that they could no longer speak?'

'I don't know.'

'You don't know?' Charles said, with a strange, shapeless smile. 'Then perhaps, Charlotte, you should make an effort to find out.'

A dense silence weighed down on them. Charlotte felt her eyes filling with tears. Her mother, who noticed, started to make a noisy clatter clearing up plates.

'I haven't finished,' Charles said, resuming with his knife and fork. For several long moments, the three of them sat in perfect stillness, listening to the sound of Charles chewing, his jaw clicking like the minutes on a clock face.

The feeling of having to perform to her father's satisfaction, to proffer arguments that were coherent and well researched, to have opinions that were confidently expressed and yet subtly formed, had lasted into adulthood. As she had got older, Charlotte had acquired at least a veneer of self-possession and she knew that she was able to hold her own in conversations with Gabriel or her peers, but in front of her father, she found herself dissolving into the same sort of mute terror. There seemed to be little point in debating a topic with Charles – he was always determined to win an intellectual argument, even if his manner was more impressive than his logic. Increasingly, Charlotte preferred not to say anything, or to steer the conversation entirely in the uncontroversial direction of what was happening in *The Archers*. When she went home for Christmas, she would try to withdraw from the dining table as soon as possible under the pretence of doing the washing-up.

So the email had come out of the blue. She noticed that he had signed off 'Charles' rather than Dad – something that he had started to do in recent years, with no warning or explanation, as if he were actively trying to distance himself from fatherhood, as if he felt that theirs should now be a relationship of equals. Charlotte disliked the habit. Because, whatever else she might think of him, she still desperately wanted him to be her father. She wanted him, more than anything, to be proud of her. However much she tried to dismiss it, Charlotte realised that his opinion mattered to her above anyone else's.

They had met for dinner that evening in a small tucked-away café behind Piccadilly Circus. The interior had not been touched since the 1950s and it felt like stepping into a film set, with the formica bar, fake leather banquettes and chrome lightshades hung low over the tables on long brown wires. Charlotte ordered the cottage pie and Charles produced a bottle of wine from his briefcase because it was a place where you could bring your own. The waiter took out his corkscrew with a flourish before noticing that the bottle was a screw-top. All three of them laughed.

'I'm never sure about screw-top bottles,' said Charlotte, hoping to make the burst of good humour last as long as possible.

'I know what you mean,' her father replied agreeably. 'But I read somewhere that modern screw-tops are so precise that a winemaker can adjust the tightness of the seal to allow exactly the right amount of air into the wine without the risk of cork taint.'

Oh dear, Charlotte thought, here we go again.

But it turned out to be a surprisingly pleasant dinner. A little strained, yes, but Charles proved to be relatively easy company. He didn't say why he had suggested meeting and Charlotte did not ask, choosing to believe that this was just the type of normal thing a father and an adult daughter should be doing.

'How's Mum?' she asked dutifully towards the end of the night.

'She's fine. She's painting the study. It's her new project.' He stopped, thought for a short moment, and then added: 'How's your friend . . . Gabriel, is it?'

Charlotte was stunned. She had never, ever spoken about boyfriends to her father. She hadn't even mentioned Gabriel's name to him, aware, as she was, that she would be forced into an immediate defensive position. 'He's very well, thanks,' she answered. And then he asked for the bill and the shutters slammed down on that brief moment of intimacy.

Later, as they made their way outside to a night sky lit up by the flashing neon Fuji and Coca Cola hoardings, there was an oddly charged atmosphere between them. As they walked, her father seemed to be standing slightly too close to her, his shoulder level with her chin, the thick felt of his coat rubbing up against the sleeves of her jacket. He was close enough that she could smell the wine on his breath, mingling with the lactose tang of the crème brulée he had ordered for pudding.

'I'll hail you a cab,' he said.

'No, honestly, there's no need. I can get a Tube from Green Park.'

'I want to get you a taxi. I'll pay.'

'It's not the money . . .' she protested, but then he turned suddenly to face her, grabbing her by the wrist so that she almost tripped over the pavement kerb. He stared at her so intently that the clear, light blue of his eyes seemed almost to dissolve into tiny pixellations of colour, before coalescing again into something darker, something hidden and unspoken. 'What?' she said and she noticed she was trembling. The bitter wind blew her hair across her face with such force it felt like a slap. There was the sound of a faraway siren, a hideous catcall that slipped gradually into the distance.

'Charlotte . . .' His hand was still around her wrist. She could feel his thumb pressing down on her veins, leaving its imprint on her flesh. He was clasping it more and more tightly, his fingers opening and closing on her arm with an insistent, uncomfortable motion, as if kneading resistant dough. She began to feel scared and then, without knowing where it came from, she started to cry. A whimpering sound bubbled up from her throat and when she heard it, she wondered who had made the noise.

'I didn't mean to hurt you,' he said and his voice was absolutely level, clear and consistent, as it had always been. 'Do you understand?'

She nodded her head, incapable of speaking. He leaned forward, taking her other wrist in his right hand, and she felt his strength and his power and his protection and his danger all at once. She felt everything that had always made her so terrified and simultaneously so admiring of him, and she knew she was trapped, yet again, in a snare of her own making. He leaned forward. She was crying. He leaned forward. He drew her close and all at once his face was on hers, his tongue squirrelling in between her closed lips, the taste of his wetness at the back of her throat. She could hear him groaning softly, as if in relief. It lasted seconds. He pulled back and dropped her wrists.

She noticed the line of his mouth was crooked and his lips shiny with saliva. She felt the familiar disgust, the sense that she was somehow to blame. He tried to reach out and touch her hair. She turned away. She didn't run, but she walked so quickly that her breath was ragged and wheezy by the time she got to the Tube. She noticed that she had stopped crying but she could feel the thudding beat of her heart all the way home.

A few days after that, Charles had been knocked off his bicycle and Charlotte had an excuse for not thinking about what had happened. She parcelled the incident up and pushed it far back into the recesses of her mind. She pretended everything was as it was. Or as it should have been. She acted out the part of a dutiful daughter with surprising facility – it was easier to like her father when he was physically incapable of action or speech, she thought dryly – and a part of her knew that this is what her mother was doing too. They were both playing their roles as they usually did and there was an obscure sort of comfort in their mutual lack of closeness; the unspoken acknowledgement of what was really going on.

And so, just for the moment, Charlotte deliberately chose not to think about that night in Piccadilly. She knew, without much self-examination, that it would lead to thinking about other, more troubling, thoughts that she did not want to admit existed. She was not ready to give shape to the darkness inside. Not yet. Not just yet.

Anne walked back into the room carrying two polystyrene cups, steam smoking out of them. 'I thought I'd get you one in case,' she said, unsmiling, her eyes cold behind the smudged lenses of her glasses.

'Thanks,' said Charlotte, sliding her chair away from the bed and taking the cup in her hand.

Neither of them said anything else. They both knew there would be no spoken apology. That wasn't their way. Instead, it would be left hanging, unresolved but tacitly dealt with by way of a silent compromise.

'Janet called while I was getting them,' said Anne.

'Oh yes. How is she?'

'Chatty as ever. She wanted to see if I would go with her to some choral concert that's happening in Wilton Place.'

'That sounds great,' said Charlotte, without much enthusiasm. 'Are you going to go?'

'I'm not sure I feel up to it, what with all this . . .'

There was a long pause. Charlotte knew she was meant to offer sympathy, that this was a tactic to get her on side, but she simply ignored it. Anne sipped at her coffee uneasily.

'The whole thing is exhausting, it really is. All this driving to and from the hospital, endless traffic and the amount of people wanting to have updates on his condition – I'm on the phone constantly whenever I'm in the house.'

'You're a saint, Mother,' Charlotte said under her breath.

'It's all right for you, Charlotte, because you have your job. You get to go to the office every day and I daresay it takes your mind off things. You have work to keep you busy. I don't have anything like that. I wish I could think of a little part-time job, just as a sideline, just to do something worthwhile. But here I am, stuck in this place with your father in limbo. Goodness knows what the doctors think is going to happen.'

Anne heard herself speaking, her voice curiously detached from her insides, a shrill and unfamiliar sound. She wasn't sure why she was saying all of this apart from a wish to make Charlotte think well of her, to ensure her daughter knew that at least she tried. Anne always felt so ashamed of never having had a proper job and was deeply admiring of Charlotte's professional success but whenever she attempted to voice either thought, it came across as a sort of festering resentment.

'Mum, you always do this.'

'I always do what?'

'This. This constant harping on about how much you have to deal with, about how you wish your life was different. You keep asking me what you should do as a part-time job and I come up with suggestions and every time I say something, you dismiss it.'

Anne shifted in her chair, her chin dropping down to her chest. Charlotte looked at her sitting by the window and briefly touched her knee, withdrawing from the physical contact almost as soon as it had been made. 'I'm sorry, Mum. I'm just . . . well, I'm worried about you, obviously, and it's been a tricky day. I think I'm a bit stressed.'

Anne looked at her daughter, at her drawn face and her anxious eyes, at the faint frown line that extended all the way across her brow, and she felt a sharp internal pain. She wanted, more than anything, to take her in her arms and feel the soft curls of her hair against her cheek.

'You should take things more easily.' Anne couldn't think of anything else to say. She was worried, if she said anything more, that the febrile peace would be broken, that she would once again unwittingly talk herself into a corner and attract Charlotte's impatience, or worse, her derision.

'I know, Mum. I know.' And Charlotte turned away from her, so that Anne could no longer see her daughter's face.

Anne; Charles

THEY GOT ENGAGED THE month before graduation. Charles went about everything in precisely the right way – asking for her father's consent, getting his grandmother's ruby ring adjusted so that it slid snugly on to her fourth finger and then, eventually, dropping to one knee in the Grantchester fields where they had taken their first bicycle ride together.

She knew what he was going to say before he uttered the words and although she had looked forward to this moment for the two years they had been together, although a part of her had known all along that it would lead to this conclusion and had imagined the joy she would feel, she was surprised to discover that her smile was the forced, slightly rubbery kind that made her cheeks ache. It hung shapelessly on her lips for a few seconds before slipping off her face like a frayed silk dress from a hanger.

'Will you marry me?' Charles had said, his face tilted upwards, his hand extended to take hers in his. He looked vaguely ridiculous in this chivalrous pose – it seemed so false, so anachronistic, somehow – and yet Anne never for one moment thought of saying anything other than 'Yes'.

But once she had uttered the word, a curious silence fell between them, and she realised quickly that Charles was looking at her expectantly, as if he wanted her to say something that displayed rather more gratitude or emotion.

'Yes, darling Charles,' she said, pulling him up. 'Yes, yes, yes.'

He stood up beside her, his shoulders level with her nose and she could breathe in the burnt tang of tobacco mingled with a slight dampness, as if his clothes had not been left out to dry properly. She snuggled into his chest and he put his arms around her, kissing the top of her head as though it was a reward.

'You'll be a good wife,' he said, and she thought fleetingly what a curiously belittling phrase it was to use, as if her wifeliness existed as a sort of separate entity from her womanliness.

'I hope so,' she giggled. And then he had taken the ring out of his inside jacket pocket and all at once she recognised a swell of excitement and was able to smile properly at last without the feeling of watching herself. It was the right decision. She thought to herself that she had never been so happy than standing here by the riverbank with Charles, a man who was desired and handsome, who was clever and self-assured, who was so physically broad that she felt protected by his sheer physicality, and a man who was now, indubitably, without question, hers.

On the walk back to Newnham, Anne convinced herself of how wonderful it all was. She had always imagined she would get married and now, here it was – the chance to tie things up neatly, to become a wife, a married woman, a person of status and maturity, to make a home, to sleep in a double bed, to be adult and calm and to gain wisdom through the years by the fireside, to settle down and have children, to grow old together, to tend to her garden just like her mother did, pruning roses with secateurs before emerging, pink-cheeked, to prepare a roast Sunday lunch that her father would always say was the best Sunday roast he'd ever tasted. It was, she thought to herself, all she had ever wanted.

So why was there this low murmur of uncertainty in her heart? Was it simply because the things one looked forward to so much always ended up being an anti-climax? Yes, she supposed, that's exactly what it was. Everyone must feel a bit like this when they've just made such a life-altering decision. It was only natural for the logical side of one's brain to question, to rein in the joyful emotions that otherwise might overwhelm her. Perhaps pure happiness always had to be diluted by common sense, she thought, in order to make it digestible. Reassured by her own explanation, Anne dismissed her caution. They should be celebrating.

She glanced sideways at Charles, his profile set against the low blue of the dusky sky.

'What are you thinking?' she asked, lightly.

'Hmmm?' He turned and looked at her vaguely.

'What's going on in that head of yours?'

'I was just wondering how quickly we can get it done.'

'What?'

'The wedding.'

'Oh,' said Anne, momentarily taken aback. Then she thought, well, why wouldn't he want to be married as soon as possible? There was no reason to wait around unnecessarily, was there? Not when they both knew what they wanted and how in love they were with each other. 'Can't you wait to be married to me?' She smiled coquettishly.

He grinned at her, ruffling her hair. 'No, that's it exactly. I need my Anne by my side. I don't want to hang around and watch you get scooped up by some other young reprobate.'

She laughed. 'That's ridiculous.'

'You have no idea how easy it is for men to fall in love with you,' he said. 'You're an unwitting flirt.'

'And you make a very poor reprobate.'

The slight unease that had settled seemed quietly to drift away. He pulled her to him and kissed her, his arms so tightly clasped around her back that she could feel his muscle and the faint outline of his rib cage pressing into her breasts. He drew back.

'But now no one else can have you.' He tickled a finger beneath her chin. 'Because you're mine.'

'Yes, Charles. Yes, I am.'

In the coming weeks, as Anne arranged the church, the dress, the flowers and the finger buffet reception, people she knew would repeatedly remark on how 'radiant' she looked. With each new person she told, she gained an incremental measure of conviction. She noticed, with her single female friends, that a transient look of mild jealousy would pass across their faces as they congratulated her and she enjoyed the sense of superiority this gave her; the sense of living life on a level that they had not yet reached. Sometimes she would stare at her engagement ring for several long minutes until its shape warped in front of her eyes and it became watery and dark, the glistening red jewel leaving its imprint on the darkness of her eyelids when she blinked. She practised her married name, saying it out loud in the mornings in front of the basin mirror and writing her signature with a new flourish of pride. She was going to be Mrs Charles Redfern and she wanted nothing more.

Everyone expected her to be happy and so, because she was used to meeting expectations, she was. She did not allow herself to question this because, after all, cold feet were natural in the run-up to a wedding and it was normal for a bride-to-be to feel nervous, a little unsure of things. Normal. Usual. To be expected. It was what she wanted. It was how it was meant to happen. It existed and it was there to be got on with. She was lucky. Lucky and, as she told anyone who would listen, terribly, terribly happy.

It was Frieda who sounded the only false note. The two of them had grown apart over the last year. It had been an imperceptible distancing and one that Anne had never quite admitted. It was, she told herself, the usual story of a university friendship forged in freshers' week: it had started out as a companionship of necessity and of mutual insecurity that, once they realised they had little in common beyond their newness in an unfamiliar place, drifted into a milder sort of acquaintance.

Charles had occasionally remarked that she didn't seem to see much of Frieda any more. Anne would reply with a sort of airy nonchalance, as if she hadn't noticed.

'You two used to be thick as thieves,' Charles said one day, sitting at his desk, which was covered with bits of paper and library books with bent, open spines. A mug of coffee had left a ring-mark on the dulled leather worktop. His battered tweed jacket was slung over the back of his chair, one shoulder sagging off the side, the arm trailing on the floor. A Roberts radio, encased in thick beige leather, was tuned into Radio 4. Although it was after 10, Anne was still in bed, her limbs stretched out with the indolence of a sunny Saturday morning.

'Oh, not really,' she said, yawning slightly. 'We don't have all that much in common.'

'I thought you got on with her?'

'Hmmm? Well, yes, I got on with her to an extent. You know, she was perfectly fine to go to parties with or to see around college, but . . .' Anne drifted off.

'But what?'

'Don't you think she's just a bit . . . well . . . melodramatic?' Anne made a face, deliberately trying to mimic Frieda, sucking in her cheeks, frowning and pouting slightly with an air of extreme seriousness.

Charles laughed, a low rumble that sounded like gravel and honey. Then Anne laughed too and went across to sit on his lap, her nightdress bunched up around her knees. Charles put his hand underneath the thin cotton material, laying it flat on the flank of her inner thigh. He stared down intently, looking at the movement of his hand shifting slowly upwards until the tips of his fingers reached the edge of her pubic hair. He bent his head and kissed her breasts through the nightdress, his fingers rubbing against her with an insistence that soon became monotone, almost repetitive.

'Charles.'

'Yes,' he said, still staring at his own hand, at the pinkness of his flesh dimmed through the gauzy whiteness.

'Not now. I've got to get up.'

He seemed not to have heard her and he carried on, prodding at her without looking her in the face, as if he were engaged in some scientific experiment that required exploring her insides. His finger slid in and out, in and out, in and out until she began to feel uncomfortable and she stood and walked to the other side of the room.

'Let's go out for a walk,' she said brightly.

Charles turned back to his desk without answering and started to leaf through a book.

They didn't go for a walk that day.

Although they were no longer close, Anne had made a point of telling Frieda her news. She did not acknowledge this to herself but, at some level, she knew that it was important to establish her ownership, to prove that Charles had chosen her above anyone else. She had always felt slightly insecure in Frieda's presence because of her inscrutability. Anne was easy to read; Frieda seemed to delight in impenetrability. She was, as Anne said to her more straightforward female friends, 'not a girl's girl'.

So one evening, at dinner in hall, Anne had taken her tray and sat down next to Frieda, the thin stainless steel cutlery rattling slightly as she did so. Frieda looked up.

'Anne,' she said, her face shuttered down, devoid of expression except for a wryness around the eyes. 'What an unexpected pleasure.'

'Do you mind if I sit here?' said Anne, feeling oddly nervous and simultaneously annoyed with herself for the sensation of anxiety. She was, she had to remind herself, an almost married woman. She no longer needed to feel the fluttering uncertainties of youth. She was self-possessed and sure of her place in the world. But still . . . Something about Frieda's straight-backed grace, the angular elegance that lent her every slight movement the fluency of a calligraphic brushstroke, seemed designed to intimidate. Frieda didn't have to say anything. Her enigmatic demeanour spoke for her. It made her appear prickly, almost stand-offish to other women. The girls in college regarded her warily and tended to dismiss her because they couldn't understand her. Gradually, through the three undergraduate years Anne had spent at Newnham, she noticed that the mere act of gently laughing at Frieda had forged an unspoken female solidarity among the others. It was never explicitly done. It was more a question of rolled eyes, raised eyebrows and a kind of humorous chiding – 'That sounds like something Frieda might say' was a sign that you were taking yourself too seriously; 'That's the sort of thing Frieda would wear' was a warning that your dress was too studiedly over the top.

A bit of it was jealousy. She appeared effortlessly refined: while the other girls opted for tight, flared trousers and sparkling false eyelashes, Frieda defied the prevailing fashion and wore men's jackets with vintage silk dresses. She read Simone de Beauvoir rather than Jacqueline Susann. And while Frieda might not have found it easy to attract close female friends, she had no trouble striking up intimate alliances with all sorts of men. Nor were they just any men – Frieda would seek out the most popular, most clever, most dashing, most creative, most sporty and most unusual men in Cambridge. Often, they were postgraduate students or tutors who were substantially older than her. Once, much to the astonished exhilaration of the Newnham third years, it had been a Jamaican immigrant who worked washing dishes in the Trinity kitchens.

Frieda would have afternoon coffee parties in her room, with fresh patisseries bought in from Fitzbillies cake shop, that seemed almost to be literary salons. The men would come in twos or threes, smoking and laughing, with rolled-up newspapers peeking out of their jacket pockets and carrying bunches of watery-stemmed flowers in blotted paper. They would rap their knuckles noisily on Frieda's door and she would open it and there would be a haze of steam coming from the coffee pot and the vague scent of something heady and scented – bay leaves, maybe, or aromatic cinnamon – and the men would disappear to the sound of urgent conversation and Frieda's knowing laughter. The women who shared Frieda's corridor would pretend not to be interested and yet, often, they would catch each other out, peering round their doors, straining to hear what might be going on in the secret world that lay beyond the walls; a world of the unknown, the adult, the illicit and the impossibly sophisticated.

'Of course I don't mind,' said Frieda, pushing her tray ever so slightly to one side to make room for her.

'Thanks.' Anne smiled, feeling calmer inside. 'I went for the gammon – what did you have?'

'Something entirely indistinguishable from what I had yester-day. I'm still not sure what it was.' Frieda gestured with her hands as she spoke and Anne noticed that her tapered fingernails were painted in a garish red polish. The bone on one of her wrists stood out smoothly from her pale arm, a small, hard ball of flesh.

'Haven't seen you for a while.' Frieda let the statement lie between them without elaboration.

'Yes, I've been quite busy actually, so I haven't really seen much of anyone,' said Anne, and she immediately heard herself sounding apologetic. 'I mean, I've mostly been with Charles.'

Frieda's lips curled. 'Ah yes. The charming Charles.' She turned to look at Anne, her dark-grey eyes like pools of petrol. 'How is Charles?'

'He's very well, thank you. Very well, actually.' Then she blurted out: 'We're getting married.'

The effect was immediate. Frieda pushed back her chair with such violence that it screeched against the dark parquet floor. She turned to look at Anne with what could only be described as a look of utter incredulity.

'Married?'

'Yes,' said Anne, obscurely satisfied to have provoked such an obvious reaction. She wondered, not for the first time, whether poor Frieda had an unrequited crush on Charles. Well, let her realise that it was hopeless. Charles had quite clearly picked Anne from the start. He was besotted with her. Just because Frieda had unlimited faith in her own allure did not mean that all men were so easily ensnared. To press her point home, Anne added: 'We got engaged a few weeks ago. We're getting married after we graduate. In the summer. There's a lovely church near my parents' house in Kent, so we thought . . .'

'But, Anne,' Frieda seized her hand and Anne was so taken aback by the force of it that she jumped, spilling her glass of water on to the table. 'Sorry. But Anne, have you really thought about this? I mean, really thought it through?'

'I . . . I don't know what you're talking about, Frieda. Of course I've thought about it. I've thought of nothing much else since we got together.'

'Oh Anne . . .' Frieda broke off and then turned back to the table, propping her chin up on her hands. 'It's just . . .'

'Just what?' Anne asked, not sure whether she should feel angry or alarmed.

'Look, I know we aren't as friendly as we used to be and that's fine – no,' she said, as Anne started to protest half-heartedly, 'don't be polite, that's fine. I understand that you wanted to be with Charles and, besides, I had my own things to concentrate on. But it doesn't mean I don't like you any more or that I no longer care for you.'

Anne sat slackly in her chair. She had never heard Frieda speak so openly or in such a burst of agitation.

'And all I want to ask you, Anne, is whether this is truly, deep down, what you want. Of course girls get married all the time. It's what good, decent, nice, middle-class girls like you do. But what about you, Anne? What about your degree? What use will that be now?'

It was something that had not even crossed Anne's mind until this moment. Her studies had diminished in importance since meeting Charles. Always conscientious, she carried on writing her essays and attending lectures, but she no longer felt particularly inspired by her subject or especially invigorated by the thought of doing well. It was true she had thought to herself that qualifications didn't actually matter much if she was going to marry Charles. He would be the breadwinner – in fact, he already had the offer of a job with a prestigious bank in the city that would put his Economics degree to good use. Anne would concentrate on making their home as lovely as it could be. She would have children and she would bring them up, just as her mother had done. This was what she had always believed would happen. Yes, of course she was good at the academic side of things, but although her school had pushed her to stay on for an extra term and apply to Oxbridge, she had never wanted it for herself. She had fallen into it and it had been enjoyable, mildly diverting, but nothing more. The best thing that had come of her three years at Cambridge was meeting Charles. That was all there was to it.

'I don't need to work,' Anne said, as if that were explanation enough.

'But what about your mind, your brain?' said Frieda, exasperatedly. 'Will you just stop using it and become a breeding machine?'

'Frieda, it's really none of your business.'

'I'm sorry. I simply want you to evaluate your options.'

Anne picked at the corner of her paper napkin. Spores of white flaked off it like dandruff. She had never felt her mind needed attention and thought it mildly humorous that Frieda was so earnestly anxious about it on her behalf. She and Charles did not have that sort of relationship. He didn't ask for her opinion and she didn't mind. He was the thinker and she was the doer. He got his intellectual stimulation from other quarters – from his friends, his books, his tutors – and relied on her for an unthinking emotional support. This, thought Anne, was the basis of a lasting and fulfilling partnership. She did not want to compete. She felt no need to. Anne was perfectly content not thinking about anything too much. But how to explain this to Frieda without feeling inferior? She knew Frieda would be horrified if Anne admitted she was quite looking forward to being a wife and nothing more.

'I'll always have my degree, Frieda. It's something I can go back to a bit later on. Just at the moment, though, I want to be with Charles. I want us to be married. I want to be his wife. I love him.'

Frieda sighed. 'And does he love you?'

Anne looked at her sharply. 'Of course he does.'

'Anne, I'm not saying this to make you feel angry. I'm saying this for your own good.' The sound of shrill laughter came from a gaggle of girls by the door. Frieda dropped her voice. 'I'm saying this because no one else will. No one else will be rude enough or plain-speaking enough. No one else will dare. Charles is not the right person for you.'

Anne began to tidy up her tray, intent on leaving as quickly as possible. How dare she, Anne thought. How dare this strange, ludicrous person sit there and be so obnoxious. And all because she thinks she's so much better than I am, so much cleverer, so much more mysterious. She can't bear the thought that any other woman could be wanted by such a sought-after man. She's jealous.

'I'm not jealous,' said Frieda, as if she had read her thoughts. She placed her hand gently on Anne's shoulder to make her sit for a moment longer. 'I warn you, Anne: that man is uncontainable.'

Anne stood up, so abruptly that a gust of breeze scattered the torn-up napkin over Frieda's skirt. She walked away, the clip-clop of her heels sounding out like bullet shots, across the dining hall. She did not say anything. From the outside, no one could have told she was furious. As she placed her tray on the shelf to be cleared away, she deliberately waved at a girl in her tutor's group. She could see Frieda, looking at her still, her eyes impassive and unmoving, each one a lacquered sphere of black. As Anne walked out of the dining room, she brushed a lock of hair off her forehead. Her fingers, when she looked down at them, were clammy with sweat.

Charlotte

*I*N THE END, SHE called Gabriel. It felt like a capitulation, but she had waited a whole night and day and couldn't face the thought of going to bed feeling so miserable.

Still, Charlotte thought, she could delay it as long as possible, just to see if he called her first. So once she got back from the hospital, she ran herself a bath that was too hot to sit in comfortably. Yet she wanted to feel the slight prickliness of the heat as if to persuade herself she still existed. She swallowed big gulps of steam, clearing the back of her throat and her sinuses. She splashed water over the bathmat and the floor as she scrubbed her arms and legs with a rough loofah that was starting to go a mouldy black around the edges.

Then she rested against the bath's smooth enamel and closed her eyes. Her hair lay gleaming, flat against her scalp, smelling faintly of eucalyptus. But she couldn't take her mind off the fact that she wanted to call or the lingering feeling of guilt about how horrible she'd been to her mother in the hospital. She picked up the magazine that had come free with her Sunday newspaper. For a few desultory minutes, Charlotte read about this year's new trouser shape and a feature entitled 'I Was Stalked By My Future Husband'. The glossy paper became crinkled with moisture. The ink started to bleed on to the tips of her fingers. Charlotte threw it aside, impatiently.

She stretched her arm out of the bath, dried her hands on the towel that hung nearby, and reached for her phone. Charlotte frequently made calls in the bath – a habit that had resulted in several mobiles falling from her grasp into a watery mass of bubbles. The staff at her local Carphone Warehouse knew her by name, such was the frequency of her demands for a handset upgrade.

No text message. Nothing. She wasn't particularly surprised. She called his number and the ringing tone sounded loudly in her eardrum, echoing off the tiled walls. It rang and rang and then clicked into his answerphone.

'Hi, it's . . . er . . . Gabriel here.'

She hated his voicemail message. That little hesitation always sounded so contrived, as if he wanted the world to think he was perpetually slightly offhand and too busy to answer your call. Charlotte hung up. Then she dialled his number again. The same ringing. The same answerphone message. She hung up. Then called again. Where the hell was he?

She ran through the options in her head. It was 10.45 on a Wednesday night. That meant it was not yet closing time – he could be having a drink in a pub with friends, she thought. But which friends? He hadn't told her he was due to meet anyone. And Gabriel didn't normally like to drink more than one or two pints on a week night. Unless, of course, he was having fun. Unless he hadn't noticed the time go by. Unless he was with someone so scintillating that he didn't want to leave.

Her thoughts started to spiral. What if he was with another woman? What if he'd got drunk and thought Charlotte was annoyed with him and had gone off with someone else out of spite? What if he'd gone out with Florence and she had persuaded him to ditch Charlotte and go back to his wife? What if he was with his wife right now, asking for her forgiveness? What if Charlotte had been monumentally stupid and naive? What if she'd trusted some- one who was fundamentally crooked inside and all those people – her friends, her mother – all of them had been right to warn her against getting involved? How could she possibly face up to them?

She took a sip of her hot chocolate in an attempt to calm down. She knew that her mind could occasionally get like this – over- heated and irrational – and that the only way to calm her rising panic was to try and talk herself out of it logically. When Charlotte worried too much as a child and was unable to sleep owing to her fretfulness, her mother had told her that if she was thinking the worst, it was unlikely to happen because the worst would always be unexpected.

She tried to reassure herself with this but it didn't work. Why couldn't she be the normal, easy-going type of woman who never gave this sort of thing a second thought? Why was she automatically suspicious, jumping to the worst possible conclusion, torturing herself with her own inadequacies? Why did she get so eaten up by insecurity when there was absolutely nothing to feel insecure about? Gabriel loved her, so why would he risk losing her? Question after question piled up inside, each one weighted down with the same unanswerable gloom. Why would he go to all that effort to persuade her he meant what he said when he could far more easily have enjoyed a string of meaningless affairs?

But then, Charlotte knew that men were unpredictable creatures when it came to the sating of their own desires. How could she possibly believe Gabriel possessed any degree of restraint when his past history proved otherwise? How could she expect any man to be monogamous when it just wasn't in their make-up? She was always being told it in different ways: in books, on television, in magazines that printed quizzes to help you work out if your lover was being unfaithful. Just the other day, a red-top tabloid had published yet another exposé of a cheating celebrity chef who was supposed to have the perfect marriage. How could she trust anyone if the untarnished surface image, the one she so wanted to believe, was actually a lie?

She felt her mind contract, the thoughts unfurling and multiplying and gradually swallowing her consciousness. She felt her chest grow tighter and she could make out the indistinct shape of something in the corner of her eye, an image that was struggling to become clear like a fuzzy photographic negative gradually shifting into focus. There was a darkened room with a bed in one corner. There was a bright, silvery flash that she couldn't quite make out. There were dark shapes and movement and the feeling of being too hot and then too cold. There was an indistinct sound, a sort of metallic tinkle and there was a pervasive smell of burnt toast. For a while, Charlotte lost her bearings, conscious only of the cold sensation of a sort of fear heightened by familiarity. She knew, without choosing to know, where this was leading.

The phone rang. Gabriel's name flashed up on the screen. Charlotte grabbed the phone with wet, shrivelled fingers. 'Hello?'

'Hi. It's me. I had a couple of missed calls from you.'

'Yes,' Charlotte replied, determined to be as aloof as possible. In the background, there was the tinny sound of a Tube platform being announced. She could make out the noise of a train whooshing past, windows rattling.

'Weeeelll, here I am calling back. What's up?'

It was typical of him to assume this air of studied insouciance, thought Charlotte, so that she was the one who ended up sounding both unreasonable and hysterical.

'What do you mean what's up? I haven't heard from you in over a day,' she said, trying to keep her voice from becoming too shrill.

'Yeah, and if you remember, that was because you walked out on me at the opening.'

'Only because you were being so sodding unreasonable.'

'Don't swear at me.'

'I wasn't swearing. I said fucking sodding.'

'I'm telling you, Charlotte, don't swear at me –' She started to protest, talking over him and getting more and more angry as she did so. 'And don't talk over me either. Do you want to listen to what I have to say or don't you?'

'If it's an apology.'

'An apology?' Gabriel raised his voice in incredulity. He started speaking more quickly, so Charlotte knew he was genuinely furious and immediately regretted having made him so. Instantly, even though they were mid-argument, she wanted to turn round and apologise and smooth it over and make everything all right. She was scared of Gabriel being angry. Scared of what it meant about her. Scared of losing him because she made him so unhappy. Scared of being such a fuck-up that she would push away the one man she had ever truly loved.

And yet, she couldn't explain it to herself, there was another side of her which wanted to push, push, push until she won the argument and forced him to admit he was wrong.

'Yes, Gabriel,' she enunciated his name with the precision of a schoolteacher talking to a naughty child. 'An apology. How do you think I felt the other night when –'

He cut her off, shouting out his words. 'Let me remind you, Charlotte, that you were the one who blew up in the middle of the evening without warning. You were the one who accused all my friends of slighting you or insulting you. You were the one who said how awful it was being "the other woman" and having to cope with awful me and my awful back history and my awful ex-wife. You always do this. You always make everything revolve around you –'

The injustice of this was so acute that Charlotte cried out, but Gabriel ignored her. 'And it doesn't, Charlotte. There are other people with other lives and other problems and they have shit to deal with, too. And I know you're going through an awful time with your father and everything, and I feel for you, I really do, but it's not a fucking excuse –'

'Don't swear at me,' said Charlotte, because it was an easy point to score.

'Don't be so childish. My friends, although it might have escaped your notice, are finding this whole separation from Maya very hard too. They've known her for years. Of course they're going to feel loyal to her. Of course they're going to find it odd meeting my new girlfriend –'

'Oh, so I'm your new girlfriend, am I? How many others have there been?'

'I don't know what you're talking about. You should listen to yourself. You know that I love you. You know that. Why isn't that enough for you?'

Charlotte, disarmed by his burst of emotional honesty, felt her throat stiffen and clog so that she couldn't speak easily. 'Why don't you stand up for me?' she asked, plaintively.

She could hear Gabriel exhaling deeply on the other end of the line. 'How could I have done more? I've done everything I said I would. I've been totally consistent in what I've said to you. I don't know how I can prove myself any more than I already have.'

'It's not about proving yourself.'

'Yes, yes, it is, Charlotte. You constantly beat me over the head with my past. Well, it happened. I don't like it, but there it is. It happened and I feel shitty about it and I wish I hadn't done the things I'd done but I hadn't met you then and I can't carry on apologising. I can't be the one who convinces you this isn't going to fail. You have to do that yourself.'

There was a long silence, interrupted only by the soft dripping of the tap.

'Are you in the bath?' he asked and his voice seemed kinder, more his own.

'Yes.' Charlotte wiped away the tears that she noticed were running down her face. She hoped he couldn't hear her crying. 'I'm sorry,' she whispered.

'Look, you don't need to be sorry. I know it's hard. Especially with everything else on your plate at the moment.'

'I'm sorry I'm so useless,' she said, aware of how self-pitying she sounded.

'Sweetheart, you're very far from useless. I just wish you had a bit more faith in yourself. In us.'

'I do have faith in us.'

'Yes, but perhaps not enough. Not as much as I have.'

She wanted to make a joke, to inject a little burst of levity into the conversation that would bring Gabriel closer to her, that would make him laugh and love her all over again, but she couldn't think of anything to say, so she just let his words hang mid-air.

'I miss you, Charlotte.'

'I miss you too,' she said, depleted of energy. 'Do you want to come over?' Since moving out from the marital home several months earlier, Gabriel had been renting out a friend's spare room in Pimlico. There was an unspoken assumption that Charlotte would never stay over. She got the impression from Gabriel that it wouldn't be appropriate, that it would raise more questions than it answered.

'No, that's a nice thought, but I'm shattered. I think I might just head back and hit the hay.'

'OK,' she said, adding as nonchalantly as she could: 'Where have you been tonight, anyway?'

'Oh, just out with Florence. She called up at work today to see if I was free, so we grabbed something to eat.'

'How is she?' said Charlotte, brushing aside her welling sensation of mistrust.

'Fine, fine. Good actually. She's seeing a new bloke.'

Charlotte broke into a grin. 'That's fantastic.'

She turned on the hot tap with her toe and Gabriel laughed as he heard the water splashing. She felt warm again and hopeful and at the same time determined that everything from now on would be better than it had been before. She shut her eyes and listened to Gabriel's voice and she smiled with relief. Her thoughts were once again back under control.

Charlotte

S HE HAD NEVER BEEN properly ill before. She had read about it
in books, of course, about the onset of fever and the chills and
the shakes that frail female heroines and governesses contracted
when they had been out in the cold for too long without a shawl.
But Charlotte had never had the flu, only colds and sniffles, and
now here she was, aged twelve, finally suffering from her first
unarguable dose of adult illness.

She felt obscurely proud despite the dizziness and the raging
temperature, as if she was going through an important rite of
passage into maturity. Her period had started a few months
earlier, much to her alarm, because the only time Anne had
tried to talk about 'becoming a woman', Charlotte had been
so mortified that she pretended she already knew all about it
from the girls at school. When the first specks of brownish-
red appeared on her knickers, she hadn't known what it was
because it didn't look like blood. She had ignored it for a while,
stuffing her pants with layers of loo roll in an attempt to disguise
the discharge. But then Anne had taken her dirty underwear
from the laundry basket to wash and, wordlessly, passed her a
packet of sanitary towels from the cupboard at the top of the
stairs that she used to store indigestion tablets and packets of
waterproof plasters.

'Here, use these,' Anne said, an impenetrable look on her face.
Charlotte took them, feeling a blush rise up her neck. She was
embarrassed but, at the same time, pleased that she was now a
woman who could share these things with her own mother.

The flu seemed to be an extension of this. One had to endure pain to become an adult, Charlotte thought to herself as she lay in the evening duskiness of her bedroom, feeling hot and cold all at once. She was exhausted and yet unable to sleep because of a perpetual throbbing behind her eyes. Her throat was dry and scratchy. The light from her bedside lamp seemed too acute, too bright, so she reached across to switch it off. This slight effort gave her a spinning head and she lowered herself gingerly back down on to her pillow, eyes closed so that she didn't have to think.

She wasn't hungry but she knew she would have to eat something to keep her mother happy. Anne had gone out earlier in the evening to one of her fortnightly bridge evenings, leaving strict instructions that Charlotte had to try and digest something – anything – to keep her strength up.

'Will you be all right?' Anne had asked, peering round the door before she left.

'Yes,' Charlotte croaked. 'I'm actually feeling a bit better.' This was not entirely true, but Charlotte thought it was the sort of thing a grown-up ill person should say. She didn't want Anne to go out but she knew she mustn't say anything because she didn't want to sound babyish. It was just that her mother was much better at looking after Charlotte than Charles was. She had a maternal sixth sense about the sort of things that were needed – a pint glass of diluted Ribena or a lavender-scented pillow to help Charlotte sleep or a bowl of home-made vegetable soup with soft chunks of comforting parsnip that melted softly on the tongue. And Charlotte had discovered that being ill brought out a protectiveness in Anne that was not normally in evidence. Over the last few days, it seemed that her mother had become noticeably more tactile. One of Charlotte's favourite things was feeling Anne's cool hand brushing across her forehead with its slightly roughened fingertips and the trace smell of lemony Fairy Liquid.

Standing at the door, Anne had smiled with an unusual tenderness, the creases on her forehead disappearing so that she looked almost pretty in the half-light.

'Well, your father is here and can make you some supper. You must try and eat something.'

'I will.'

'Good. You're an excellent patient.' Anne turned away with a little wave of the hand and Charlotte was left feeling both proud and, all of a sudden, a bit alone. She sensed a small vibration of panic in her stomach and propped herself up on her elbows.

'Bye, Mummy,' she said, as loudly as she could manage so that her mother would hear it before she disappeared. She stared at the closed bedroom door, half-willing Anne to come back through it.

But instead, Charlotte could make out the sound of her footsteps going down the stairs and then a muffled conversation with her father in the kitchen below and the starting-up of a car engine and then she was gone.

She said she felt like toast for supper.

'Nothing else?' asked Charles. 'Are you sure?'

Charlotte nodded.

'All right then. A round of toast coming straight up. Do you want anything on it?'

'Just butter, please.'

But then, after a few minutes of clattering downstairs, Charlotte had smelled an unmistakable acrid smoke and realised that her father had somehow managed to burn it, in spite of the toaster dial always being turned to the same setting. She heard him shout something and assumed it was a swear word. She tensed her shoulders and clasped her two hands in front of her mouth and started to pray that Charles would not be in a bad mood this evening.

'Please, dear God, let Daddy be all right,' she whispered to herself. 'Please don't let him be angry. Please protect him and make him into a better person and a better Christian.'

She breathed out in relief and then, as a guilty afterthought, added, 'And please look after Mummy too.'

The praying was an odd thing. She had started it after being presented at school with a small, red Gideon's Bible by a visiting speaker who came to tell them stories about long-ago children who had read and prayed each day and ended up living wholesome lives. The idea of this spiritual routine greatly impressed her and she felt excited to have been given a gift without it being her birthday or Christmas, so she left school that day with a favourable opinion of religion and, although neither of her parents went to church, Charlotte had begun to read a passage from her Bible in bed each night before she went to sleep. She liked the way the translucent pages felt underneath her fingers, like tracing paper. She found the ritual stilled her.

From that, it had seemed like a natural progression to start praying, but she knew it wasn't right to pray for yourself or things you secretly wanted, so she generally asked God to protect her parents and thanked him for a wonderful home when so many others were homeless. Occasionally, she added in a reference to world affairs – the famine in Ethiopia or the terrorist attacks in Northern Ireland. She always remembered the rainforests and the animals in danger of going extinct because she was a member of the World Wildlife Fund and had a panda-shaped membership badge that was one of her most prized possessions. Charlotte found the process of praying extremely calming and often fell asleep in the middle of her recitations, waking up in a state of panic because she had forgotten to mention something that required her attention.

She was still praying – eyes squeezed tightly shut, hands pressed together – when she heard Charles walking up the stairs. She quickly unclenched her hands, the palms sticky with sweat. She was mortified at the thought of her father catching her at it. She knew that he would think it was silly and that she would be unable to explain it to him logically. She knew that he would be more approving if she told him she didn't believe in God, but she couldn't do that however desperately she sought Charles's praise. It would feel wrong, disloyal somehow. It would feel sinful.

Charlotte felt her heart beating more quickly as his steps approached and mentally prepared herself for a polite exchange in which she would have to act gratefully for whatever food he had managed not to incinerate. She felt a tickle at the back of her throat and coughed to dislodge it, but then she couldn't stop and she was still coughing when Charles walked through the door, crouching so as not to hit his head on the door-frame and precariously holding a tray in two hands. The tray made a clinking sound of trembling crockery.

'Here we are,' he said in a self-consciously cheerful voice that didn't suit him. 'Sorry it took a while. The first round of toast burnt. I think your mother must have changed the bloody dial setting without telling me.'

Charlotte nodded her head in what she hoped was a non-committal show of understanding. She sat up in bed, positioning the pillow behind her back and flattening the folds of the duvet over her lap so that Charles could put the tray down in front of her. She saw that he had made her two slices of undercooked toast and sliced them each in half – into rectangles, not the triangles you got in hotels. He had slotted them into a silver toast rack that Charlotte had never seen before. Normally she had her toast in a single slice, buttered with a thin sliver of Marmite on top. Charles had attempted to butter it but because the bread had not been in the toaster long enough, the knife had left slapdash holes in the dough. Big yellow globules dotted the crusts. There was a pot of honey and one of thick-cut marmalade on the side of the tray. He had poured her a glass of water and made her some tea that she hadn't asked for, incongruously served in a dainty cup and saucer rather than her usual mug.

Although it was not quite what she wanted, Charlotte could see that he had made his own peculiar sort of effort.

'Thank you,' she said. She smiled and it felt forced so she relaxed her lips rather too quickly and hoped he hadn't noticed. She waited for Charles to leave the room and go downstairs. Normally he liked to spend the early evenings catching up on the day's newspapers in his study and Charlotte knew not to disturb him.

Instead, he took the small velvet-upholstered chair from her desk and drew it up beside the bed. He sat down even though the chair was far too small for him and his gangly limbs were folded up like a big insect, knees touching the edge of the mattress. He seemed all at once to be very close to her and Charlotte felt uncomfortable and then, immediately, ashamed of herself. He was only trying to be nice.

But she found she had a lump in her throat now and didn't want to eat in front of him.

'Aren't you having any?' Charles asked.

'Oh. Yes. Lovely.' Charlotte picked up a limp bit of toast and took a tiny bite. She chewed it for a long time.

Charles was staring at her and she felt his pale blue eyes bore into her like pinpricks of heat. She spread some marmalade on the second slice, taking care to leave the bitter shreds of orange peel in the jar. She bit into it and found that the sweetness tasted good against her tongue. She managed to finish half the toast and the cup of tea. She put the glass of water on her bedside table 'for later,' she explained.

'Thank you,' she said again, raising her eyes briefly to meet Charles's silent stare. 'Just what I felt like.'

He smiled at her, the corners of his lips twisting. Still, he said nothing. Charlotte wasn't sure what to do. Her arms began to feel cold beneath the thin cotton of her T-shirt nightdress, so she handed him the tray to take away, hoping that Charles would go back downstairs, but instead he took the tray from her and bent down to put it on the carpeted floor. As he sat back up, his hand brushed against her arm.

'You're freezing,' he said, the shadow of his smile still on his lips. He left his hand there and stretched his fingers right round her bicep so that he was holding on to her and she could feel the imprint of his thumb on the soft skin just beneath her armpit.

He's only being nice, she thought to herself, attempting to quell the rising sensation of unease. She tried to laugh and lighten the atmosphere, but it came out as an awkward, dry choking sound.

'Mmm. The top half of me feels all cold and the bottom half feels too hot.'

There was a pause.

'Poor little thing,' he said and it was such a strange turn of phrase, so entirely unfamiliar in its gentleness, that Charlotte's heart started to quicken again in her chest. He was not usually the type of father to say paternal things. It felt wrong. It felt somehow menacing.

'Let's cool you down.' He leaned across and slowly drew back the duvet, folding it back at the end of the bed so that Charlotte lay uncovered, her bare legs exposed to the night air. She looked down at her thin ankles, the skin scuffed over the knobbly bone where she had tripped over in the playground at school. She noticed that her nightdress had bunched up around her thighs and she pulled it down as far as it would go. There was an oversized picture of Mickey Mouse on the front that stretched into distorted outlines as she pulled at the hem with both hands. She swallowed and found, to her embarrassment, that she made a loud gulping sound. Still Charles looked at her, his eyes unwavering, his pose both static and monumental. She felt small next to him; small and insignificant.

Now that she had no duvet, Charlotte started to shiver, but she didn't want to say anything because she was scared of offending him when he had tried so hard to look after her and because she didn't know what was expected of her. Instead, she started to talk to herself in her head and, after a while, she realised she was praying but it wasn't her normal prayer. 'Please, dear God, let everything be all right,' she was saying to herself, over and over again and slowly, she found herself lulled by the rhythm of repetition.

Charles started to rub his hands up and down her legs. At first, the warmth of it felt nice but then, the pressure of his touch changed perceptibly so that he was no longer rubbing her skin with brisk practicality but rather stroking it, tracing the skinny outlines of her kneecaps with the tips of his fingers. Charlotte flinched involuntarily. Charles looked up at her and his eyes seemed to have acquired a translucent film, as if they were no longer quite focusing on what was in front of him.

'Ticklish?' he asked, his voice viscous as treacle. Charlotte nodded, unable to reply. She felt dizzy, as if she was about to cry but had no tears. She didn't know what was happening or what she should be doing but she knew that, whatever the outcome, she would be a grown-up. She wasn't going to be babyish. She was a young woman now and had to deal with the unexpected. Perhaps this was all part of the process of becoming an adult. But the thought was not as comforting as she wanted it to be. 'Please, dear God, let everything be all right.'

Charles's fingers were edging up her thigh so that she could feel them brushing against the worn elastic of her pants. He's only

94

trying to be nice, she told herself. His fingers kept stroking: up and down, up and down, up and down. He was no longer looking at her. His head was bent down, his shoulders slouched over the bed and he seemed to be following the progress of his hands with his eyes. There was something at once both intimate and detached about it, as if he were looking at himself playing the piano, watching his fingers stretch to reach the keys of an arpeggio.

And then, something odd happened to Charlotte. The room around her dissolved into blackness and there was nothing left apart from the sound of her own breathing, the beat of her heart and the tight dark sensation of shut eyes and silence. She stopped. She stopped feeling. It was as though her insides detached themselves from her body and then she was being lifted up, floating to the highest corner of her bedroom ceiling, out of harm's way. She thought of the scene in *Mary Poppins* where the characters found themselves suspended in mid-air, enjoying a cup of tea high up above furniture and the image made her giggle.

She looked down at her own body in her bed and was struck by how tiny she seemed, how faraway and powerless. Her arms were lying slackly on each side and she had pushed her head back against the pillow so that she was looking straight up at the ceiling. Charlotte stared at the shell of her own empty self and felt relieved that she was no longer down there. She felt safe up here.

She could see the top of Charles's head. She could see his hands moving gently up and down her legs, from the contours of her upper thigh down to the blistered heels. Her nightdress was pushed up over her hipbones, the image of Mickey Mouse wrinkled into countless creases. She lay there tense, rigid, drained of being.

There was the smell of burnt toast.

In the days that followed, Charlotte found that she could not clearly remember what had happened. The evening seemed to smudge in her memory, becoming part of the general blurriness of her remembered illness. It sank into the confusion of fever, into the vivid, too-bright sense of everything having been heightened and slightly surreal. The images seemed to shift and break apart in front of her like eggshell shards in a bowl of gloopy albumen.

The next morning, she woke to find her mother was back *in situ* and her father had gone to work. When he returned in the evening, he seemed back to his distant self, as if nothing had changed. Charlotte was unsure of her own recollections: she could not clearly remember what exactly had gone on and, because of this, she did not want to talk about it with her mother for fear of ridicule.

When she tried to clarify the chain of events in her own mind, she found that she could not put her finger on precisely what had been so terrifying about it. She had been cold and Charles had rubbed her legs to keep her warm. Removed from the immediate context, it seemed to Charlotte that it could have been a perfectly innocent, caring gesture. It was just that it had seemed wrong – both the look he had given her and the sense that he had become something other than himself.

But perhaps she was so unused to his touch that she withdrew from it rather than welcoming it and it was this that was the source of her discomfort. Perhaps she was at fault rather than her father. She began to admonish herself: instead of being worried by his closeness, she should have been mature enough to receive his affection in the spirit that it was intended. He was unused to showing his love, she thought, which was why, when he tried, there was a vague unease about it.

She ended up thinking that she should have made the most of Charles's undivided attention, an attention she normally craved but felt ill equipped to deserve. Usually, she never felt clever enough in answer to his questions across the supper table. She never knew how to impress him or make him laugh. She was never quite entertaining enough to divert him and she felt the pressure of this enormously.

Generally, Charles would talk to her in adult terms – explaining a complex scientific theory he'd read about in the paper or holding forth on his latest political opinions – and he would expect adult answers that she could never give him. She felt that she let him down, each unanswered question becoming a small admission of her own failure.

And now, here he was being nice to her, being attentive and tactile and unquestioning and actually looking after her – all the things she most wanted – and instead of being pleased, she was upset!

So although there was much she did not understand about the adult world around her, Charlotte steeled herself to accept its occasional confusions with grace and intelligence. This, she felt, would set her apart from other children. This, she knew, would meet with her parents' approval.

And, the more she thought about it, the more she convinced herself that, after all, there was nothing so very wrong in what her father had done.

That was the first time.

Janet; Anne

*J*ANET HAD GOT TICKETS. And when Janet had got tickets, it meant there was simply no escape. She was one of the most efficient bookers and makers of reservations that Anne had ever encountered. No sooner had Janet heard a play mentioned on the radio or read about a forthcoming museum exhibition in the paper, than she got straight on to the phone to call the relevant box office, credit card details at the ready, pen and paper beside her in order to jot down the reference number.

Janet didn't like those new automated voice systems where you had to speak loudly into a computer. She took delight in telephonic exchanges, drawing the person on the other end of the line into meaningless conversation about the terrible weather they were having.

By the time she put down the phone, Janet felt that a rightful order had been restored to the world. She would fish out her diary from her eco-friendly canvas-weave shopping bag, flick through the months until she got to the correct day and then she would write in the details of this new event in small, precise handwriting. Her days were delineated in black ballpoint, each one wrapped up like presents to be opened, and dotted at regular intervals through the year in order to eke out maximum pleasure. It left her with a sense of calm satisfaction – she had done something: she had arranged An Outing.

Needless to say, Janet always booked two tickets. She convinced herself this was an altruistic gesture – she would bestow a treat on an appreciative friend – but, if she was being really honest with herself, it was more a way of ensuring companionship. People felt less ready to turn down an invitation if there was money involved, and the lure of a free ticket was often enough to make even the most reluctant guest say yes.

But Janet was not overburdened with friends to ask, so the tickets often went to nieces or nephews who would slouch around galleries with her out of a barely concealed sense of duty. Sometimes, the second ticket went to waste. Once, she had been forced into the undignified position of attempting to sell a ticket for a sold-out musical outside the theatre. She found herself surrounded by touts, each one in a large black puffer jacket and knitted hat, shouting out their wares like market traders.

'You all right, love?' one of them asked, hawking up a globule of phlegm and spitting on to the pavement. Janet shrank back in disgust.

'Oh, oh, yes, thank you,' she stuttered, feeling so embarrassed and out-of-place that she almost started crying.

'You want me to sell that for you?' The tout extended his hand, the yellowed tips of his nails poking through a pair of grey fingerless gloves. Janet looked at him in surprise.

'Well, that would be kind. Are you sure?'

'Course, love. I'll have it sold for you in a jiffy.'

And he had. Within five minutes, a harassed-looking businessman with a bundle of Cellophane-wrapped roses under his arm was handing over £40 in exchange for Janet's ticket. 'There you go, darling,' the tout said, passing on the two crisp £20 notes.

'But it only cost me £35.'

'Spend the extra on ice cream,' he said, with a wink. But Janet insisted on giving him the £5 excess. He looked a little offended, but he took it nonetheless, and she pushed her way into the foyer feeling strangely exposed. It was an experience she never wished to repeat.

Most of the time, of course, Janet could rely on Anne to come with her. She knew Anne was almost as lonely as she was, although she also knew that Anne would hotly deny this was the case. Anne could be prickly, yes, and give the appearance of ingratitude, but Janet felt, at some level, she needed her friendship even though she would never actually say so. The two of them needed each other. They both needed to believe life was more than it was. They needed to cancel out each other's solitariness, even if all it meant was a simple physical togetherness that was worn lightly, that was accepted without question because to question it would be to admit what lay beneath. To question it would be to strip back the skin of their mutual compromise.

So Janet would always book two tickets. More often than not, Anne would say yes in spite of herself.

This time, it was one of those dubious shows that involved an ageing raconteur holding forth in front of an appreciative gaggle of people who should know better. It was called 'An Audience With . . .' and featured a silver-haired man called Richard Vickers who had achieved minor fame as the presenter of a humorous quiz on Radio 4 that required contestants to speak for a whole minute on a random subject without hesitation, repetition or deviation. Janet had called round at Anne's home one evening after she had returned from the hospital to ask if she wanted to go.

'I know you like the show,' Janet said brightly, sitting at the wooden kitchen table and fiddling with the coaster beneath her mug of tea. 'And it's at the Cambridge Arts Theatre, so I thought we could make a day of it.'

Anne found, to her surprise, that the prospect didn't fill her with quite as much dread as it usually would. Perhaps it would be nice to have something to relieve the tedium of hospital visits and tense exchanges with Charlotte. There had been no change in Charles's condition for over three weeks. The doctors were starting to talk gently about persistent vegetative states and 'quality of life'.

She glanced across the table. Janet was wearing a new voluminous brown cardigan that she had bought in the sales but which didn't suit her at all. It made her look fatter than she actually was and accentuated her short arms and large bust. Her face, powdered and lipsticked with the normal carelessness, seemed a mask of trembling desperation, almost of nervousness.

'I suppose it would be all right not to go to the hospital for one day.'

'Of course it would be, Anne. You've been running yourself into the ground these past few weeks and you thoroughly deserve some time off.'

There was a pause. Anne turned away, patting her hair down, so that she didn't have to maintain eye contact. The fact that she wanted to go seemed almost like a defeat that she wasn't quite willing to admit to herself. When she spoke, she was deliberately offhand.

'Yes, well, all right, Janet. I'd like to.'

There was a delighted squeal from across the table.

'Thanks for thinking of me,' Anne added, even though she knew there was no one else Janet was likely to have thought of first.

'Oh, that's terrific,' said Janet, sitting back in her chair with two hands clasped around her mug, her hunched-up shoulders finally relaxing into the shapeless cardigan. She took a sip of her tea and Anne noticed there was a genuine gleam of happiness in her eyes. She was moved by this. How wonderful, Anne thought, to be able to gain such joy from something so insignificant. How touching that Janet seemed to value these tiny shreds of friendship so highly. She would give anything to experience the same degree of uncomplicated optimism, the same wholesome faith in life. She used to be able to, thought Anne, filling up Janet's mug from a dribbling teapot. She wondered what had happened to make her so dried-up inside.

It reminded her, oddly, of the wording of a prayer she had learned in the run-up to her confirmation, something about the faithful 'not being fit to eat the crumbs' from under God's table. The phrasing had lodged itself in her fifteen-year-old mind. She had an image of a powerful God-like figure sitting at a vast, polished dining table with a shepherd's crook in one hand, breaking up a big loaf of bread with the other, crumbs of it falling on to the ground and being meekly gathered up by a crowd of enthusiastic pygmies, crawling over each other like ants following a trail of honey.

Anne sometimes felt as though she scattered her morsels of affection on to the floor just like this, to be hoovered up by Janet with her customary, slightly pathetic, gratefulness. It gave Anne the occasional twinge of guilt, but it also left her with a sense of power over someone else that she had never before experienced and that she had come to cherish. In every other area of her life, Anne felt she was controlled by other people – by Charles's domineering manner, by Charlotte's conscious detachment, by shop assistants and bus conductors and parking wardens who saw her as a worn-out housewife with grey hair and nothing more. Her love had never been returned as unconditionally as she had bestowed it and now it was too late to hope for this to change.

With Janet, Anne knew she was in a position of dominance, and she exploited this. She knew that Janet's affection for her outweighed its reciprocal measure. After a lifetime of giving too much love only to have it scorned or dismissed or broken by the person to whom it had been entrusted, it felt good to be on the other side. She convinced herself that this was not cruelty so much as a deliberate thoughtlessness: she liked Janet to an extent – despite finding her (and she felt bad about this) so intensely irritating – and she knew that Janet liked her and got pleasure from their friendship. As long as this was the case, she couldn't see the harm in her behaviour. They were both getting something out of it, weren't they?

So they went to Cambridge, catching a fast train from King's Cross station at 9.15 on a Saturday morning. It was the first time Anne had been back to her university town since a Newnham College reunion over fifteen years ago that had promised more than it delivered. Anne had rather hoped to dress up and impress the old familiar faces with tales of Charlotte's academic success and domestic bliss with Charles, but hardly anyone she recognised had come. She ended up sitting next to a dour woman who did something incredibly dull in flour imports and had only two conversational topics – the fragility of the flour markets in times of financial uncertainty and the world's most challenging hiking hotspots.

This time, Anne found she was looking forward to the prospect of showing Janet round her old haunts. When Charlotte was applying to universities, Anne had dearly wanted her to try for

Cambridge but Charlotte had refused point blank, even though her grades would have been good enough.

'Don't you want to go there?' asked Anne, mystified.

'No, Mum. Why would I want to do exactly the same as you and Dad?'

'It wouldn't be exactly the same,' she replied. 'You'd be able to make it your own. It's a wonderful opportunity, Charlotte, and you might end up regretting –'

'No,' Charlotte butted in. 'I don't want to be where you and Dad were.'

And that had been that. Charlotte ended up going to Leeds, doing some ridiculous degree in media studies that seemed to mean nothing at all.

The train pulled out of King's Cross and the drizzle-dampened concrete gave way rapidly to terraced houses with creosoted fences bordering the railway line. Anne wondered idly if The Currant Bun coffee shop, where she had spent many a happy teatime with Charles in the early days of their courtship, was still there. And the dark little pub, tucked away by Jesus Green, where they had once got drunk on a Saturday afternoon without intending to. And the Grantchester fields where he had proposed, although she doubted that they would get time to go there.

Anne drifted off into a pleasant reverie as the buffet trolley came rattling up the aisle. She bought herself an overpriced bottle of still water and treated Janet to a hot chocolate. In a fit of exuberance, she asked for a packet of shortbread biscuits at the last minute and didn't get much change out of a £10 note. She unwrapped the shortbread and offered some to Janet, whose face broke into an uncomplicated smile.

'Ooh, yes please,' Janet said, dipping a shortbread finger into her steaming plastic cup. 'Lovely.'

'Might as well treat ourselves,' said Anne, with uncharacteristic jollity.

Janet beamed. It made Anne feel – not happy, exactly – but good. She felt like a good person.

But when they got there, nothing was as it had been. The Currant Bun had turned into a Starbucks and was filled with tourists wearing anoraks and back-packs talking loudly over their guide-books. The pub was still there, but the doors were shut up and one of the windows had been cracked and hastily stuck together with a length of dirty plastic tape. When they went to Newnham and Anne tried to show Janet her old room, the porter – an unfriendly man with small, hard eyes and flesh spilling over his shirt collar – had not allowed them in because they had no proof of Anne's alumna status. She had to content herself with pointing to the rele-vant window from the road, but she wasn't sure which one had been hers and, although she feigned a certain level of interest, it was clear that Janet had minimal enthusiasm for finding out.

It started to rain, an imperceptible dampness at first that fell harder and harder, covering their cold faces with a thin sheet of wetness. They had hoped to walk along the Backs and look at the colleges, but this plan was swiftly abandoned as the weather worsened.

'Let's find somewhere cosy for lunch,' said Janet, zipping up her lightweight red mackintosh.

'Right,' said Anne, annoyed at both the weather and the use of the word 'cosy', which she hated beyond all reason.

They tramped back to King's Parade, but every restaurant or café they passed was full of people, the windows fogged up with condensation. At one unappetising Italian chain, a queue of forlorn-looking customers had formed underneath the dripping awnings outside.

'How long do we have to wait for a table?' Anne asked a young waiter sporting a diamond earring and a shaved head.

'Dunno. Could be as little as half an hour. We're busy.'

'Yes,' said Anne in a clipped voice. 'I can see that.'

They seemed to walk for hours in ever decreasing circles of dispiritedness. Even Janet's perpetual good humour seemed to be starting to flag.

'It would be so nice to sit down, wouldn't it?' Janet said wistfully as they passed a grotty Wetherspoon's pub that had no free tables.

Eventually, they had to admit defeat and return to the Italian restaurant, where they joined the queue. The waiter Anne had spoken to earlier came up to them carrying a clipboard.

'You back then?' he said with an insolent grin.

'Evidently,' said Anne.

'Right, you're looking at a forty-five-minute wait. What's your name?'

'Forty-five minutes?' Anne said, incredulously, her voice rising. 'You said half an hour.'

The waiter scowled. Janet laid her hand gently on Anne's arm. 'I'm sure it's not this young man's fault,' she said, smiling with a benevolence that served only to heighten Anne's bad temper. 'My name's Janet and we'll be happy to wait for when the next table becomes available.'

The waiter snorted derisively. 'Janet. How you spelling that?'

Anne groaned and shook her arm free. Janet spelled out her name with painstaking politeness and the waiter left, leaving the two of them in a stilted silence.

'There,' said Janet as if she'd just put a plaster on a child's knee graze. 'All done.'

'Good for you.'

Janet smiled pleasantly into the mid-distance and started to hum an indistinct tune. The queue moved more quickly than either of them had anticipated and they were soon seated at a cramped corner table just by the door, so that every time someone walked in, the two of them were assailed by an icy blast of East Anglian wind.

'Shall we share a bruschetta?' said Janet, putting on her reading glasses.

'I think you pronounce it brus-ketta.'

'Oh,' said Janet, her lips quivering. 'I'm sorry.' Janet started to concentrate intently on the menu, the tip of her tongue poking through her thin lips. She was still humming when the waiter came to take their order. Anne deliberately skipped the starters and asked for the basil pesto pasta. She caught Janet's eye and saw her look momentarily bereft that Anne had ordered the plainest thing on the menu, ignoring the fact that it was meant to be an 'occasion'.

'I'll have the same,' Janet said in a small voice before closing the menu and passing it back to the waiter with an ingratiating nod of the head. The pasta, when it came, was surprisingly delicious.

'It seems they must have an Italian chef even if the waiting staff are very much English,' said Janet. There was a smudge of lipstick on her upper teeth.

'It's pretty difficult to ruin a bowl of pasta,' Anne said, and it came out more harshly than she meant it to, so she added in a conciliatory tone: 'But it is very good.'

It struck Anne, not for the first time, that the exchanges she had with Janet were more hesitation than conversation. They seemed constantly to be missing each other's targets, misfiring and misinterpreting and then attempting to compensate while both knowing it was never going to work. It frustrated Anne immensely. She wished Janet were more capable of standing up for herself. But then, if she had possessed that quality, perhaps she would no longer have been the unquestioning, accepting presence that soaked up Anne's moods like a good-natured sponge.

There was even more queuing to get into the theatre because Janet had insisted on getting there forty-five minutes early 'to avoid the rush', blithely unaware that every other sensibly minded fifty-something woman within a certain radius would have had exactly the same idea. It was clear, once they had shuffled like battery hens to their seats in the stalls, that Richard Vickers's fanbase consisted almost entirely of a gaggle of middle-aged ladies clutching their programmes with sweaty-palmed anticipation and the sort of trembling elderly gentlemen that had reached the stage in life where one starts wearing slippers as shoes. The mosquito hum of their hearing aids sounded through the theatre like a vibrating tuning fork.

For a few moments before the lights dimmed, Anne looked around her and was horrified to think she might fit in here. She wondered briefly whether she actually looked old to outside eyes even though she still felt relatively young on the inside. She was terrified of becoming the sort of woman who doesn't realise she is dressing inappropriately – the kind who prides herself on fitting into the same clothes as her daughter or the kind who grows her hair slightly too long, unwittingly emphasising its thin lankness.

In recent years, Anne had become frantically worried that the flesh on her upper arms was sagging, hanging off the bone like a crumpled plastic bag filled with groceries that would swing from side to side whenever she clapped. She had taken to wearing longer sleeves and altering her hand gestures so that they were no longer quite as free or expressive when she talked. Although Anne had thought these changes dramatic, no one else appeared to notice, and this had depressed her even more.

She began to realise that she had turned into the sort of woman that people no longer look at. Charles had stopped looking at her in that way many years before. But it was more the impervious nonchalance of strangers that upset her: the workman who no longer whistled or the postman who no longer winked. She found she couldn't, as she used to, trade on mild flirtation to guarantee an upgrade on a flight or talk her way out of a parking ticket. It wasn't that these unconscious strangers were being rude or unkind; it was because they had simply stopped thinking of her as a sexual being. To them, she looked dignified, upstanding, middle-aged. On her good days, she could appear well dressed, striking, even handsome, but only with the unspoken suffix 'for her age'. She was not desirable. Not any more.

It was a desultory sort of evening. Richard Vickers came on to the stage and was greeted by polite applause, to which he responded with a camp wiggling of the fingers on his left hand. In his right, he held a microphone. 'Thank you, thank you,' he said in his whispery voice, the lights picking out a faint halo of face powder and hairspray. He made his way across to a chrome bar-stool, hoisted himself on to the seat and crossed his legs primly before launching into a seemingly endless stream of not-very-entertaining anecdotes. He was wearing, Anne noted, a pair of slip-on shoes – something that she always distrusted in men – and a double-breasted blazer with old-fashioned brass buttons and a salmon-pink handkerchief poking ostentatiously out of the breast pocket. He looked like a golf club stalwart, Anne thought dismissively, a man whose idea of bliss was a fortnight in Tenerife.

All around her, people were chuckling good-naturedly. Janet had a glazed smile fixed permanently in place, occasionally clapping softly when a punchline tickled her. There was a dreary question-and-answer session, in which members of the audience posed deferential queries as to what so-and-so 'is actually like in real life?' or whether he would consider such-and-such 'the highlight of his career?' And then it was mercifully over and they were filing out into the foggy evening air.

Once on the train, seated opposite each other with a table between them (Janet had, of course, booked the tickets in advance), Janet looked at Anne with an expression of tentative hopefulness.

'Did you enjoy it, Anne?'

'Yes, of course,' she replied, not altogether truthfully.

'I'm glad,' there was a stilted little pause. 'I hope it – well, I hope it took your mind off things.' Janet left the sentence hanging.

'It's difficult to take my mind off things entirely,' said Anne.

'Yes. I imagine it must be.' There was a weighted pause, as Janet geared up to say something else. 'Having Charlotte around a bit more must be nice.'

Anne snorted. 'Hardly nice. It would be far nicer if her presence weren't required. If Charles weren't lying there fighting for his life.'

'Well, of course, I only meant . . .'

'I know what you meant, Janet,' said Anne, cutting in. 'I didn't mean to snap. I suppose I'm rather at the end of my tether.'

'Of course you are,' said Janet, and her calmness surprised Anne. 'Are you still unsure about this Gabriel chap?'

Anne's shoulders tensed, so that she felt her muscles tighten all the way up through her neck to the upper curve of her cheekbone. Without warning, she felt she was about to cry. Horrified at the thought of losing control in front of Janet, she made a great show of foraging around in her handbag for a tissue with which to wipe her glasses. She told herself to calm down and took a couple of surreptitious breaths. She collected her feelings in a neat pile and folded them away, like a fresh stack of ironed laundry. She looked at Janet levelly.

'I don't think he's right for her,' she said quietly. 'And I don't know how to tell her.'

'Do you mind if I say something, Anne?' said Janet, reaching her hand across the narrow table and pressing the tips of her fingers down gently on the inside of Anne's wrist. The fragile touch felt alien to Anne's skin and it recalled that odd sensation she got sometimes when she was rooting around for a pair of socks and her fingers brushed suddenly against the waxy texture of a drawer lining. She nodded.

'Well, I'm not sure that talking to Charlotte would do all that much good, dear. I do think that you can't choose who you love and –' Janet broke off and leaned forward, so that the thick gold chain she wore round her indeterminately baggy brown jumper swung against the table's plastic edge. 'Anne, you should know that better than anybody,' she said quietly.

Anne slid her hand away and hurried out of her seat to the train lavatory, opening the door into a grim grey cubicle with damp tissue paper balled up in piles on the floor. She looked at herself in the scratched mirror above the sink that was edged with the black spider's scrawl of nameless graffiti. She met her own eyes in the reflection. A woman with brittle grey-brown hair, sensibly bobbed to just beneath her ears, her skin dulled with the slight powderiness of age. Her mouth was tightly drawn into an anxious hyphen across her jaw and the faint wrinkles that ran down her chin seemed to tether her disapproving lips in place like tent poles.

Anne took her glasses off and let them hang on her chest. They were suspended by a cheap fake-silver chain ordered years ago from a catalogue that specialised in small necessities. At one point in her life, she had thrown these catalogues unthinkingly in the bin without removing them from their plastic wrappers. Now, she relied on them. When did that happen, she thought, aimlessly. When did she get old? She placed her hands on the edge of the sink, leaning her weight forward and dropping her head so that she no longer had to look at herself. Tears dropped fatly on to the burnished stainless steel.

It didn't work, she told herself. Janet was right. No matter how hard she tried to convince herself otherwise, she knew that she still loved him. She missed him. In spite of herself, she thought angrily, in spite of everything that bastard has done, she missed him.

Her loneliness made her shudder with a sort of distaste. However hard she tried, she still could not escape him. He was indelible;

spread across her body like a dark tattoo, the inky rivulets sinking into the granular surface of her ageing skin so that she was no longer sure what flesh was hers and what flesh was his.

She had chosen him over everything: her friends, her life, what could have been her career, and even – yes – her own daughter. She stopped herself thinking then. Stopped herself short. She did not want to go back to that time, that day, that moment when her betrayal of Charlotte had become irrevocable. It was there, always there, disturbing the surface like blotches of damp seeping through fresh white emulsion, but she did not acknowledge it. Because to acknowledge it – to calibrate the precision of what she had or had not seen, to click the blurriness of that single image into a sharper focus – would be the final destruction. She would not do it, however much it cost her.

Anne waited a few moments before returning to her seat. She spent the rest of the train journey in silence.

Charlotte

'*D*ON'T YOU LOVE ME?'

'Of course I love you.' Charlotte rolled away from him under the duvet. She lay on her side, silent and cold, drawing her legs up to her chest with her arms and pressing them tightly to her. She wanted to make herself as small and impenetrable as possible. She closed her eyes, wishing she wasn't there.

Gabriel shifted beside her. She felt him prop up his head with one arm and could sense his perplexed semi-frown, the slight crinkle he got between his eyes when he wasn't wearing his glasses. She knew he was confused and upset, but she didn't have the energy to help him through it, to tell him why, to explain what couldn't be explained. She heard him sigh loudly and then swing his legs down to the floor, easing himself up with knuckled hands and walking out noisily to the loo. The bedroom door handle creaked as it always did when it was pushed too roughly.

Charlotte drifted into a mild sleep, waking with a jolt when she felt Gabriel's weight depress the other side of the mattress. He turned towards her and placed his hand gently on her right shoulder, drawing her towards him so that she was forced to look at his face. She saw that he was trying both to conceal his frustration and to convey a feeling of tenderness and the effort of reconciling these two opposing forces had made his mouth vaguely misshapen, so that it looked somewhere in between a smile and a grimace. The corners of his lips were twisted like the thin metallic strips used to tie up freezer bags. Charlotte felt a sweep of emotion. She kissed the tip of his nose.

'I'm sorry.'

He stroked her hair. 'I just don't understand. Perhaps if you could make me understand it would be easier.'

She said nothing.

'We've been together now for almost a year and I love you more than anything else in the world. And you've led me to believe that you feel the same way, so . . .'

'I do feel the same way.'

'And you haven't suddenly become an evangelical Christian or anything, unless you're hiding it well.'

Charlotte laughed and nestled her head into his chest. She could hear the thick beat of his heart and imagined it pumping blood around his clean, clear arteries and veins. The image gave her comfort, made her feel oddly secure. He seemed so strong, so perfect, so unblemished.

'Is there something wrong with me?'

'Of course there isn't!' Charlotte protested, her voice muffled by the soft curlicues of his chest hair.

'Because otherwise there's just no explanation that I can think of for why you wouldn't want to have sex with me.'

Charlotte drew back against the wall so that they were no longer touching. The words were out. Vocalising the thought had given it a certainty, a permanence that she had hoped to avoid. She thought if neither of them mentioned it, if they just went on doing what they were doing, smiling at each other politely through the translucent screen of a gradually building silence, then it could for all intents and purposes be categorised as 'normal'. All couples went through dry spells, didn't they?

Charlotte remembered a recent conversation with her newly married friend, Susie, who had admitted that she and her husband had been unable to have sex on their wedding night. They'd booked the honeymoon suite in a nearby spa hotel and the staff had thoughtfully strewn rose petals over the bed in the shape of a giant red heart. There was a bottle of champagne chilling in a free-standing ice-bucket. A few weeks before, Susie had spent almost two hours at a luxurious lingerie emporium in central London where the assistants had fussed over her with a measuring tape and pineapple slices and glasses of white wine until she capitulated and bought an absurdly expensive 'wedding trousseau' that consisted of a complicated arrangement of ribbons and ivory satin and underwired padding, all designed, so the assistants gushed, 'to make your husband realise he's a very lucky man'.

And then, after all that, the two of them had been so tired, so tipsy, so disembowelled of energy by the stress of the occasion, that they'd passed out without the necessary physical consummation. Charlotte remembered Susie telling her this shortly after the wedding, accompanied by gales of laughter.

'I mean, how bloody useless!' she had said, giggling. 'After all that effort!' Charlotte laughed along with her but couldn't help thinking that she would be profoundly depressed if her wedding night turned out to be the same, literal, anti-climax.

For Charlotte, the act of sex had become a means of valuing herself. Until Gabriel, she had not been used to receiving compliments about her appearance from boyfriends. Charlotte did not seem to be the sort of woman who invited these easy snippets of flattery although she was never quite sure why. She had asked one of her boyfriends about it once and he replied, without a trace of either hesitation or irony, 'But Charl, you're so capable.'

'Capable?' She made a face. 'Thanks very much.'

'I mean, I wouldn't have thought it's the kind of thing you'd value hearing.'

She thought about this for a second and wondered how on earth she gave such an outward impression of confidence in herself when she felt so differently inside.

'Every woman wants to hear she's pretty,' she said, quietly.

'Well, you are.'

'What?'

He sighed. 'Pretty,' he said, not raising his eyes from the newspaper he was reading.

It had always been like that. Charlotte had never wanted to ask for a compliment – too needy, she thought with a shudder, and ultimately, too trivial to mean anything – and yet she had secretly been desperate to hear how desired she was. Perhaps, she reasoned, these reluctantly emotive men believed that voicing a thought about her aesthetic qualities unnecessary when it was obvious that she looked nice.

When she was a child, she remembered bursting into tears when she brought home a report card from school that was liberally sprinkled with As and impressive test results. Her mother had read it, nodded her head, and handed it back to Charlotte without a word. Anne seemed surprised to see her daughter crying.

'What's wrong?'

It was rare for Charlotte to be able to work out exactly how she felt, to be able to express it in a fashion that would convey the precision of her emotion, but this time, she knew exactly what to say.

'You never say well done,' she said, in a raggedy voice that meant she had to stop herself mid-sentence and take a deep breath to continue. 'Even when I get As. My teachers tell me more than you do.'

Anne raised her eyebrows ever so slightly so that a faint, horizontal line appeared across the top of her brow. She seemed momentarily lost for words. 'Charlotte, you always do so well . . . I suppose I just expect it of you. And I know that your teachers think you're terribly impressive so I suppose . . . I suppose I think that they're telling you all that you need to hear and I don't have to.' She took Charlotte's hand in hers, clumsily, so that Charlotte's fist was still clenched and Anne had to extend her fingers right round this tight ball of her daughter's frustration. 'It's obvious to me how clever you are,' she added, softly.

But while Charlotte's success might have been obvious to her mother, it wasn't obvious to her and she needed someone to tell her. She regarded this need as a weakness, but it persisted nonetheless.

In the same way, she knew she was pretty because there were brief moments when she was able to look at herself dispassionately and see that the construction of her face held together in a relatively pleasing fashion – the blunt, upturned nose, the spray of freckles, the dark brown hair that hairdressers remarked was unusually thick, the light blue eyes that her friends said made her look vaguely Nordic. But all of this was a logical sort of reasoning: she was presented with the available evidence and she could draw a rational conclusion in much the same way as she could understand, objectively, that Gabriel loved her. Feeling it – actually knowing it without having to force herself to go through the motions of acquiring knowledge – was a different matter entirely. She did not feel beautiful. She needed people to tell her, to put it into plain words that could not be misunderstood. She needed something that could not be argued with.

When this was not forthcoming from a boyfriend, sex had become a substitute for speech. If someone was having sex with her, she reasoned, if the act of penetrating her was making the other person orgasm, then she must be attractive to them. It was a fact and the possession of this fact made her feel relieved and strangely confident for a few brief hours. Because the capacity to make a man weak with sexual desire was also a sort of power. In the past, if she had ever been angry or upset with a boyfriend, she would transmute this unconsciously into sex. She would become deliberately unresponsive. She would not cry out or dilate her pupils in an approximation of longing. She would not wrap her arms around his neck or her legs around his back. She would not touch him beyond the necessary. She would stare coldly into his eyes as he worked his way into her and she would clench her insides to trap him there. She would look at him, in the moments after he came and she felt his stickiness leak out on to the sheets, and she would sense the re-establishment of her superficial dominance. She did not need him like this. She could choose.

Paradoxically, such actions usually had precisely the opposite effect from the one she intended – her unusual submissiveness and wordless acquiescence seemed to turn men on far more than anything else she would do; more than all the sucking and kneeling and stroking and caressing and thrusting and panting. Often, Charlotte would feel as if she was looking on from the corner of the room at a convincing performance, rather than being carried away with the mutual abandon we are all taught to crave. It seemed as if sex was a conglomeration of images learned from movies and magazines. It, too, was never truly felt inside.

With Gabriel, it had been different. The images were all still there, but they were rearranged in such a way that she suddenly comprehended what they stood for. The sexual archetype, which had previously been painted out in monochrome, all at once became a blaze of colour.

'So this is what sex is meant to be like,' Gabriel had once said in the early days of their relationship, a laconic post-coital smile on his face.

'That was incredible,' said Charlotte, unable to escape the cliché of self-congratulation.

'You're incredible.'

Sex with Gabriel had been a shining discovery. Charlotte had expected it to be good, and it was, but it was more than that. It was – and she hated herself for sounding so trite about it – meaningful. It made them stronger, brought them closer. It was an expression of total honesty: no hiding, no pretence, no anxiety that either of them was being judged. She knew that neither of them had ever had sex like it and, for the first time, she felt she wanted to bring him pleasure rather than going through the motions because it was expected of her. She felt no distaste when she took his cock in her mouth. He was the only man whose cum she had ever swallowed. She was not scared of him.

Or at least, she hadn't been until a few weeks ago. Then, inexplicably, things had shifted without either of them noticing, like the transfiguration of a landscape by a glacier's creeping progression. Charlotte had stopped wanting to have sex. Neither of them thought much of it at first. It lay, unspoken, between them. They still kissed and cuddled and did all the other things that old swimming-pool posters would categorise as 'heavy petting'. But there was no penetration. Whenever they got to the stage where it seemed to be the inevitable next step, Charlotte placed her hand softly but insistently on Gabriel's chest and pushed him away with a smile and a shake of the head. He had accepted this for over a month without questioning her. But now, the shapeless feeling of unease had solidified. Gabriel was looking at her expectantly. Charlotte had to say something.

'I'm sorry,' she said, more sulkily than she meant to.

'You don't need to be sorry. I just want to know what's going on. What's going on in here?' He tapped the side of her head.

How to tell him? How to tell him that the reason she didn't feel comfortable was directly related to that dinner with her father, to that profound internal misery that was gnawing away at her? How to begin to tell him all that had happened? She couldn't. She could barely explain it to herself. She did not want to think about it more than she had to and she refused to let it define her. She imagined it polluting her life, a black swarm of flies blotting out the sun. If she did not admit it, it could not exist. If she did not acknowledge its power over her, it had none. Whatever 'it' was.

She looked up at Gabriel's face, at its open sweetness: the large brown eyes that appeared bigger without glasses, their uncomplicated roundness reminding her fleetingly of those manga cartoon characters who seemed to swallow up the world around them in a single gaze. He was a decade her senior and yet, in this single moment, she felt so much older than him, so much more lived-in than this man-child who held her tight and did not for one second guess at the darkness that lay beneath. How could she drag him into the murkiness? It would endanger all that she most needed in him: his purity of intention, the honesty and directness of everything he said and felt.

'I think I'm just a bit stressed,' she said finally, and she knew that he was not convinced by this half-hearted attempt at dismissal. So she played the joker card, the one she knew there was no answer to other than affection. 'You know, with my father and everything going on at the hospital and there's still no change in his condition. My mother's driving me mad but I know it's not her fault.' Charlotte took a deep breath, scratching the tender flesh of her inner elbow with one finger so that dry flakes of her eczema scattered over the pillow. Gabriel took her hand softly and held it away from her. Her fingernail, when she looked at it, had a thin red-brown line of blood at its tip.

'Don't do that, you'll make it worse.' He drew her into him so tightly that she could feel the strong protrusion of his veins against her back. 'I'm so sorry, Charlotte. I've been incredibly selfish, I know I have. Of course this is going to have an impact on you. I don't know how you've coped and here I am, I should be supporting you and instead, well, instead I'm demanding sexual satisfaction when clearly it's the last thing on your mind.'

'You've been wonderful,' said Charlotte, who meant it. 'Truly, you have.'

'I haven't. I don't feel I've done enough, but you say you don't want me to come with you to the hospital –'

'I don't,' she said, sharply. 'I really don't.'

'I'd do anything for you. You know that.' He cupped the back of her head in his hand. She felt immediately guilty for having made him feel sympathy for her. Although Charlotte rarely admitted it, she knew that she felt little compassion for her father, lying there in his semi-dead state. She could pretend, of course. She had been used to doing that for most of her life. She could go and sit by his bedside and even take his hand on occasion and she could talk in a blithe and essentially meaningless fashion and, in a curious sort of way, it was a release. It was the sort of relationship she had always wanted with her father – easy chit-chat, unrestricted by the weight of knowledge that bore down on their shoulders like the heavy steel girders that kept you in place on rollercoaster rides. It was the only time she had ever felt wholly free of his judgement. She no longer craved his approval or pride because she knew he was incapable of giving it. She no longer felt the queasy trickle of threat that had run through much of their communication. She didn't mind being alone with him any more because he couldn't touch her, in any way.

How could she tell Gabriel all of this? She couldn't. Not yet. Perhaps not ever. And so, because it was easier than verbal language, because it would mean she didn't have to explain, she kissed him fully on the mouth and switched off the part of her mind that was screaming no and when it got to that pinprick moment when sex seemed the unavoidable conclusion, it was Gabriel who pushed her away, tenderly, with a smile and nothing else. She smiled back, relieved. They went to sleep, curved towards each other, their heads and toes touching like brackets at each end of a sentence.

Anne; Charles

I T ALL STARTED TO go wrong almost immediately. Looking back at the early days of her marriage, Anne was always struck by how quick the change had been. There was none of the gradual slippage that she might have expected, none of the neat narrative clues that would have made sense of the sudden shift in tone. There was no little give-away sign, no scent of perfume on his shirt collar, no sleeping in separate beds, no slow drip drip drip of the tell-tale disintegration that pushed couples apart from each other in books or soap operas. It seemed simply as if Charles had shut a door, flicked a switch, drawn a line; as if, having married her, she was packaged neatly into a box labelled 'wife' that he no longer had to bother with. He had achieved the conventional marriage to the pretty bride without much effort, and it felt to Anne as if he had accomplished what he had set out to do and could put it to one side. It was as though he had met some internal target, as though he viewed the act of marriage as a chore to be ticked off on a list of necessities so that he might be liberated to get on with the rest of his life. Being married, for Charles, was enough. He didn't need it to mean anything.

The wedding day went exactly to plan. The village church near her parents' home was filled with so many sweet peas that Anne fancied she could smell their marzipan pungence as soon as she emerged from the pigeon-grey vintage car in her white silk dress.

'I'm so happy, Daddy,' she said to her father as he proffered his arm, guiding her over the grassy divots and the stone slabs engraved with ancestral names.

'I'm glad, darling. He's a very lucky chap.'

And the funny thing was, she had meant it absolutely. She had spoken with a complete lack of guile, an unthinking, almost clumsy, admission of her own good fortune. Although there had, on occasion, been the infrequent moment of quiet anxiety over the last few weeks, she had attributed such thoughts to the stress of arranging seating-plans and hymn sheets. On the day itself, she felt no qualms. She felt utterly calm, safe in the knowledge of her own radiance and certain of her future.

In the porch of the church, she stood for a few seconds rearranging the train of her dress and she could hear the murmured anticipation of the congregation, the half-spoken conversations, the muffled laughter, the atmosphere of something being about to happen, at once both heavy with expectancy and light with excitement. She felt a tremor of satisfaction that they were all here to see her in this moment. In one hand she held a bouquet of blotted blue and dusty pink spring flowers. She lay the other hand gently on her rib cage, pressing her palm down on the comforting rough-smooth texture of the raw silk bodice. She could feel her heart beating out a frantic rhythm. Her dress was buttoned so tightly she could hear a small gravelly wheeze every time she breathed in.

'Ready?' asked her father.

She smiled and nodded, holding the bouquet carefully in front of her with both hands. The organ started up.

They drove to Normandy in her parents' ancient black Austin for a week's honeymoon. It rained almost every day: a thick, clouded sort of wetness that saturated the landscape until the fields seemed to liquidise and evaporate into the sky so that the horizon was smudged into nothing and the surroundings became an endless flat streak of grey. At first, Anne had thought that the ceaseless tapping of rain on the slate roof of their stone cottage might be romantic. Their bedroom was situated up a rickety wooden staircase, squashed under the eaves so that Charles hit his head every time he got up in the night to go to the loo. The windows weren't watertight, so the whole place smelled of damp curtains and the mustiness of mothballs.

'It's our very own impoverished writer's garret,' said Anne as cheerfully as she could.

'Yes,' said Charles. 'Impoverished is the word.'

But he didn't sweep her up in his arms or take her to bed in a fit of unbridled passion or any of those things that she expected. Whereas previously, Charles had always been the instigator of sex, Anne now found herself in the uncomfortable position of neither receiving his advances nor wanting to ask for them. She didn't feel confident enough to question him and so she dismissed her vague dissatisfaction as a pointless worry. Perhaps everyone felt like this on their honeymoon, she told herself.

On the third morning after their arrival, Anne woke up to find that Charles was no longer beside her. There was a hollowed-out shape in the mattress where he had been sleeping, but the sheets were cool enough to suggest he had been gone for some time.

'Charles?' she said, sleepily.

There was no answer. She slipped on a pair of socks and walked gingerly down the staircase. Downstairs, there was a single room with a small brown sofa in one corner, surrounded by a bookcase stacked half-heartedly with thin paperbacks. The newspaper they had brought with them from England lay messily folded on the seat of a threadbare armchair, the front page dominated by headlines about the conviction of six IRA men for a pub bombing in Birmingham. At the other end was a square table covered with a waxed red-and-white checked tablecloth. The front door just beyond it opened straight on to the tiled kitchen floor. There was no sign of Charles.

She crept back upstairs, telling herself there was nothing to worry about and yet still feeling a rising tide of panic. She realised that she had no idea of how to act. Here she was, suddenly adult and married, on her honeymoon with a husband who had turned out to be more of a mystery to her than she had ever imagined. She felt foolish, like a child trying on her mother's high heels with no notion of how ridiculous, how naive she appeared to the outside world.

Why had no one told her what to expect after the wedding? Why had no one said that marriage was a strange new world where you had to forge your own way with no advice, no parents to hold your hand and guide you through? Why did no one talk about how anti-climactic it was, how very depressing it was to feel so . . . so . . . Anne searched for the right word in her head and realised that what she most felt was not blissfully happy or perfectly content but trapped. Why hadn't she imagined she might feel like this? she asked herself hopelessly. She had been so focused on the engagement, the build-up and then the wedding itself that she had forgotten to think about what might come afterwards. Now here it was and she didn't know how to deal with the change in circumstance.

She got back into bed, keeping the socks on to warm up her frozen toes. She drew the eiderdown over her head and shut her eyes tightly in the hope that she could trick herself into going back to sleep. She remembered those nights as a child when her parents would come in late from a party and she would pretend to be asleep as they kissed her goodnight, and she felt tears sting her eyes. When she noticed she was about to cry, Anne gulped loudly in shock. This should be one of the happiest weeks of her life and here she was, miserably missing her parents. It was quite ludicrous, she admonished herself sternly. Charles was bound to be back soon – he had probably just popped out to find some croissants and coffee for breakfast.

The thought of breakfast was strangely reassuring – the sound of greaseproof paper being unwrapped, the smell of freshly baked bread, a pot of apricot jam the colour of amber, the gentle steaming hiss of the coffee pot. Her stomach rumbled. She was sure that was it. Charles had gone to get breakfast. Pacified, Anne went back to sleep, thinking that the noise of the front door opening would wake her up to Charles's imminent arrival.

He didn't come back all day. A thick dusk was settling over the dampened fields when the front door clicked open. Anne, lying on the bed upstairs, trying to read her book, tensed in alertness. 'Charles?' she said, and she realised it was the first word she had spoken for hours. Her voice sounded scratchy in the gloom.

'Yep,' he said loudly, and there was the sound of drawers being opened noisily, the banging of cupboard doors and a chair squeaking against the floor.

Anne didn't know what to make of it. She came downstairs, wondering if he had been held up in an accident or had got lost somewhere – anything, really, that would reasonably explain his lengthy absence.

Charles was sitting at the table, leaning back with his legs splayed out untidily. Half a baguette lay on the tablecloth, its crumbs scattered over the floor. The other half had been jaggedly torn off, and Charles was eating big chunks of the fluffy white dough, chewing with his mouth open and tearing off another bite before he had swallowed the first. He appeared ravenous.

'Hello,' he said, through a fine haze of spittle. Bits of bread were lodged in his cheeks: lumpy protrusions pushing through the tautness of his skin. He smiled and Anne felt instantly calmed. It was all right after all.

'Where were you?' she said, walking up behind him and putting her hands tentatively on his shoulders. He made no motion to turn and look at her. She could smell a combination of tobacco smoke and grease on his clothes, as if he had been sitting in a stuffy little café. The faint crenellations of his upper lip were stained red. It looked like wine.

'I went out.'

'I gathered that,' said Anne, with a jauntiness she did not feel. She could hear herself slipping into her mother's voice, as if she could find a sort of safety, a sense of how to act from simply adopting someone else's intonation. 'Where did you go, darling?'

Charles finished off the half loaf of baguette and licked his fingers. He got up without answering her and poured himself a glass of water from the sink. Anne felt foolish, standing there in her socks, unsure how to proceed. She twisted her hands together, clenching and unclenching fists, digging her fingernails into her palms. He looked at her levelly, lifted up the glass as if toasting her and then laughed, a low, dry sound like the put-put of a motorbike starting up in the distance. He brought the glass to his lips and tilted it back so that he downed the water in one single succession of noisy gulps.

'I couldn't sleep,' he said, finally. 'So I thought I'd explore.'

'Oh,' said Anne, after a moment. 'You should have woken me and I could have come with you.'

He snorted. There was a perceptible sneering curve to his upper lip. 'It wouldn't have interested you – tramping around the countryside. Besides, I know you like your sleep.'

Anne sat down at the table, attempting to hide her own bafflement. Should she be angry or understanding? Was this normal or was this unfair? What was her response meant to be? She decided to be conciliatory, almost jovial. This was a triviality. He had gone for a walk and left her to sleep. If anything, it was evidence of a degree of thoughtfulness on his part. All right, she might not have acted in exactly the same way and she had expected that they would spend every minute of their honeymoon together, but perhaps that was unrealistic. Not everything could be the romantic idyll one hoped for. She shouldn't make such a fuss.

She smiled at him. 'Well,' she said, 'I'm glad you're back now.'

'Yes, yes,' he said, nodding his head exaggeratedly. 'I'm back. That's the important thing, isn't it? Back to my wife, waiting here for me patiently like the good little spouse she is.'

There was something mildly threatening about his tone and yet he was still smiling, walking towards her, his arms outstretched as if nothing had happened. She didn't know what to make of this confusion of signals – the aggression of his voice combined with the apparent affection of his gestures – but she fell into his arms with a relief that bordered on gratefulness. He took her chin in one hand, pushing her face roughly to one side before kissing her cheek, pressing down on her so strongly that she could feel his stubble bristling uncomfortably against her chin. She forced herself to giggle. 'Ouch,' she said, trying to release her face from his grasp. She found that she couldn't. After several seconds, he let go of her. She started back towards the stairs. 'I'm just going to put some decent clothes on,' she said, finding suddenly that she had to control her voice to keep it from shaking.

'I don't think you should bother with clothes.'

'What do you mean?' she said, lightly.

'I mean, I don't think you should bother with clothes when I'm only going to take them off.' He glared at her. Much of his face was in shadow but his eyes were accentuated by the fading light, glinting like glassy blue marbles in the half-dark.

She didn't reply, but turned and walked up the stairs, each step creaking under her footfall. He followed close behind, putting one hand in the small of her back so that it felt as if he were pushing her forwards.

Upstairs, Anne sat mutely at the edge of the bed, the mattress springing softly beneath her. She took off her socks and the sight of her bare feet struck her as both pathetic and slightly absurd. She focused on the curved outline of each pink-white toe, pressed against the caramel-brown floorboards as Charles got undressed. She could see his erection poking through the thin cotton of his underpants as soon as he stepped out of his corduroy trousers, folding them with incongruous neatness and placing them carefully on the top of the chest of drawers.

'Turn over,' he said, tonelessly.

Anne turned over so that she was lying flat on her belly, her arms splayed out like a sacrifice.

'On all fours.'

She pushed herself up by the palms of her hands, the bones in her knees clicking loudly in the gloom. He positioned himself at her rear end, placing his cold hands on either flank of her buttocks. Quickly and without warning, he shoved his penis deep inside her, groaning as he moved deeper towards her core. Anne heard herself whimper. For a brief moment, she told herself this was what she had wanted – at least they were having sex like honeymooning couples were meant to – but then, with each new thrust, she felt herself switching off her thoughts one by one. There was no point in thinking any more. She just had to accept. Accept and survive.

Charlotte

CHARLOTTE HAD AGREED TO meet Gabriel after work for a drink in their pub. She knew it was a conscious effort on his part to re-inject their relationship with its early sense of thrilling opportunity, to ease the silent strain between them so that they could get back to normal. Whatever normal was, she thought dryly as she ordered a glass of the house white.

'Chardonnay or Sauvignon?' asked the barmaid, a careworn forty-something with dyed blonde hair and a purple T-shirt that revealed a baggy expanse of white marbled midriff.

'Erm,' said Charlotte, weighing up which one would be comparatively less awful. 'Sauvignon, please.'

The wine, when it came, cost £3.80 and smelled of glue. She took a sip and went to sit in a corner table, sliding into the dark wooden bench as carefully as she could so as not to spill any. She always seemed to be carrying too many bags and it was as she was trying to rearrange them under the table that she heard her phone beep with a text message. 'Running a bit late. Be there soon. Sorry. I love you x G.'

She looked at her watch. It was already 7.30 p.m. and she had been late herself. Annoyingly, she had just finished the novel she had been reading on the Tube and now had nothing to look at apart from a crumpled, slightly soggy copy of the *Evening Standard*. She flicked through the pages in a desultory fashion, the smell of stale beer rising unmistakably from the newsprint. There was a story about a minor royal on page three talking about a charity trek up Kilimanjaro. There was some of the usual boring news about

Tube strikes and planning disputes. Soon, she was reduced to completing the quick crossword on the back page. When she had done that, she started on the Sudoku panels but didn't get very far as her mind was wandering. She checked her watch again. 7.50. Charlotte felt her frustration mount and she knew this wasn't a good sign: if she didn't talk herself out of this impending gloomy mood, the evening would be blighted from the start. She knew what she was like: soon her mind would be playing tricks on itself, deliberately thinking the worst, purposely making herself feel insecure and untrusting and sad and angry all at once. At five to eight, Gabriel walked in the door accompanied by a cold gust of evening air, his eyes frantically scanning the room with a harassed expression, his hair windblown and his raincoat dishevelled.

He saw her and smiled, his shoulders relaxing.

'There you are,' he said, walking over. 'I'm so, so sorry.'

'It's fine,' said Charlotte, even though she knew her voice implied it was anything but.

'What are you drinking?'

'Paint stripper.'

He forced a smile. 'Oh dear. Well, can I get you something different?'

'No, don't worry. This cost me £3.80, after all. I refuse to be defeated.'

He looked relieved then, and the atmosphere lifted slightly.

'OK. I'm just going to the loo and then I'll get a drink.' He removed his coat and dumped it beside her, stooping down as he did so to kiss her on the lips. 'Hello, gorgeous,' he said, and Charlotte felt herself enveloped by warmth. She smiled. It was going to be all right.

'Hello, you.'

He walked to the tiny box-room that doubled as a lavatory at the back of the pub and Charlotte noticed he had left his briefcase on the seat next to her. It was open and there was a hardback book inside. Still looking for something to read, she took it out and saw that it was a second-hand copy of *Great Expectations*, the title picked out in black sans serif letters against a white-and-red cover. She opened the cover and saw '£5.50' scribbled in pencil in the upper right-hand corner of the flyleaf. She turned the page and her stomach lurched. A cold, creeping dread trickled down her spine.

'To my darling Gabriel,' read the handwritten inscription. 'To remind you of our wet weekend in Cornwall, keeping warm by the open fire. And to remind you how much I love you, always. Your loving wife, Maya.'

The handwriting was black and round and flowing, the letters curved and plump against the brown-yellow of the paper. It was an artistic sort of writing, its elegance heightened by its apparent careless ease. It was the kind of handwriting Charlotte wished she possessed, the kind that made her feel instantly inferior and pedestrian. She knew it was ridiculous, but looking at that dedication and thinking of all the intimate subtleties that it suggested, she found herself wishing that Maya's handwriting were easier to dismiss. If she only wrote with teenage silliness, dotting her 'i's with round circles, making the letters squat and unglamorous, expressing something straightforward and unromantic, Charlotte would find it far less threatening. Instead, it seemed simultaneously sophisticated and intelligent. There were three kisses underneath her name, a row of xs scattered like bullet-holes across the page.

She saw Gabriel approaching the table, a pint in one hand, a glass of wine in the other, taking great care not to spill anything as he wove between the higgledy-piggledy tables.

'Here we are,' he said, putting the drinks down and sliding in beside her on the bench. Then he noticed the book open in front of him and Charlotte could see his eyes register the dedication. She saw that he swallowed loudly and then quickly started to assess whether he had done anything wrong, taking a sip of his pint to play for time. A thin line of foam, like the trace of white bubbles left behind by a wave on a beach, formed across his top lip.

'So,' he cleared his throat, 'you've found my copy of *Great Expectations*?'

'Evidently,' said Charlotte, her voice clipped.

He closed the book and slipped it back into his bag. And then he waited, silent, bracing himself for what was coming next.

'Do you want to tell me about it?'

'Not particularly,' he said, a spikiness to his tone.

'Really? You don't want to tell me about your glorious weekend in Cornwall, snuggling up together in front of roaring open fires?'

'For Christ's sake, Charlotte . . .'

'Because I'd be interested. No, honestly, I'd be extremely interested to hear all about the wonderful times you had with your ex-wife.' She spat out the last word angrily.

Gabriel kept his voice quiet and level, whispering urgently as he always did when he wanted to portray himself as the reasonable one.

'Perhaps you'd like to tell me what exactly you were doing rifling through my briefcase?'

'I wasn't rifling –'

'Because I don't think that is the behaviour of someone who is meant to trust me – no, more than that, someone who professes to love me –'

'And I don't think that someone who professes to love me should be carrying around romantic trinkets from another woman.'

'I wasn't carrying it around –' He noticed his voice was getting louder and made an effort to regulate it. 'I was rereading a favourite book –'

'Oh, it's your favourite book, is it? How charming. How sweet that you got to share that with her.' She heard her voice coming out in a stream of vitriol and she hated it but at the same time, she couldn't stop. She felt so unbelievably angry and her distress was so righteous, so unfettered, that she couldn't help but allow all her irrationality to boil over, steaming out of her like a hot–cold cloud of liquid nitrogen.

And the thing was, she knew it was irrational. She had books that ex-boyfriends had given her and had written in, but the difference was that she would never carry them around with her to read. She would care enough about Gabriel's feelings not to take the risk that he would see anything that could hurt him. But beyond that, she thought, hissing and spitting with internal rage, the difference was that she had never bloody well been married.

Gabriel stared at her. She kept his gaze for several silent seconds, then dropped her eyes and took a substantial glug of wine.

'I forgot that she'd written in the book,' he said, talking slowly. He sighed. 'I suppose when you're in a relationship, even if you're not meant to be with the person you're with and on some level you acknowledge that, deep down . . . I suppose the thing is that you carry on making gestures, however hollow they might be because you're play-acting, in a way. It doesn't mean anything –'

'Of course it means something. She talks about how much she loves you "always".'

'But the point is, Charlotte, that I'm not with her, am I? I love you. I'm with you.'

He laid his hand over her clenched fist and stroked her fingers, coaxing them out, unfurling them so that she found herself holding his hand and it felt warm and soft against her skin. She didn't look at him.

'I'll stop reading it,' he said with a smile. 'I've read it so many times anyway that it's getting to be a bit boring.'

But for days afterwards, Charlotte found herself becoming increasingly obsessed with the idea of Maya. The handwriting seemed to have given Gabriel's ex-wife a life of her own, a shape, a sense, a hint of the sort of woman she might be. Until now, Charlotte had been able to treat her as a two-dimensional cut-out, a woman whom Gabriel did not love and, therefore, a woman who possessed none of her qualities or attractions or talents; a woman who need not trouble her.

The discovery of the book had challenged all those assumptions and shown them to be hopelessly superficial. Because the truth was that however he felt now, Gabriel had loved Maya once; had loved her enough to marry her; had believed that this love would last a lifetime. And wasn't the inevitable conclusion therefore that Maya and Charlotte probably shared some common attributes? That Gabriel had 'a type'?

A love of books, for instance, when previously Charlotte had thought that her long, wine-fuelled literary discussions with Gabriel were specific to their relationship. She had flattered herself that she possessed a cleverness, a kindred taste for the intellect that must have been sorely lacking in his former partner.

Or something as trivial as liking open fires. Or buying second-hand editions of *Great Expectations* in out-of-the-way charity shops or jumble sales. All of these things Charlotte had believed were in some way hers. They were what made her charming and unique. And now she felt she couldn't do any of them without somehow recalling the spectre of the woman who went before.

The thought gnawed away at her. She found herself rifling through Gabriel's wallet when he wasn't looking, scanning its contents for clues pertaining to his past life. She checked the text messages on his phone when he was in the bathroom, in a curious, half-paranoid frenzy. She wanted to find something incriminating to justify her suspicions, to prove that she had been right all along to mistrust him, but the bigger part of her simultaneously dreaded discovering he had been lying.

It turned out that there was nothing remotely sinister in either his wallet or his phone, but still she could not entirely escape the low buzz of discomfort. So she did something she could not explain, even to herself. She scrutinised Gabriel's driving licence and memorised the home address. She recognised the road name – Ellingham – as a residential street in the part of Shepherd's Bush that most locals like to convince themselves is actually the slightly posher part of Hammersmith.

One Wednesday lunchtime, when the two company directors huddled into a small office for something they grandly called a 'board meeting', Charlotte scurried to her car with her Pret à Manger chicken sandwich in one hand, the keys in the other. She felt absurdly underhand, like a bad spy being chased by a nebulous gang of assassins sent out on the orders of a podgy man with a white cat on his lap. She hastily opened the door and clambered in, slinging her bag and the sandwich into the passenger seat. An empty cup of coffee lay crumpled on the floor and as Charlotte looked at it, she found herself wondering whether Maya's car was as unkempt as hers. If, indeed, she had a car. Perhaps, thought Charlotte, she was a terribly worthy environmentalist who cycled everywhere looking impossibly glamorous with toned limbs and a special luminescent tailored jacket.

She turned the key in the ignition and set off. Within fifteen minutes, she was indicating to turn into Ellingham Road. She drove carefully over the road humps, scanning the passing front doors for numbers. As she got closer to number 12, she felt her heart beating noisily against her rib cage. Then, suddenly, there it was: a door painted duck-egg blue, a neat front garden that was mostly patio and a windowbox with straggly red geraniums. Charlotte parked as close as she could and waited, munching on her sandwich, her eyes trained on the door.

Although it was lunchtime, Charlotte had picked up from Gabriel that Maya worked from home on Wednesdays. She was an interior decorator and worked on a word-of-mouth basis for private clients. She was, Gabriel had said unthinkingly, incredibly good at what she did. At the time, Charlotte had filed away the comment as yet another thing to try not to be hurt by, but now it came back to her with its full, prickling force.

No wonder the front of the house looked so well-tended. She compared it to the windows of her own ground-floor flat, the paint peeling, the wood rotting, the panes of glass covered in a thin layer of grime and, in one spot that she had not got round to cleaning, the amoebic mark of a stranger's spittle.

Halfway through her second sandwich, the blue door shifted backwards. At first, Charlotte couldn't make anything out apart from the dim shadow of the hallway and the sound of a woman's voice.

'OK, yeah, sure,' came the voice. It sounded upper class but accessibly so; the sort of casual, consonant-dropping poshness that only the truly privileged can carry off. It sounded like the voice of a person who had been privately educated but who prided themselves on their liberal egalitarianism. It was the voice of someone who felt they had nothing to prove, a person comfortable in their own skin. 'I'll see if I can pop round first thing tomorrow if that suits you?' the voice continued. 'Great. OK, darling. Speak later.' Then, there she was, walking out of the house, snapping shut a mobile phone and slipping it into an expensive-looking handbag. Maya was petite, shorter than Charlotte and with smaller proportions – slim shoulders, tapered waist, a gentle curve of bust. She was wearing several different colours that shouldn't work together and yet somehow did – a coral pink blouse with delicate puffed sleeves, a pale grey skirt that stopped above the knee. She had bare, tanned legs with just a shading of calf muscle and extremely high heels in the same patent black leather as her handbag.

It surprised Charlotte to see that she was blonde. Her hair was bobbed to just below her ears, curled under as if it had been professionally blow-dried, and highlighted. Her face was striking rather than beautiful: she had a strong jaw and an aquiline nose, but she had good cheekbones and an aesthetically pleasing dip where her cheek slid into her chin. Her make-up was impeccable: glossy lips, subtle bronzer and neatly arched eyebrows. The top three buttons of her blouse were undone, revealing a flash of pert cleavage. She looked like the kind of woman most men would find sexy and most women would think was a newsreader.

Analysing it objectively, Charlotte could see that she was naturally prettier than Maya but she could also see that she made less of an effort to appear so preternaturally groomed. She couldn't work out if this was a good thing or not. And however reassuring she should find it that they looked so different physically, Charlotte instead felt it was rather worrying. If that was the type of woman Gabriel had loved so much he ended up marrying her, then what was she? A mousy alternative that he was taking for a test drive? Was it the superficial dissimilarity that so attracted him to her, as if – fresh from his divorce – he wanted to try out the exact opposite for a while, just for the hell of it?

But the worst thing of all was that Maya, with her easy phone manner, her colour co-ordination and her inherent sense of style, appeared so confident, so powerful and so very much in control of things. She did not look like a woman whose beloved husband had walked out on her. And, all at once, Charlotte started worrying that it was not Gabriel who had done the leaving, but Maya. What if he had been lying to save face? What if he was still in love with his ex-wife but had to ignore it, push it to one side and pretend it no longer mattered? What if . . .

Just at that moment, Maya turned her head to look over her shoulder, the hair swinging back slickly to reveal the contours of her face. She seemed to stare directly at Charlotte without seeing anything. They looked at each other for a second, uncomprehending; two women disconnected and yet inextricable. Then Maya turned and carried on walking.

It had only lasted for the briefest of seconds, a barely perceptible crease in the flatness of the day, and yet something about it stayed with Charlotte. It reminded her of another memory, another moment, another uncomprehending stare. She couldn't put her finger on it, but it made her feel strange; unsettled and sad. It was something about the look through the windscreen, the fact that Maya had shown no recognition or understanding despite the level of Charlotte's own intensity.

It was only when she had revved the engine and was backing out of the tight parking space that Charlotte remembered. The vision came to her with such shattering force that her bumper crashed into the car behind.

It was her mother. It was Anne, looking at her, meeting her gaze without acknowledgement. It was Anne's eyes that seemed so cool, so weirdly detached, so impassive. Her mother was looking at her and her eyes were blank, vacant, dug like deep holes into her face. And it was Charlotte, cowering in the corner, small, lonely, scared, who was asking her for help.

Anne; Charlotte

ANNE HAD A FAVOURITE doctor at the hospital. His name was Dr Lewis but he insisted that she called him George. 'It makes me feel less old,' he explained. Anne, to her embarrassment, heard herself giggling.

Dr Lewis was young with florid cheeks and an imposing physique that looked as though it might run to fat in later life. His black-brown hair was curly and slightly too long, hanging just below his earlobes so that he resembled a 1970s footballer. But he was undeniably attractive. There was something about his manner – reassuring, authoritative, kind but not overly familiar – that she responded to. She felt that he did not patronise her. He did not, like the nurses, call her 'dear' or 'sweetheart' or 'love' or any of those infantilising terms of professional friendliness that she so hated. Instead, he scrupulously referred to her as Mrs Redfern. She had never asked him to call her Anne.

They were sitting in Dr Lewis's office. It was a small room overlooking the river, furnished in shades of pale birch. Thick certificates and medical textbooks populated the shelves. A photo frame stood on the desk, its face turned inwards so that Anne, to her frustration, could not see whether the picture it contained was of a wife, a girlfriend or a child she never knew he had. There was a wilted rubber plant in a pot by the window, its leaves dusty.

'You should spritz some water on that,' said Anne, pointing vaguely at the plant.

Dr Lewis looked momentarily mystified and then turned to follow her gaze. 'Oh,' he said, his face breaking out in a smile.

'Yes, I know. I have been rather remiss. I'm not a natural gardener. You?'

'Yes,' she replied. 'I mean, I'm not brilliant at it. But I like growing things. I find it calming.'

It felt as though she had confessed something deeply intimate. Why was she wittering on like this, she wondered? Dr Lewis was a busy man. He had better things to do than talk about gardening.

'Sorry. You wanted to talk to me about Charles?'

'Yees,' said Dr Lewis, stretching out the single syllable and steepling his hands. 'There is no easy way to say this, Mrs Redfern . . .'

'You don't need to worry. I'm quite prepared.'

He nodded his head politely, as if acknowledging his relief that she was a superior sort of woman who wouldn't get hysterical but who could be trusted to remain calm, dispassionate and logical. Anne drew herself up in her chair, taking a deep breath and steeling herself to remain impressive at all costs. She wanted Dr Lewis's good opinion.

'I know that we've had a few conversations over the past weeks about your husband's condition. We are now getting to the point where difficult decisions need to be made,' he paused, allowing this to sink in. Anne met his eyes with level coolness, waiting patiently for him to continue. 'In general, the longer the coma, the less likely it is that the patient recovers. Mr Redfern suffered a severe brain injury and has now been in a comatose state for six weeks. He exhibits no voluntary movement or behaviour. We did all we could to reduce the swelling and bleeding in the brain, but the prognosis is – and I'm sorry to have to tell you this – extremely poor.' Another pause. 'It is my professional opinion that Mr Redfern will never fully recover. The risk is that he will spend the rest of his life in a persistent vegetative state unless –'

'Unless we switch him off,' said Anne, matter-of-factly.

Dr Lewis looked taken aback. 'I wouldn't put it quite in those terms,' he said, an understanding smile creeping across his face. 'And naturally, we will continue to give him the very best level of care as long as you consider that the best course of action –'

Or as long as the private health insurance keeps paying, thought Anne.

'It might be time for a conversation with your family about what would be in his – and, indeed, your – best interests.'

She had known it was coming, of course. She watched too many of those prime-time medical dramas not to realise the implications of Charles's prolonged absence from consciousness. But there was something about hearing it explained to her in such stark terms that shocked her. Suddenly, Anne found herself confronted with the reality of making a choice, rather than simply carrying on as she had been, obscuring any thoughts of the future with the deadening monotony of routine. She realised she would have to talk to Charlotte. The thought of it filled her with dread.

The chat with Dr Lewis meant that she was home later than usual. It was 3 p.m. by the time Anne got back and her stomach was grumbling noisily. One of the most irritating things about getting older, she found, was her increasing inability to go for more than a couple of hours without a regular portion of food. Someone had once told her it was to do with blood sugar. She rather feared it was simple greed.

She had just got the bread out from the fridge to make a ham sandwich when the doorbell rang.

It was Charlotte. The surprise of seeing her daughter on the front doorstep, arriving unannounced in the middle of a Wednesday afternoon, was so startling that Anne was momentarily unable to speak.

'Hi, Mum,' Charlotte said. Anne noticed that Charlotte was trying to smile, to pass off this unexpected visit as an entirely natural turn of events, but that the smile was tight like overstretched elastic.

'What on earth are you doing here?' It came out as an accusation when she had meant it to be robustly affectionate.

'I thought I'd surprise you.' Charlotte walked inside, wiping her feet on the doormat. She strode down the hallway, her old leather handbag slung over one shoulder and looking as though it needed a polish. She didn't turn back, so Anne was left standing foolishly in the open air, holding the door in one hand as she tried to get her thoughts in order. She closed it carefully and padded down the hallway to the kitchen in her socks – she always took her shoes off to avoid trailing dirt through the house.

'I was just making a sandwich,' she said, raising her voice in what she hoped was a suitably nonchalant fashion. 'Would you like one?'

'No thanks,' said Charlotte, who was leaning with her back against the Aga, her arms folded in front of her chest. 'I've just had one.'

'Let me take your bag –' said Anne, reaching towards her. Charlotte seemed to flinch and draw back and then, deliberately checking her abruptness, passed the bag over. Anne gripped its straps tightly, willing herself not to do or say anything stupid that might push her daughter further away. She placed the bag carefully on the sideboard. It was so rare that Charlotte ever dropped in. It felt to Anne as if an exquisite faun had appeared in the middle of a dense forest and the slightest noise of snapping twigs would scare her off.

Charlotte stood silently, staring abstractedly out of the window and into the garden.

'I've just come back from the hospital,' said Anne, trying to make conversation. 'I had a chat with that nice doctor – you know the one? Dr Lewis?'

'Mmm.'

Anne tittered self-consciously. 'He's such a nice man. And so young. I don't know if he's married or has a girlfriend, but –'

'Mum, don't.'

'Don't what?' said Anne, her hand with the butter knife freezing mid-air.

'I know what you're trying to do.'

'What?'

'All this talk about the eligible Dr Lewis –' she put on a funny voice when she said his name. 'I know you're trying to pair me off with a man you deem suitable.'

Anne was genuinely affronted. 'I was doing no such thing. I was just saying how nice he was.'

'Well, Gabriel's very nice too,' Charlotte said, before adding, under her breath but loud enough that Anne could hear, 'if you'd give him a chance.'

Anne carried on buttering her bread furiously, but the butter was too cold and made big holes in the dough. It was impossible, she thought bitterly, simply impossible to do or say anything that would please her. She might as well not even try.

'You're in a very bad mood all of a sudden.'

Charlotte didn't reply.

'Why aren't you at work?'

'Board meeting. They let me have the afternoon off.'

Anne didn't believe her. There was something about the tense set of her shoulders, the square, determined jut of her jaw that suggested she was upset about something. And when Charlotte got upset, she became stubborn and recalcitrant. Anne decided not to pursue the conversation any further and took a slice of ham out of a plastic packet, laying it neatly on top of the bread before folding it in two. She took a small bite, catching the crumbs in a cupped hand, and waited for Charlotte to say whatever she had come to say. She was mildly anxious that her daughter might confess to being pregnant, but she wasn't prepared for what came next.

'Did you ever think of leaving him?'

At first, Anne couldn't think who she was talking about: Gabriel? Dr Lewis? And then the realisation dawned: she was talking about Charles. She was stopped short by the question but she was not surprised by it. Part of her had been expecting it, just as part of her had been expecting Dr Lewis to tell her it was time to let go.

'No,' she said, calmly. She took another bite. She could have said more, but she didn't yet know where this conversation was heading, so she stopped herself, waiting for Charlotte to set the next parameters.

Her daughter turned to look at her and Anne could see all at once that her eyes were watery and squinting with something in between anger and hurt.

'No?' said Charlotte, her voice quietly incredulous. 'Not even after everything he put you – us – through?' Her voice dropped to a whisper.

'What do you mean?'

'You know what I'm talking about.'

Anne took two small steps backwards. It was a barely perceptible movement, but the tiny physical retreat enabled her to adopt her usual cool detachment when faced with the unpredictable squalls of emotion. She took herself out of the sphere of sentiment, removed herself from its clawing grasp, and acquired a lacquered coating of impenetrability. When she spoke, her words were deliberately dry, denuded of intensity. She spoke as if Charlotte were no longer her daughter – at least not recognisably so. She had to do this, otherwise she would feel too much and it would all dissolve in front of her – all the carefully constructed half-truths and acceptances would crumble. She could not, for this moment, allow herself to love her daughter too much. She had to gather herself together. She had to buy some time to think.

'Charles was – is – not perfect,' she found herself saying. 'No man can lay claim to that particular character attribute. But I made a decision and I stuck by it.'

Anne paused. And she thought about what she had said and she truly believed it. She had to – otherwise, what had any of it been worth?

'Which was?' Charlotte said, staring straight at her, her face impassive.

'I meant what I said when I took my wedding vows. Marriage is not something to be disposed of, thrown away, when things start to go wrong. It's something your generation doesn't seem to understand.' That hit home, Anne thought, looking at Charlotte wince as she made the inevitable connection to Gabriel. 'And really, dear, I don't see that it's any of your business.'

She took another bite of her ham sandwich and it was this studied gesture of normality, this seeming trivialisation of everything that had been said, which finally pushed Charlotte over the edge.

'None of my fucking business?' she hissed and the swear word was so unexpected that it lay there between them, slick as an oil spill.

'Don't swear, darling,' said Anne, witheringly. 'It doesn't suit you.'

'Don't call me darling,' Charlotte countered. 'It doesn't suit you.'

'I really don't know why you're so upset. You turn up, unannounced, in the middle of a weekday when you should be at
work. You storm in and then you expect me to answer all sorts of
personal questions –'

'It's not just about you, though, is it, Mum?'

'My marriage is absolutely about me,' said Anne with a stiff
control. 'It is about me and about Charles and it always has been.'

'No, Mum, no,' said Charlotte and her voice rose just as the
tears started to trickle down her cheeks. 'It was about me too.
That's the whole point.'

Without thinking, Anne stretched out her hand to wipe away
the wetness from her daughter's face.

'Don't touch me,' said Charlotte, her voice hoarse. 'Just don't.'
She picked up her bag and walked out of the kitchen and Anne
could hear the click-clack of her smart work shoes against the hallway floor and she knew Charlotte was walking away from her and
yet there was something that stopped her following. She let her go.
The front door slammed. The ham sandwich lay uneaten on the
sideboard.

Anne picked up the butter knife, still greasy and smeared with
yellow, and hurled it across the kitchen. Its handle thumped on the
cupboard door beneath the sink. The knife rebounded, skittering
across the red tiled floor before coming to a stop a few inches from
her foot. She looked at it lying there for a long while.

Charlotte walked out of the house in tears, her breath coming in
uneven, sobbing spurts. She hated crying in the street like this,
hated feeling so pathetic and helpless. She had no tissue with her
– it was the sort of thing Gabriel always had, neatly folded in
his jacket pocket – so she had to wipe her face with the edge of
her sleeve and this childish gesture made her feel even worse. She
couldn't understand how her mother could be so cold and simultaneously so desperate to be close to her. She knew that Anne loved
her with a claustrophobic, almost cloying intensity but she also
knew that this didn't come naturally to her mother – rather, it was
something Anne had acquired in the last few years as the realisation dawned that she hadn't given Charlotte enough affection

when it most counted. Never naturally tactile, Anne had taken to touching her at every opportunity – attempted hugs; uncomfortable kisses on the cheek; a tentative stroke of the arm that felt so horribly premeditated it made Charlotte shiver with a sort of distaste. It all seemed so insincere, as if Anne were trying to make up for lost time by giving her daughter all the built-up love at once; as if someone on a diet had denied themselves what they most desired for years and then, one day, decided to gorge on chocolate and litres of full-fat cream.

But co-existing with all this mad love was Anne's startling capacity to remove herself, to choose detachment when faced with too much truth. Was it a defence mechanism? Maybe, thought Charlotte, but how could she stand it when her own daughter was standing there, crying, asking her for help?

By the time she got to her car, Charlotte had wiped away most of her tears and was able to see clearly enough to get the key into the door. She took a few deep breaths and told herself to calm down. It had been a curious lunchbreak, she thought to herself dryly: first the shock of seeing Maya, then that sudden serrated glimpse of long-forgotten memory, then the strange confrontation with her mother. No wonder she felt overwrought. She must try to collect her thoughts before returning to the office. She sniffed loudly.

'Charlotte?'

She turned, half-expecting to see her mother standing behind her, arms outstretched in apology. But instead, it was Janet, dressed in a vast grey poncho that appeared to be made out of the sort of thick, South American wool sold in craft market stalls labelled 'alpaca'. Janet, short and plump, seemed almost drowned in it. Only her round head and stocky legs protruded. The sight of her, with her uncertain smile and kind eyes and her ludicrous clothes, instantly made Charlotte feel better.

'Janet,' she said, hoping it was not obvious she had been crying. 'How are you?'

'Oh I'm fine, thank you.' Janet beamed. 'Have you popped in to see your Mum?'

'Yes. There was a board meeting at work, so I, um, had a few hours spare.'

Janet nodded her head, her watery blue eyes never leaving Charlotte's face. 'That's nice of you,' she said. 'I'm sure Anne really appreciated it.'

Charlotte snorted. 'I don't think so.'

Janet looked perplexed and then, without a word, an arm jutted out from beneath the capacious grey folds and she took Charlotte's hand in hers. Janet was wearing thick, fingerless gloves and the wool felt scratchy against Charlotte's skin, but not unpleasantly so. In fact, there was something about that simple gesture that was exactly right: just reassuring enough. Charlotte smiled.

'It must be such an awful time for you,' Janet said. And then, after a moment: 'I hope Gabriel is looking after you?'

Charlotte was surprised that Janet remembered his name. She had never spoken about him to her. Her mother must have said something. She was obscurely touched that Janet had made the small effort to remember his name and to get it right.

'Yes. He is. He's been really great.'

'That's good. I'm so glad you have someone like that in your life – someone kind and supportive.'

There was a small silence.

'Your mother loves you very much,' said Janet, so softly that her words were almost blown away on the breeze, 'even though I know she doesn't always show it.'

Charlotte looked at her, both disconcerted and comforted by Janet's atypical outspokenness. What an extraordinary thing to say, thought Charlotte. This woman whom she had always half-dismissed as a bit of a joke, a perfectly pleasant sort of busybody, a nice, lonely middle-aged woman on the lookout for friends, but not one that Charlotte would ever have imagined possessed this sort of insight. Perhaps she had underestimated her.

'Anyway,' Janet said, dropping Charlotte's hand and briskly rearranging her poncho. 'You and Gabriel must come round for dinner when you have a free evening.'

'I'd like that,' said Charlotte and she realised that she meant it. 'I'd really like that.'

Janet was conspicuously thrilled. 'Wonderful, wonderful! You let me know some dates that would suit you and I'll get Anne round and we can make a night of it. I'm so glad I ran into you like this – I've been meaning to ask for ages.'

'I'm glad too.'

'Well,' said Janet, stroking the front of her poncho as if smoothing down bobbles of fluff. 'Well,' she said again. A shaft of sunlight appeared from the drizzle-grey sky and glinted off the side of Janet's spectacles.

'I'd best get back to the office, Janet, but it was lovely to see you.'

'You too, Charlotte. Drive carefully.'

Janet stood on the pavement as she got into the car. Charlotte waved at her through the windscreen and when she drove away, she could see Janet still standing there, a small grey blob of familiarity gradually receding into the distance.

Anne; Charles

THE TRENEMANS WERE HAVING a wine and cheese party. Anne had secretly been dreading the evening for several weeks, ever since Cynthia Treneman had popped round and knocked on the door, shouting 'yoohoo' in her irritatingly piercing sing-song. 'Just wondering if you and Charles can make it round for a little soirée we're planning,' she said. 'It's going to be a wine and cheese evening. Terribly sophisticated!' She laughed with a shrill tinkle. Anne tried to laugh along with her, but found that the smile stuck on her lips.

She had said yes to Cynthia because it was generally viewed as 'the done thing' to be sociable on this street. The neighbours, who were all young-marrieds with small or about-to-exist children, prided themselves on their extended friendship group. They turned up faithfully to bridge nights and birthdays, to dinner parties and housewarmings, to weekend barbeques and ironically themed Hallowe'en evenings. The same faces, smiling, smiling, chatting, chatting, holding glasses of tepid wine and making the same familiar jokes as if trying to convince each other they were still happy and urbane and cosmopolitan, still capable of drunkenness and flirtation and the unthinking excesses of youth, still at the heart of a swinging social scene when, in actual fact, they were like flies trapped in honey, sliding into the sticky morass of suburban normality.

Cynthia was a small, busty woman who wore twinsets in varying shades of pastel, always neatly accessorised with a single string of pearls, and discreetly dyed hair. She spoke in a series of exclamation marks and laughed through her teeth. When Charles and Anne had first moved to this street in Kew shortly after returning from their honeymoon, it had been Cynthia Treneman who was the first to introduce herself, bringing with her a bottle of Blue Nun wrapped up in tissue paper that appeared to be fragranced with a cloying floral scent.

'To help you settle in,' Cynthia had said, each syllable weighted down with an ingratiating meaningfulness. 'Welcome to Carlton Avenue!'

Charles thanked her so profusely that Anne could not help groaning inwardly at his obvious insincerity, but Cynthia was charmed. Soon she was giggling and slapping his arm playfully with her bejewelled hand. 'Stop it!' Cynthia screeched, apropos of nothing in particular. 'You're so naughty! Oh, Anne, how do you cope with him?'

Not all that successfully, Anne thought to herself dryly. In the weeks and months since their wedding, Charles had increasingly set himself apart from her, becoming more and more aloof with each day that passed. It was not that he was unkind, exactly, it was just that he seemed to have no particular desire to spend much time in her company. At weekends, he would occasionally disappear for the day without explanation, returning for supper in a state of contained agitation. He would sit down at the table and eat vast quantities of food, washed down with glugs of wine, refusing to speak until he had finished, as if recharging himself. On one occasion, she had noticed small green burrs stuck to the back of his tweed jacket and she wondered if he had been walking somewhere in the countryside. On another, he had scaled the façade of the house and entered through the attic window. Anne had screamed when he appeared in the kitchen, terrified that he was a burglar.

'Did you forget your keys?' she asked, her hands shaking.

'No,' he replied. 'I just felt like showing it could be done.'

But at times, he could be extremely affectionate, surprising her with a sudden kiss between the shoulder blades as she washed up or presenting her with a small blue jewellery box containing a silver bracelet engraved with their initials. Both the disappearances and the demonstrative gestures came equally out of the blue so that, afterwards, Anne would always wonder if she had invented them. There was a randomness to his behaviour that she could never understand.

For the most part, Anne had learned not to question his mysterious absences for fear of pushing Charles further away or angering him unnecessarily. Instead, she convinced herself that all married couples needed their own space. The best that she could do for Charles was to allow him his and to be there when he came back. Besides, she reasoned, he was the breadwinner and he needed to be able to relax on his own terms – his job in the city was time-consuming and pressurised and allowed them both to live in four-bedroomed, red-bricked splendour within walking distance of Kew Gardens.

The house was Victorian and sat squatly on its haunches, set back from the road by a small patio dotted with stone flower tubs. The front door was patterned with dusky panels of stained glass and opened on to a tiled hallway. Off to the left, a green-carpeted sitting room with a bay window was dominated by a large fireplace and over-plumped sofas. The kitchen had a cream Aga along one wall and French doors opening on to a long stretch of lawn.

Anne had never entirely shaken the feeling of being a stranger here. The proportions of the house were so vast that it felt like being a child playing make-believe adult games, but Charles had insisted they would need the space when they started having children.

'It's a family home,' he said confidently when the estate agent showed them round.

Anne smiled with acquiescence. She attributed the slight shiver she sensed on her skin when she walked the corridors to the fact that the house was filled with other people's furnishings. It would be far more homely once she'd been able to make it her own.

But even after they'd moved in, Anne discovered that the sofa she bought at John Lewis – a neat two-seater upholstered in a cheerful, floral pattern – was swamped by the largeness of the sitting room. The comfortable armchair that her parents had given her, inherited from some long-lost aunt with a taste for battered leather, suffered a similar fate: it looked like doll's house furniture in a giant's home. In the end, the sitting room stayed more or less as it had been – green and grand and yet simultaneously stuffy, like a cordoned-off museum piece in a stately home – and neither of them used it much unless they had people round. It started to radiate the unmistakable mustiness of abandonment, the slightly stale scent of wood polish and damp carpets. The chintz sofa ended up in the kitchen. The leather armchair, Anne put in the smallest bedroom that doubled up as Charles's study.

They had been living there for eight months and, in that time, had hosted only two social events for their neighbours, which Anne knew was generally regarded as a disappointing performance average. Most couples around here managed one dinner party every other month, interspersed with less formal gatherings where not-quite fashionable music would be played on record players and the food would consist of cocktail sticks threaded with cubes of cheese and pineapple. Of the two, Anne much preferred the latter because she knew they never lasted as long – it was perfectly acceptable to 'make an appearance' at one of these drinks parties before insisting one had to be somewhere else – but with dinner parties, Charles tended to linger into the early hours, getting progressively drunker and more sociable as the evening wore on, so that she often found herself hanging around far longer than she intended, attempting to catch his eye in a meaningful fashion that would not be interpreted as rudeness by the other guests. The evenings were never as fun as she was meant to find them.

And now they had agreed to go to the Trenemans' and there was no way out of it. Anne was already feeling nervous. Looking at the clock on the kitchen wall, she noticed that it was just after 7 p.m. and Charles was late back from work, despite promising that he wouldn't be. She started scrubbing down the worktop surfaces with a dishcloth to take her mind off her unease, even though she had already cleaned them a few hours before. Then she cast a critical eye over the windows above the sink and noticed the tell-tale silvery screeds of a spider's web in one corner. She took out a feather duster from the cupboard beneath the stairs and ferociously jiggled it so that the threads broke off and collapsed in a tangle on to the windowsill. Then she stretched a layer of cling-film over several bowls of coronation chicken that she had made earlier in the day and placed them in the fridge, with a view to eating them at intermittent intervals through the coming week.

She looked at the clock again. 7.10. She sighed. There was no point putting it off any more. She would have to get ready.

Anne made her way upstairs to their bedroom and sat down on the pink velvet stool in front of her dressing table. She started brushing her hair methodically, staring at her face without quite seeing it. Although these days she increasingly found herself feeling faded, drained and empty, she acknowledged that she still looked striking in the mirror's reflection. She had lost a bit of weight recently without really trying and her cheekbones appeared more prominent, so that her face seemed somehow to hang better. She was lucky in that her features were regular and symmetrical – almond-shaped eyes that disappeared into almost-squints when she laughed, pale, fluid lips that were just fleshy enough not to appear stretched and a high, smooth forehead. Hers was an obvious attractiveness. It struck you immediately and then sat there, not having to prove itself. It was not especially interesting – you did not have to work to appreciate it – but it was easy, straightforward and pleasing to look at. When Anne smiled, it still gave her a vivacious air that others found charming. But she noticed that her smiles now never quite reached her eyes. They seemed glazed, somehow, as if drawn on to her face.

Her life had become a daily routine of nothing much and although a part of her had always craved this habitual domesticity – had hoped, in essence, to find security in it – she had never envisaged it being shaped by an absence of ease. She had always imagined a happily mutual marriage, where Charles would go out to work and return, pleased to see her and grateful for the meal on his table, while she would take pride and delight in making things nice for him, in keeping house, in feathering her nest in preparation for children. But it hadn't worked out like that. Anne wasn't yet pregnant despite Charles's regular advances – he appeared to regard the business of procreation as another mindless task to perform, another index card to be filed away – and she found that she felt alone and bored. Not having children felt like a profound failing, an emptiness that spoke of her worthlessness as a woman, especially as she found herself surrounded by smugly fecund females popping out babies with disheartening regularity. In the darkest moments, the moments that she hardly ever allowed herself to contemplate, she felt terribly sad.

Anne found the best way to deal with it all was to pretend it wasn't happening. There was nothing much she could do about it now and she felt ashamed for having self-righteously ignored Frieda's warnings. She made an oddly conscious decision not to follow her thoughts to their worst conclusions, instead erecting a mental dam against the flow of her half-buried misery. She acted as if the superficialities – the surfaces she had made so pretty and clean and sweet-smelling – were indicative of greater meaning. She surrounded herself with the trappings of happiness and did not question them. Disconcertingly, she found that no one else questioned them either and, in this way, Anne was able to convince herself that the appearance of something was the best substitute for its actual existence. She found that her mental neatness started to manifest itself on her outward environment – she cleaned the house with ferocious efficiency, had two baths a day and took great care with her make-up.

Anne started to apply her face powder, dabbing it on to her skin with a thin pad clogged up with years of use. It smelled lightly of vanilla pods and flour and it gave her a twinge of hope, a light fragrance of expectation. She spritzed some perfume – Yardley's White Linen – on her wrists and on the nape of her neck just beneath her hairline, something that her mother had taught her to do because it was meant to last longer that way. With an eyeshadow brush, she painted a slick of beige across her lid, accentuated by a small triangle of darker brown on the outer edges. She covered her lashes with a thin coating of mascara – dark brown because black looked common – and then swept her cheekbones with pale blush. She sat back to examine herself with a critical gaze and then she heard the keys turn in the front door. Anne looked at her watch: 7.25. They were due at the Trenemans at 7.30 for 8.00, which meant that, depending on Charles's mood, they might just make it.

She took a deep breath and smiled so she would sound more cheerful than she felt.

'Hello, darling,' she said, her voice slightly raised.

'Hello.' There was the sound of scuffling and muttering downstairs, of his coat being taken off and his briefcase being put on the hallway floor. Then she heard him walk into the kitchen and open the fridge. What was he doing? she wondered. He knew they were going out – surely he wasn't making himself something to eat now? But then she heard a clattering of china and knew that he'd taken out one of the bowls of chicken. There was a silence which meant he was probably eating and then, shortly afterwards, the sound of him making his customary gin and tonic. Anne got up from the stool and walked downstairs.

She entered the kitchen and saw Charles facing away from her, standing over the sink and looking out of the window at the garden beyond. It was autumn and the leaves from a tall oak tree were in constant fall, leaving a thick layer of brittle brown-red covering the lawn like a spilled glass of beer. He did not turn round even though he must have heard her footsteps. She tried to interpret what this meant about the mood he was in and found that she couldn't.

'Hello, darling,' she said again, feeling slightly stupid for repeating herself. He turned to her.

'What time are we due at the Trenemans'?' he asked, taking a sip of his gin and tonic. The ice cubes bumped noisily against the side of the tumbler. So at least he'd remembered, Anne thought with relief.

'Cynthia said 7.30 for 8.00 so you're just in time,' she said brightly.

He crunched an ice cube noisily between his teeth and then looked at his watch, an unnecessarily shiny silver Rolex that he had bought himself when he started his job.

'Right. Well, I'd better have a shave.' His eyes met hers, unsmiling. 'Is that what you're wearing?'

Anne glanced down at her dress. It was a patterned empire-line cotton smock in emerald green. Two strings hung from the neck, each one ending in three small silver balls that jangled as she walked. She had bought it recently on a trip to Sloane Square because she loved the depth of the colour and because wearing it made her feel other than who she was. It was an exotic dress, a dress that breathed optimism and laughter and youth. It was the sort of dress she used to wear. It felt good against her skin.

But now, looking at it out of the light of the shop changing room, she saw it suddenly through Charles's eyes and worried that it appeared absurd, too ornate and over-the-top for an evening at the Trenemans'. Their neighbours would no doubt look at her askance, as if she had ideas above herself, as if she was trying to make them feel foolish in their provinciality simply by wearing something quite so unapologetically impractical. She bit her lip, feeling sick inside.

'I thought so, yes,' she said, her voice uncertain. 'What do you think?' And she forced herself to give a gay little twirl, like a fifties film star.

'It's very . . .' he broke off for several seconds. 'Adventurous.' He swallowed the rest of his drink in one quick motion, put the glass down on the side of the sink and walked past her without saying anything more. After a few moments, she heard the sound of a basin filling with water upstairs.

She felt dejected, as if the air had been sucked out of her. She didn't know whether to change or not. If she changed, she would be equally nervous that Charles wouldn't like the new outfit and a part of her would feel pathetic, as if she had no mind of her own. But if she stayed in the dress, she knew it would make her uncomfortable all night; she knew she would constantly be questioning her own taste and wondering if everyone was looking at her with secret disapproval. In the end, she walked into the hallway and took down a long black cashmere cardigan from the coatrail to wear over the top. The dazzling green of the dress now appeared dulled against the dark fabric. She felt her eccentricities had been sufficiently disguised.

Then, noticing the bottle of Gordon's still open on the counter, she poured herself a large tumbler of gin. She debated adding a splash of tonic but, before she had time to decide, she downed the glass in a single slug. Anne felt the clear liquid spiciness trickle down her throat and slam into her stomach. Her gastric juices bubbled and twisted with the sudden heat of alcohol. She poured herself another glass and knocked it back. By the time Charles came down, freshly shaved and wearing a new shirt, Anne felt pleasurably numbed against the evening.

Cynthia's husband, Giles, opened the door. 'Well, hello there, Redferns!' he said with half-mocking jollity. He was a florid-faced man who drank too much, the redness of his capillaries getting more intense with each glass of Burgundy. Tonight, the veins in his nose were criss-crossed like contour lines on an ordnance survey map. Anne took this to mean he was already pretty far gone.

'Hello, Giles,' she said, smiling and leaning in to kiss him on the cheek. His skin felt clammy against hers. He hugged her for slightly too long and pushed himself slightly too close to her so that she had to step away first.

'Annie! Looking lovely as ever.' He made a great show of taking her by the hand and standing back to admire her. 'You are a lucky bugger, Charles,' Giles said, pumping him by the hand and drawing them into the heat and the party noises. There was the sound of tinkling Richard Clayderman piano music coming from within and the occasional staccato burst of laughter.

'Come in, come in. Cynthia's just doing the rounds with a particularly good French brie.'

Anne glanced at Charles and, for a brief moment, they shared a look of pure camaraderie at the awfulness of the situation they found themselves in. Charles took her hand and gripped it tightly as they walked into the Trenemans' sitting room. She felt absurdly thrilled at this small, physical gesture. In one stroke, all the insignificant strain and build-up of the evening dissolved into nothing. He did love her after all.

Cynthia beetled up to them in a flurry of hairspray and pale purple angora. 'Anne! Charles! So pleased you could make it!' She air-kissed Anne and then made a semi-lunge for Charles, leaving a wet smudge of lipstick at the corner of his mouth.

'Cynthia, you're looking spectacular,' Charles said with a wolfish grin. 'Thanks so much for having us over. It all looks wonderful.'

He sounded so unutterably genuine that Anne found herself casting an eye round the room in case she'd missed something. But no, there were the usual suspects in evidence – the Gordons (Tina and Max), the Chethursts (Gwen and Tommy), the Stenhams (Julie and Terry) and the Cockburns (Marcus and Antonia). Marcus caught her eye and raised his wine glass with an almost imperceptible leer. Anne winced involuntarily. He was a strange little man, whose hair was always overgrown and whose collars were always unwashed. For some reason, he had taken a particular shine to Anne from the moment they'd moved to Carlton Avenue. It had become something of a joke in their social circle because, at parties, he would trail after her with a hang-dog stare, totally ignoring his mousey but well-meaning wife.

Tonight proved to be no exception. Almost as soon as Cynthia had plied them with chunks of refrigerated brie (served on a red napkin triangle), Marcus shuffled across the room, his shoulders hunched forward with intent. When she looked round, Anne found that Charles had disappeared.

'So, how have you been keeping, Anne?' Marcus said, passing a hand through his greasy hair so that a light sprinkling of dry skin scattered on to his shoulders like dust. His breath smelled tepidly of old vegetables and cheap wine.

'Very well, thank you, Marcus,' Anne said, a vague smile fixed in place. 'How's Antonia?'

'Oh, she's fine.' He glanced in the direction of his wife, who was gripping her glass of orange juice with two hands, her eyes darting nervously around the room. Giles, noticing her isolation, immediately strode up to Antonia with a tray of cheddar. He wasn't a bad sort really, thought Anne as she watched Giles engage her in a vociferously one-way conversation.

Marcus was standing so that his shoulder brushed against her cardigan, saying something complimentary about Anne's dress. Anne zoned out, giving him non-committal but polite answers while letting her mind wander over other things. She wondered what she and Charles would do this weekend, whether he was going to do his enigmatic disappearing act or whether she could tempt him into a few hours of togetherness. Perhaps they could go to Petersham and have a picnic on the riverbank like they used to in Grantchester, she thought. Perhaps they could re-establish some of their old, easy intimacy. Perhaps she could cook him a favourite meal. But then she realised she had no idea what his favourite meal would consist of and, besides, she knew she was a terrible cook despite her best efforts, and then Anne felt curiously flat all over again, the faint flicker of lightness she had experienced when Charles took her hand suddenly doused by the cold dankness of the reality of their life as it now existed. She blamed herself for not being able to keep his attention. He was too charming, too clever, too good-looking for her and he always had been. She was an unpolished pebble next to his dazzling diamond. She was meant for men like Marcus: men suffocated by their own accumulations of disappointment, men who never expected to do much more than fail, who treated anything mildly good as a happy accident, who were crumpled by the expectations of others and who would not demand anything other than the chance to claim her as their own. Men who would not challenge her sense of self. Men who could be understood and contained by their own limitation. Men with dirty shirt collars. Men whom she didn't love.

She took a large sip from the glass of wine that had appeared in her hand. It mingled with the gin she had drunk earlier, enveloping her in a cloud of fuzzy detachment. She noticed that her eyes were not focusing quite as sharply as they should and that her tongue felt slightly too big for her mouth. She scanned the room, trying to find Charles's familiar outline but she was overwhelmed by the noise of braying couples, the clink of bottle against glass and the bright swirl of her green, green dress against the Trenemans' patterned white carpet. She felt a sudden urge for water.

'Excuse me,' she said to Marcus, who was looking at her with great significance, his eyes attempting to search out reciprocation where there was none. She was familiar with how that felt, with the cruel unrequitedness of it, and she felt a pang of sympathy for him. 'Sorry, I just need to get some water.'

Marcus nodded his head limply, accustomed to the sensation of defeat, and turned back towards Antonia without a word.

Anne made her way to the Trenemans' kitchen along the corridor, steadying herself by tracing the walls with the flattened palm of her hand. The air seemed to expand and contract around her, painting the evening in surreal, dream-like shades. She must have drunk more than she thought and she hadn't eaten since breakfast – there never seemed much point in digesting a proper meal when Charles wasn't there.

The kitchen was tucked away behind the stairs, around a corner at the end of the corridor. The door was closed but a narrow line of light was filtering through the gaps where the edges did not quite meet the frame. There was muffled laughter coming from inside and something that sounded like hushed squeaking. She wondered idly whether the Trenemans' two young children – Camilla and Timothy – had crept downstairs to polish off the leftovers, sipping on half-finished glasses of wine with an illicit, adult excitement. She smiled at the thought of this as she pushed open the door.

A bright yellow light poured out of the room, temporarily blurring her focus and numbing her sense of what was going on. She found she had to take a step back before she could work out what she was seeing, consciously removing herself from the immediacy of the scene so that the oddness of it could be filtered through her mind.

There were two figures huddled together, one male, with his back to her, and one female. The woman was half-sitting, half-standing against the lip of the sink, her pale purple angora cardigan in a state of disarray, her knee-length skirt hitched up over her thighs so that the material had become stretched out of shape, her flesh straining and spilling against the hem that was cutting into her skin. The woman's plump legs, shiny with the sheen of nude stockings, were spread apart. The man was pushed up against her, one arm round the woman's back, the other hand pressed up underneath her skirt. The woman was giggling and simultaneously trying not to. Her eyes were shut in an approximation of helpless lust, the lids smeared with bright blue shadow. The man was laughing softly, shushing her and then groaning, softly at first and then more loudly as his hand worked its way further up the skirt. She squirmed at his touch, wriggling underneath his weight and then she seemed to surrender herself to it and the giggles transmuted into a series of high-pitched chirruping noises.

For several moments, the couple did not realise they were being watched. The man's arm was pumping up and down. The woman was panting noisily, her cheeks glistening, her hair coming undone. Then, mid-squeal, the woman opened her eyes. Her face slackened in horror. Her mouth dropped open. She looked at Anne standing in the doorway and then looked away.

'Charles,' the woman said, but still the man's arm kept moving. 'Charles,' Cynthia said, her voice more calm and adult than Anne had ever heard it.

'What?' His arm stopped moving. He was wearing his favourite tweed jacket, the one with patches that Anne had sewn on when his elbows wore through the tattered fabric.

She stared at the familiar outline of his broad shoulders, at the thickness of his hair, at the back of his head, his neck, the places she had touched and caressed and thought were hers alone. She stared at them with such intensity that she felt she could almost touch and smell him. She stared at him and willed him back to how he used to be, to how she had once imagined him. She stared at him and hoped, beyond hope, that she wasn't seeing what was in front of her. And she realised, all at once, that this couldn't be explained away and the knowledge of that felt like a rock being thrown into a deep, deep well, the echo of its fall sounding in the pit of her stomach.

He turned, at last, to look at her. She saw the blueness of his eyes and she saw that there was nothing beyond them. Wordlessly, Anne walked into the centre of the kitchen, still staring at them, trapped in their farcical embrace against the sink. She looked at them for what felt like a long time, her breath coming and going with disquieting regularity – in and out, in and out, in and out – the soft, whistling sound of it displacing the dead air in the room, shifting its atoms to one side, squeezing out the weight and shape and heat of what surrounded her so that there was nothing left except a bright blank numbness.

For a brief suspended moment she wondered if perhaps she was going to scream, or slap Cynthia around the face, or hurl a glass against the wall so that it would shatter into a thousand shrapnel splinters. And then she knew she wasn't going to do any of these things. She swallowed the scream. She stilled her hand. She stifled the physical impulse to react.

She had lost faith in her own judgement, in her own ability to read a situation, to decipher what it meant. Her confidence had been chipped away, small slivers of certainty chiselled off over time so that all that was left was a single, fragile shaving blown about in the breeze of other people's movement. She had lost her naive ease of self, the unquestioned assumption that the world was a fundamentally good place and that she was owed her own happy existence in it. She had lost it without noticing what was happening and now she had no one left to blame but herself and her own youthful arrogance. She had been so conceitedly confident, so irredeemably smug when she got married.

She did not want to run back to her parents and admit defeat. She did not want Frieda to have been right. She did not want to be the wife whose husband had been caught in an embarrassing tryst with the bubbly next-door neighbour, a woman inferior in both looks and intelligence; a woman so different in outlook and personality that it seemed to overturn everything Anne had once thought about her own attractiveness. She wanted to believe in what she had once taken for granted and, for this to be achieved, she had to sacrifice this new, uncomfortable knowledge. She had to push it to one side and pretend she had never seen it. Because, above and in spite of it all, she still wanted Charles. And although she hated herself for this, although she despised her own weakness, she knew with insurmountable certainty that this was the single most important fact of her existence. She was in love with him and she always would be, however trapped it made her. She couldn't explain it. But there was something that pulled her fatally towards his power, as if the blackness of him drained everything else of colour.

No one spoke.

Anne turned and walked out of the kitchen. The swish and jangle of her dress made a weirdly tinny sound as she moved. She took her coat from a pile hanging over the banisters. She let herself out of the front door and walked back down the road to their house.

That was when the bitterness started to bloom inside her, a bruise spreading inexorably outwards, staining her consciousness. Gradually, over the coming weeks and months and years, Anne started to realise her own personality no longer existed as a separate entity. The wholeness of her identity began to divide and scatter into tiny pieces that drifted noiselessly into the atmosphere. She was losing herself, sinking slowly into the silt, waiting for Charles to come back to her, waiting, waiting, waiting for the affirmation that she had been right all along.

Charlotte

CHARLOTTE HAD ONCE ADMITTED to Gabriel that she had never raised her voice in anger to either of her parents. They were talking about something entirely unconnected, drinking strong mugs of foamy coffee at their local café – the sort of place that was slightly too smug for its own good: its bread was 'artisan' and you had to sit at a rustic-style communal oak dining table – and he asked her to remember the last time she had argued with her family. Charlotte took a small bite of her heart-shaped shortbread biscuit and reflected for a few seconds, a small line appearing between her eyebrows as she thought. 'I don't think I ever have.'

Gabriel's mouth dropped open.

'What?' he said incredulously, dropping his teaspoon for effect. 'You must have argued with your parents. Everyone argues with their parents.'

Charlotte laughed. 'I can't remember a single time I've ever raised my voice at them.'

'You've never raised your voice at them? Charlotte, my darling –' He took her hand in his and it felt warm, like fresh-baked dough. 'You've got serious problems.'

And it was true that Charlotte could not remember ever having shouted at either Anne or Charles, despite often feeling so angry towards them. She could remember clearly the feelings of pent-up rage, but she did not have a memory of ever having translated that rage into anything external. She had never once lashed out.

'You shout at me all the time,' said Gabriel, kissing the tips of her knuckles. He had a small speck of foam from his cappuccino at the corner of his lips. Charlotte wiped it away with her forefinger.

'Mucky.'

'Yes,' he said. 'I'm terribly mucky. I'm also very dirty-minded.' Then he got that look in his eye and Charlotte knew that they would spend much of the afternoon in bed, with the blinds down against the outside world, cocooned in the lovers' luxury of doing something not-quite-right in the middle of the day.

But afterwards, she kept coming back to that conversation. Why was it that she felt able to shout at Gabriel – to scream and be unreasonable and emotional and irrationally passionate all at once until it was out of her system – in a way that she wasn't able to with her own parents? She came to the conclusion that part of it was to do with fear. She was always frightened of upsetting the febrile equilibrium at home, of unwittingly ripping a hole in the tightly stretched film of unspoken accusation that lay between her and her parents. If it was unspoken, it meant that all three of them could pretend it didn't exist. It meant that they could go on acting like a normal family even if the performance had no depth. What mattered was the appearance: both to the outside world but, more importantly, to each other.

There was another, more ingrained fear that Charlotte found it difficult to acknowledge to herself and that was the fear of her father. It was a terror that mingled with admiration and a desire for affection, so that Charlotte could often not distinguish between the knotted-together threads of frayed emotion. The thought of facing him down, of accusing him, of telling him exactly what he had done to her, was impossible. It left Charlotte with a sense of nauseous trepidation. He would be able to out-argue her, as he had always done. But he was also in a position of power: he could withdraw his love.

The realisation horrified her. For as long as she could remember, Charlotte had valued herself according to the value placed on her by others. It was a curiously exhausting way to live a life. She cared what passers-by in the street thought of the way she looked, just as she cared what the girls at school had made of her dress-sense.

She laboured under the constant apprehension that people were laughing at her, making fun of her on some level that she did not understand, keeping secrets from her. As she had grown older, she had developed a means of arguing herself out of such feelings with the application of objective logic. She could talk herself into believing, quite rightly, that most people had more important things to worry about than what particular shade of eyeshadow or denier of stocking she was wearing on any given day. And then she found that the whole process was much easier if she didn't respect the person – if Charlotte could dismiss their opinions as immaturity or stupidity or intolerance. She tried, as much as she could, to do this with Anne. She felt – erroneously perhaps – that she could out-think her own mother, that her way of looking at things was somehow more philosophical, more rational than Anne's breezy expectation that the world would arrange itself around her.

But her father remained unassailable. He represented, for Charlotte, the purest type of intellect – an intellect that did not impose limits on itself for fear of being cruel to or damning of others. This made him self-centred, arrogant and bullying. But it also made him a rigorous thinker, an inveterate charmer and a man whose good approval still meant everything to his own daughter. She wanted, so very much, to hate him and yet she found herself simultaneously drawn to him, ineluctably, like a small river current sucked to the brink of a thunderous waterfall.

What else was she apart from her father's love? What else was she worth? How could she possibly tell him all this? How could she make him understand, make him pay for what he had done when part of her had craved his attention all along?

And because she was unused to speaking about what she actually thought, she became, over the years, less and less able to work out what it was she felt. It left her horribly confused. Occasionally, with Gabriel, she thought she was angry only to discover she was in tears and that her overriding feeling was one of impenetrable sadness. Frequently, she found she was in the middle of an argument she had instigated, fighting for all she was worth, only to realise that she wanted it to be over as quickly as possible, that she didn't mind admitting she was wrong if only they could kiss and love each other again. Gabriel said she was the most defensive person he had ever met. Charlotte knew that her defensiveness was merely a disguise for the deep-down dread that she would lose him; that he would discover, after all, she wasn't worth what he had thought.

Charlotte was again pondering the conversation with Gabriel when she drove to the hospital one Sunday morning. She didn't normally go on her own, but Gabriel had arranged to meet Florence for brunch and Charlotte couldn't bear the thought of seeing her in the morning, with the whole day stretching threateningly before them.

'What if she wants to hang out with us all afternoon?' Charlotte had asked him the night before. He laughed.

'She won't. She's got the busiest social life of anyone I know. We're very lucky she's squeezed us in.'

But Charlotte hadn't wanted to go. Part of her felt resentful that Florence was intruding on their lazy weekend time of togetherness, but she knew that it would annoy Gabriel if she admitted this, so she kept herself in check and said nothing. He was allowed to have friends independent of their relationship, she told herself. She just wished the friend in question wasn't Florence. So she had invoked the hospital visit as an excuse, knowing that Gabriel couldn't possibly object.

'Do you want me to come with you?' he offered, even though she knew it was the last thing he wanted to do.

'No, that's very lovely of you but I'll be fine. It's quite relaxing in a way. I've probably had some of the most meaningful exchanges I've ever had with him since he's been comatose.' She grinned, assuming a levity she did not feel.

Gabriel seemed relieved. They still weren't having sex and she knew that it bothered him, that he found it increasingly difficult to be in her physical proximity without the question of it nagging away, deadening the air between them. She hadn't told him about her encounter with Maya, only too aware that he would think it evidence of a borderline personality disorder. Instead, she had pushed it to one side in her mind but the knowledge of it, the depressing constancy of comparison, hung over her thickly.

'OK, sweetie. I'll see you later then?'

'Yep. See you later.'

Charlotte had driven to the hospital on her own, knowing that Anne wouldn't be there – Sunday morning was her sacrosanct time for listening to *The Archers* and doing the week's load of laundry. She found that, once behind the steering wheel, negotiating an endless series of traffic lights that turned from amber to red just as she reached them, she felt unaccountably upset. It was one of those dry, overcast and slightly misty London days when the air seems to lie flat against you, pushing its weary greyness close to the skin. Everything Charlotte looked at through the windscreen made her more depressed. As she crossed over Putney Bridge, it seemed as though she were being taunted by happy vignettes of other lives lived: the families pushing buggies along the riverbank; a toddler in small Wellington boots kicking muddy dirt up from the track; rowers with ruddy cheeks, carrying boats into the water on their muscular shoulders; fat Canada geese waddling into the shallows; coffee shops playing earnest CDs of world music; and tinny, bright cars driven by twenty-something couples rushing off to Sunday lunch at cheerful pubs. Everyone had their place, negotiating the soft ebb and flow of an easy weekend.

Charlotte sighed. 'Come on,' she said out loud. 'Stop being so self-indulgent.' And she turned on the radio to Capital FM so that her ears were soon filled with the thumping bassline of assorted pop tunes she was embarrassed not to recognise.

She got to the hospital shortly after 2 p.m., despite her best efforts to make it half an hour earlier. She went through the usual rigmarole – the disinfectant squeezing, the effortful smile at the nurses, the long walk down the beige corridor – until she reached her father's door. As she turned the handle and walked in, she was seized by a sudden certainty that he had woken up. For a brief second, Charlotte was convinced she had seen Charles sitting up rigidly in bed, staring at her with hollow eyes and a terrible smile on his face, arms twisted as if the bones had snapped and were no longer pinning the flesh together. In her mind's eye, he looked like the skeleton that had once so terrified her on the ghost train ride at a theme park on a family holiday when she was little – an eerie figure rigged with wires to jump out of a coffin at precisely the most stomach-lurching moment.

It was such a lurid vision that Charlotte started to sweat lightly, a moistness breaking out along the top of her cheeks as it always did when she was nervous. She blinked violently, noticing the slight scratchy dryness of her contact lenses as the room readjusted into focus.

Charles was lying, as normal, with his eyes closed, his arms straight down against his sides, the outline of his toes poking through the bottom of the blanket. As she got closer, Charlotte noticed that his nasal hair had grown and that one, thin, wiry black strand was shivering lightly in the breeze, so that it looked almost as if he were breathing on his own. He looked bizarrely well: there was a gentle flush of rosiness on his face, and his arms remained strong despite the intravenous diet, the veins twisting down his pale flesh like thick cable.

She noticed that she had not yet taken off her coat. She shrugged herself out of the heavy sleeves – it was a tweed woollen thing with the weight of a dead animal's pelt but it was not yet quite warm enough to move to her spring raincoat – and tossed it on to the wooden-framed armchair. She stayed standing over her father, looking at him, etching out every detail of his face in her mind. There were his high cheekbones, so defined that a flirtatious house-wife had once asked him if he had Cherokee blood in his family tree. There were his thin, crisp lips that, in consciousness, could twitch and snarl and smile and kiss in the same fluid movements. There were his eyelids, lightly flickering against the imagined blue, blue, blue of his irises. There was his hairline, receding in a heart-shape from his large brow, faded gold with pockets of speckled grey. There was his nose, broken twice from university rugby matches, now grown into a crooked nobility. There was Charles, in all his glory. And yet also absent, as if the fundamental essence of him was slowly being scrubbed away, the sharpened edges sanded down so that he no longer terrified or impressed with the ferocious power he once had. She was not scared of him. Not like this.

Charlotte did not, as she usually did, take a seat next to him. Nor did she start into her habitual recitation of the week's events.

Without Anne there, she felt no need. Instead, Charlotte stood in silence, hearing her own breathing mingle with the pumping motion of the life support.

The unhappiness came back to her then, in a savage gust, a sudden squall of internal pain. She felt on the verge of retching and yet also as if she was about to burst into uncontrolled laughter. She craved the lightheadedness that a cigarette would give her, although she never normally smoked. She wanted a sort of obliteration.

She walked across to her father's bedside, unaware of what she was doing. Lightly, she lifted up his right hand, holding it out from her as she would a bit of wet seaweed on a beach. It was heavy in her loose grasp, the fingers hanging down like the legs of a dead animal. After a few seconds, she released her hold, letting Charles's hand drop with a soft thud back on to the blankets. She looked around her, half-expecting someone to ask what she was doing. When no one did, she found herself lifting up his hand once again, holding it for a moment and then letting it drop. His flesh felt cool and thick and weighted down. She repeated the exercise with the hand three times and, each time, it gave her a small sense of victory.

'Not such a strong man now, are you?' she heard herself saying, her voice oddly flat and blank. His hand looked weirdly disembodied, a detached scrap of anatomy like the marbled chunks that drop off ancient statues: an arm here, a foot there, a piece of finger exhibited on a museum plinth as something that had once belonged to a bigger whole.

Still standing, she flattened her palm against his cheek. It felt flabby, and when she jiggled her hand from side to side, she found that his flesh wobbled with the movement. This sign of weakness gratified her and she smiled. Leaning into him, she stretched her other arm over the bed, catching her sleeve on the plastic tube running from his nose. She pressed her left hand to the opposite side of his face so that she was holding his head like a lover, in an intimate sort of caress. Half-crouching over him, her face was close enough to smell him – he smelled of chemicals, a tangy aroma of pharmaceuticals mingled with stale sweat. The smell both repelled her and made her want to lean closer. A strand of her hair hung lankly across his chin.

For a moment, she did nothing. Then, after a beat of silence like the pause before a flick of a switch, she slapped him gently across his jaw with one hand, feeling the reverberations of this physical jolt on the other side of his face. She tensed, listening for the sound of a nurse with her hand on the door handle. She could hear nothing except for the occasional muffled footfall.

And then, without knowing why or how it happened, Charlotte felt her mind contract. It was as if she had slashed an internal mental artery and her thoughts came gushing out, leaving behind a pallid nothingness, a blank, empty screen. Suddenly she was screaming, screaming things that she did not know she thought or felt, things that made no sense other than that they were noise and she needed, more than anything, to make some noise, to rip the silence apart, to feel its brittle glass screens disintegrate into a violent shattering. Noise. Blankness. Hate. Rage. Tears.

'You fucking bastard. You fucking, fucking bastard. You ruined me. You fucking ruined me.'

And as she screamed, she found that her hands were hitting and punching and slapping and scratching and clawing. She thumped his right temple with a clenched force she never knew she possessed and found that instead of his head bouncing back, it lay slackly on the pillow, turned to one side. She started pummelling his stomach through the sheets, bringing her fists down on to him in a wild blur. They made a strange sound like a car door slamming shut. Still, she shouted; shouted with spittle and spray, shouted to goad him into a reaction, to force him to stand up and slap her back, to hold her wrists firm in his hands until she stopped struggling. Still, he did nothing.

She lashed out with elbows, knees and fingernails. She hit his chest with the flank of her forearm, bringing it down on him like a guillotine blade. The mattress juddered beneath, the bed slid to one side. She gripped his neck in her two hands, pressing down on his Adam's apple with the balls of her thumbs, squeezing the tendons so tightly that her fingers started to ache. One of her earrings fell on to the pillow, a burnished gold disc against the starched linen whiteness. Her hair stuck to her forehead. Her armpits felt damp with effort. And then she was crying, the tears coming without sound, simply falling down her face and on to the white sheets, leaving behind dark spots like raindrops in snow. Her words became howls, insensible cries and she was hiccuping at the same time so that everything sounded strangulated and sticky and she realised there was no point, no point at all to any of this, that it was too late, that she hated herself for being so cowardly, that no one was ever going to explain and nothing was ever going to make her feel better. There was nothing here. There never had been.

She heard the door open, the sound of feet rushing to her and then she felt thin but powerful arms pulling her back, restraining her, holding her in a vicious embrace, telling her to calm down, pulling, pulling, pulling her off her father even though she tried to grab hold of the bed, legs flailing in protest, the screams still sounding loudly inside her head.

Still, his eyes were closed. Still, he did nothing.

Still.

Anne

A NURSE FROM THE HOSPITAL phoned Anne at home. The nurse obviously didn't know quite what to say or how to explain the reason for her call. Anne could sense her discomfort almost from the first breath of the conversation.

'Mrs Redfern?'

Anne stifled an exhalation of impatience. She thought it was terribly rude for someone not to start off with a gentle 'Hello', introducing themselves and, briefly, the reason for their call. It was one of her pet peeves. When Charlotte had been younger and her schoolfriends rang up to speak to her, Anne would always notice the ones who had been well brought-up: the ones who said who they were, engaged Anne in a small exchange of politeness and then – but only then – asked to speak to Charlotte. The ones who didn't display such elementary good manners were mentally blacklisted. If they rang during mealtimes, there was no hope for them. Anne had a frighteningly long memory for perceived slights.

'Yes,' said Anne. 'Speaking.'

'Oh, hello. Um. It's Sanjita Rana here, I'm a nurse at the hospital. At London Bridge.' There was a pause. 'Where your husband is being cared for,' she prompted, unnecessarily.

'Is there anything wrong with him?' asked Anne. There was a flustered coughing sound on the end of the line.

'Well, no, not exactly.'

'What do you mean "not exactly"?' said Anne. A combined sense of impatience and anxiety started to prickle the surface of her skin.

'The thing is, Mrs Redfern, we have your daughter here.'

'Charlotte?' she said, stupidly, as if she had countless other daughters to choose from. Anne looked at the wall calendar that she hung on a corkboard in front of the phone. It was Sunday. Anne thought it was strange that Charlotte had gone to visit Charles at the weekend – normally she chose to spend all her free time with Gabriel. That's odd, she thought, but the thought hung, unfinished, in her mind. She brushed it aside and waited for the nurse to continue.

'Yes. She asked us to call you.'

Silence.

'She . . . the thing is, there was a little bit of an incident earlier. Nothing to worry about, nothing at all,' the nurse continued, with an over-eagerness that suggested she was compensating for something. Anne felt herself shiver. She looked down and saw a ridge of goose-bumps form along her upper arm. 'Your daughter came into visit your husband and there was, well, there was . . . an altercation.'

'I don't know what you mean.'

She could hear the nurse twisting the telephone cord in her fingers. When she started to speak again, it was in a low tone that was an almost-whisper. In the background, Anne could make out the familiar hospital sounds: the shuffling footsteps, the creaking trolley wheels, the beep and buzz of countless life-prolonging machines.

'Your daughter started to hit him.'

'Hit who?' said Anne, stupidly.

'Hit your husband. She, um, she hit Mr Redfern.'

There was a pause. Anne's throat went dry. She swallowed, gulping noisily. She breathed in slowly through her nose, held the breath internally for several seconds, and then breathed out, counting from one to five with as much control as she could muster. She had read somewhere this helped you to relax but it didn't seem to work.

'I see.'

'He's fine,' said the nurse, a little too quickly. 'It wasn't all that serious – a few bruises, maybe, nothing more permanent. But . . .'

'Yes?'

'Your daughter seemed very agitated. We had to –' she searched for the right word, 'we had to intervene.'

'I see.'

'She was very upset. We had to give her something to calm her down. I'm afraid she was disturbing the other patients . . .'

'That's fine. I understand.'

The nurse seemed relieved that Anne was taking it all so calmly, not seeking to apportion blame. She started to talk more easily, a hint of briskness creeping into her voice.

'Once she gathered her thoughts a bit, we asked her if she wanted us to call someone and she gave us your number. I'm sorry for the intrusion.'

'No, no, I'm glad you told me.' Standing in her kitchen, pressing the phone's receiver into her ear, Anne was struck by how displaced everything seemed, as if she was watching it all through a thick, dream-like lens. The curved outline of the Aga looked strangely precise; the red-tiled floor too shiny. Looking out of the window to the garden beyond, it appeared too vivid; too sharply in focus. She felt untethered, detached. She felt her reactions slowing, the air around her becoming thick with thought; the weight of it pressing down on her chest.

'Well,' she heard herself say, 'thank you for letting me know.'

She started to put the phone down and then she heard the nurse speaking again, a tinny noise like television interference. 'Sorry, I didn't catch that.'

'Oh, I'm sorry. I was just wondering if I should tell your daughter you're coming to collect her?'

'I don't think so.'

The nurse didn't know what to make of that. Anne could almost imagine her mouth gaping open.

'Oh, right,' she stumbled. 'It's just . . . well, it's not my business, but I think she'd like it if you did.'

'How do you know?'

'I'm sorry?'

'How do you know she'd like it?' Anne said, carefully enunciating every syllable. 'Have you asked her?'

'She asked us to call you,' said the nurse, desperately.

'I appreciate your doing so. But I imagine Charlotte has her car at the hospital and so, you see, it wouldn't be practical for me to come too.'

'I really think . . .'

'I don't care what you think,' said Anne with clipped rapidity, the words coming out too quickly now to stop them. 'These are things you know nothing about.' Anne put the phone down with such force she could feel the reverberations in her hand. Then she walked into the drawing room and sat down on the sofa that she had never liked but that she had simply grown to live with.

She was taken aback by the nurse's phone call but, while news of Charlotte's outburst was discomfiting, Anne found she was not surprised by it. She supposed, looking back, that it had been building up for years, ever since . . . well, ever since that day.

She thought that day had been dealt with, the brutal truth of it concealed, hidden, disguised from their everyday consciousness. She thought it had been best that way: that enforced ignorance was a means of coping with the ugliness of real knowledge. But now, here it was to be confronted all over again and Anne simply didn't know if she could bear it. It was too much. The past was too dazzling to look at; too blindingly bright and uncompromising.

She folded her arms in front of her chest and sat there, breathing with a heavy regularity, looking straight ahead at the mantelpiece above the open fire, filled with silver-framed photographs and invitations that had gathered a thin coating of dust. She let her eyes rest on the group picture at the far right end of the mantelpiece. It was a black-and-white shot of the three of them that had been taken on the day of Charlotte's graduation.

Charlotte was wearing a formal university robe and standing outside the terraced red-brick house that she had shared in her last year with friends. She was laughing at something beyond the edges of the frame, caught mid-smile, her eyes looking sideways, not quite focusing on the photograph being taken. Her hair had been blow-dried especially for the occasion but the wind was mussing it up, so that a few strands of it had come loose and were partially obscuring the side of her cheek.

On her right, Anne stood, smiling firmly in a fitted two-piece suit, clutching a slender, oblong-shaped bag in one hand. With the other, she was reaching out for Charlotte but not quite touching her. It looked as though she was trying to alert her to something, to protect her, but hadn't made it in time. The hand was suspended there, frozen in blurry celluloid.

But it was Charles who dominated the picture, standing on Charlotte's left, his arm expansively thrown round his daughter's shoulders as she laughed. He wasn't smiling exactly but he looked – what was it? – he looked proud, but there was a sheen of possessiveness to it, as if he were somehow claiming his daughter's success as his own. He appeared totally static, the only figure sharply in focus, immobile and monumental, aware of his own importance without having to prove it. He just was.

There they were, a triumvirate of almost-togetherness, trapped in the freeze-frame of how someone else had seen them. Who had taken the photo? Anne couldn't remember. She had always thought it odd, afterwards, that it was in black and white. It seemed so old-fashioned now that most people used digital and even newspapers had front-page photographs printed in a blaze of coloured brilliance.

She looked at that photograph for a long time. She sat on the sofa, her eyes analysing, recalling, filing away every small detail. The foggy blueness of evening crept through the bay window. The occasional speeding whir of car wheels sounded in the distance. Anne did not notice. She wanted simply to think; to think and be alone.

Anne; Charles

S O. SHE WAS PREGNANT. She sat, hunched forward on the edge of the loo seat, an unopened box of Tampons on the floor beside her. She had been late before. There had, in the four years of their marriage, been countless false alarms when she had been forced to suspend her temporary flicker of anticipation and replace it with the coolness of fact, carrying on as if nothing had happened because, in effect, nothing had. But this time, it felt different. She knew. She simply knew. And yet this knowledge, so hard-won, so long fought for, did not bring her the unquestioned joy she had expected. Instead, Anne felt herself fill up with a sense of resignation, mingled with fear. It was not fear of motherhood, she realised, lifting herself up from the lavatory and pushing down the handle to flush, it was fear of Charles's reaction.

Charles had always indicated that he wanted children although, as with so much of their marriage, they had never actually talked about any of the practicalities. And then it had taken so long for her to conceive and so much had happened in the interim that Anne was no longer sure what he would feel or, indeed, what she felt herself.

She walked into the bedroom, clasping one arm across her stomach without thinking. She drew the curtains to shut out the daylight and lay down gingerly on the bed, slipping off her shoes and pulling up the duvet over her stockinged legs, the brush of cotton making a swishing sound against the sheerness of silk. She felt cold and tired and far, far away, as though sinking to the bottom of the ocean, the daylight gradually rippling into a thousand fluid molecules of darkness. She fell asleep.

When she woke, several hours later, she was gripped by an immediate sensation of panic and guilt. Anne looked at the alarm clock on the bedside table. It was six in the evening. Charles would be due back any minute and she hadn't prepared his supper. She sat up in the bed, brushing her hands through her tangled hair, smoothing down her skirt as best she could. She stood up too quickly and her head surged with a dizzy blackness so that she almost lost her balance. What had she been doing in bed in the middle of the day? Why had she allowed herself to drift off like this? Slowly, the knowledge of what had happened started to seep through in fragments and she began to remember. Her heart began thumping wildly and she broke out in a sweat. She looked at her hands and saw that they were trembling. She opened the top drawer of the bedside table and took out a plastic bottle of pills, pushing down the lid as she turned it so that the catch released. She tipped out one of the small white oblongs into the palm of her hand and then, after a few seconds' hesitation, another one. Anne swallowed them with a single, dry gulp. She had got so used to taking them that she no longer required any water. A soothing numbness enveloped her. After several minutes, she felt herself in a pleasurable daze, the panic loosened like a helium balloon that was floating, un-tethered, to the ceiling. She supposed she would have to give these up now that she was expecting a child. Her eyes filled with tears at the thought but she did not feel sad.

She went to splash cold water on her face. Downstairs, she heard the distinctive murmur of a car engine being switched off. There were footsteps and then the turn of a key in a lock and then the sound of her husband taking his coat off in the hallway. She would have to tell him, she thought, the idea forming unclearly in her mind. And the curious thing was, she had no idea how he would react. For some reason, this struck her as immensely funny and she started to laugh. She looked at herself in the mirror. A trickle of mascara was running down her cheek and she wondered why and then she saw that she was crying at the same time and that seemed even funnier and she carried on laughing, unable to stop until Charles walked through the bathroom door.

'What are you doing?' he asked, an expression of distaste curling at the corner of his lips.

Anne looked at him and suddenly it all seemed so simple. The laughter stopped as abruptly as it had started.

'I'm pregnant,' she said. She reached for the loo roll, wanting to blow her nose but she somehow misjudged the distance so that she tripped and fell to her knees.

'About time,' Charles said. He walked across to Anne, still sitting in a strange heap on the floor, and then he tore off several sheets of toilet paper and handed them to her, folded up in a wad. 'Clean yourself up.'

She looked up at him and she noticed that his face was totally blank, a sheet of nothing. She could not read it. She could not understand what it meant. She tried to grab hold of his trouser leg with her hand but he stepped backwards so that she could not reach him. Then he turned and walked out of the room.

Charlotte

*T*HAT DAY.

There had been a gap of several months before anything like it happened again. Even then, Charlotte was not sure whether it was right or wrong or swimming fluidly somewhere in between that she couldn't quite pin down.

Once, she had been sitting on the floor in front of the sofa, watching television. Anne was upstairs, having a bath. Charles had walked in and instead of going to his normal armchair in the corner of the room, he came and sat on the sofa directly behind her and started gently kneading her neck with his fingers.

Charlotte tensed. She closed her eyes, half of her trying to enjoy what she told herself was a friendly physical contact between father and daughter, the other half simply wanting it to be over with.

He didn't say anything as he stroked her neck, gradually applying more and more pressure until she felt him pushing down on her tendons. Then, quick as a flick-knife, he slid one hand under the neck of her loose knitted jumper, his fingers lightly tracing the outline of her nipple, the tips twitching as if fiddling with a tuning dial. It took less than three seconds. Then he withdrew his hand, stood up and disappeared. Nothing was said.

Another time, he had walked in unannounced when she was in the shower on a Sunday morning. She jumped as she heard his footsteps, but he didn't do anything except sit on the laundry stool, looking at her, his legs bent together at the knee, as she washed her hair.

Occasionally, he would come to say goodnight as she lay in bed and Charlotte learned to tilt her head sideways at the very last minute so that the kiss landed on her cheek or, if she hadn't acted quickly enough, at the very edge of her mouth. For hours afterwards, she would feel the imprint of his saliva at the corner of her lips, a wet mark of conquest.

She still didn't tell anyone because she wasn't sure that there was anything to tell. She felt acutely the lack of her own maturity – she was not old enough to know whether this was normal and she did not want to risk admitting her own childishness; she did not want to be made a fool of for her own stupidity. She wanted to deal with things in an adult fashion and not be a crybaby. And, when it came to it, she couldn't explain what it was she was uneasy about. There had been no momentous physical action, no dramatic crossing of the line that she could look at, objectively, and say to herself, 'Yes, that was wrong'. She had always been awkward around Charles and imagined that perhaps his subtle physical touches, and her reaction to them, were simply a further extension of that awkwardness. There was the smallest sliver of recognition, deep at the bottom of her, that part of her liked being the focus of his attention, but she rarely admitted this – every time the thought floated to the top of her consciousness, she turned away from it, as if swimming out of a patch of sea cooled by the shadows of rocks.

At school, she tended towards isolation so there were no close friends that she could ask. At home, there were no uncles or male adults of comparable age to whom she could compare Charles's behaviour. The closest she got was her parents' neighbour, Giles Treneman, but she only ever saw him when he was red-nosed and drunk at the end of a party when he seemed extremely affectionate and tactile to any woman who crossed his path. So Charles's strange demonstrations of quasi-paternal intimacy carried on, occurring at random intervals, weeks and months apart and generally when Anne was out of the house.

But the last time it happened, it was different.

He had been driving her to school one morning because there was a bus drivers' strike and Anne had arranged to do her fortnightly charitable stint in the Red Cross clothes shop in Kew. Charlotte felt uneasy, as she always did when she was alone with her father, but she tried not to think about it over breakfast, chewing slowly on her muesli, swallowing it down even though she felt slightly sick inside. There was a science test today that she was silently dreading.

At the other end of the pine kitchen table, Charles sat with his face entirely obscured by a copy of the *Daily Telegraph*. Bits of him emerged from the other side of the newsprint, like shards of a Cubist portrait: the clean half-moons of his fingernails, a lump of shoulder and the top of his head, the golden hair thinning perceptibly. Occasionally, he would clear his throat or grumble over something he was reading. Every few minutes, he would turn the page and fold it back and there would be a loud sound of crackling paper and he would take a sip of tea before resuming his careful examination of the day's news.

Charlotte glanced nervously at the clock above the Aga. It was already ten past eight. They were going to be late.

'Daddy?'

'Mmm.'

'Shall we get going?' she asked, trying to sound offhand.

As soon as the words were out of her mouth, she realised it was the wrong thing to say. He folded up the newspaper and put it to one side, staring at her coldly as he did so.

'We've got plenty of time,' he said, pouring himself another cup of tea. 'It's hardly going to matter if you're a few minutes late.'

Charlotte chewed her lip. It probably didn't matter to him very much, but it mattered to her hugely. She hated being late for school because she would be forced to explain to her form teacher, the humourless Mrs Dryburgh, exactly why, and she would have no excuse other than her father not seeming to care.

But there was nothing she could do except sit there in painful anticipation as he finished his breakfast and then listen as he walked upstairs to brush his teeth and go to the loo, all of which seemed to take far longer than it needed to. When he finally emerged, it was 8.20 a.m. By the time they were on their way, it was almost half past. Assembly started at 8.45 sharp. Charlotte started praying that they would make it in time. She fiddled with her watch, circling her finger in an anti-clockwise motion around its plastic face as if she could make the minutes go in reverse.

She was so anxious that she didn't, at first, notice the change in atmosphere or the fact that Charles had turned the car radio off so that they were now sitting in silence. They had stopped at a red traffic light. She wound a piece of hair round her index finger, stroking the soft ends of it across her upper lip like a paintbrush. Charles turned to look at her.

'So,' he said, his voice warm. 'What are you up to at school today?'

She dropped the strand of hair from her mouth, not wishing to look childish. She wondered whether to tell him about the test and then decided against it – Charles regarded science as a particular forte and tended to launch into incomprehensible mini-lectures about compounds and neutrons at the slightest encouragement. Because he never made any attempt to speak down to her, preferring to express himself in the complex language more suited to an adult audience, Charlotte could never fully understand what he was saying. She would try so hard to follow the gossamer trail of his rapid intellectual conjecture that the effort of it left her feeling simultaneously exhausted and more stupid than she had at the start.

'We're doing a project,' she said finally.

'What sort of project?'

'It's about evacuees in World War II.' She didn't elaborate any further.

The light changed from red to flashing amber to green.

'That sounds interesting,' and as he spoke, he took his left hand off the steering wheel and reached across to her seat, laying his hand on her upper thigh, the weight of it pushing through the dense grey material of her uniform skirt. He cleared his throat. Charlotte held her breath, as if her complete immobility would stop his hand from moving. She struck a deal with herself in her mind: she could cope with this if his hand didn't move. She could cope if he just left it there. There was no need to worry as long as his hand stayed exactly where it was.

She became transfixed by it, staring until the flesh started to blur in front of her eyes like a glinting stone swallowed by a tide of muddy water. She recognised the elements of a hand – the marshmallow pinkness, the near-symmetrical dips in between fingers, knuckles like knots – and yet could no longer connect it with her father's body.

In this way, she detached herself. So although she registered the fact that they had turned right instead of left at the T-junction that led to school, she did not question why and nor did she feel particularly perturbed that this detour would make her even later. For some reason, it had ceased to bother her. It had stopped mattering. All that concerned her was the movement of that hand.

She was dimly aware of the tick-tick-tick sound of the indicator.

Tick-tick-tick.

Tick-tick-tick.

And then they were turning into a residential cul-de-sac that she had never seen before and Charles was parking with his customary precision, deftly manoeuvring into a space. The car stopped and he removed his hand from her thigh to put on the handbrake.

Charlotte breathed out, a softly controlled exhalation designed to draw as little attention to herself as possible, as if she could by sheer force of will convince her father she was not worth noticing.

He parked at the end of a row of cars so that when Charlotte looked out of the windscreen she could see a stretch of pavement bordered by detached red bungalows, each one marked by the plasticine sheen of newly built houses. There was a small shop on the corner with a newspaper rack outside. She noticed that the same newspaper front page she had stared at across the breakfast table was slotted in the top shelf, its pages battered down by the wind, the text shimmering in front of her eyes. She focused on the reassuring familiarity of the smudged newsprint.

Charles undid his seatbelt.

Click. Swish.

Then he twisted his body all the way round in the driver's seat until he was looking at her directly. Charlotte kept staring out of the windscreen. The rub of his trousers against the seat gave a muffled squeaking sound as he moved.

He put his hand back on her leg, this time at the hem of her skirt and he pushed it, gradually inching it upwards until he reached the edge of her knickers. He leaned over, pushing the other side of the skirt up so that it made a neat horizontal, bunched up just below her midriff. He dropped his eyes and looked at her naked legs, her white underwear, for what seemed like several silent minutes.

He breathed in and out through his nose and there was a slight whistling noise with each heavy lungful. Charlotte started counting.

One.

Two.

Three.

And then, so quickly that she had no time to react, he wound his hand round her neck and pulled her to him, kissing her fiercely on the mouth, the tip of his tongue prising her lips apart.

Something broke.

'No!' Charlotte shouted, pushing him away with both her hands.

Charles snapped back, his eyes dilated with shock. His face seemed to lose all its definition, the edges melting like a rubber mask in heat, the pallid skin collapsing in on itself. He bore an expression that Charlotte could not, at first, work out. And then she realised it was terror that she was seeing. He seemed to be frightened.

And just at that point, Charlotte noticed that he was no longer quite looking at her, but sideways, out through the windscreen. She followed his gaze. She looked out. And there, instead of the newspaper and the corner shop and the Lego-brick houses, was her mother.

It seemed so bizarre, so totally surreal, so dream-like that Charlotte shook her head, trying to make the mirage disappear. But when she looked up again, Anne was still there, her hair tied up in the recognisable yellow-striped headscarf that Charlotte had given her for Christmas two years ago.

She was looking straight at them, looking at Charlotte through the glass with an expression of horror on her face, her lips shrivelled into a gasping 'o'. She was carrying a shopping bag in one hand. By her feet, there was another, wrinkled polythene bag that

Anne seemed to have dropped and its contents – old jumpers, hats and shoes – were spilling out on to the street.

Nothing seemed to be making any sense. What was she doing here? What had she seen or not seen?

The thoughts sprung up in Charlotte's consciousness like pinballs released from a machine, clattering and buzzing through her head, disappearing before she could understand them. And yet amid the confused helter-skelter of her emotions, Charlotte had one, single, coherent thought that pushed through the others: her mother was here. She was safe. Anne knew. There was no need to try any more, no need to pretend or conceal or convince herself it was all right. It was out in the open. There would be no more lying. There would be no more half-guesses or stuttered attempts at normality. She did not have to hide.

But then, in the space of a shallow breath, it changed. The horror that Charlotte had seen on Anne's face seemed to slide like shale slipping off a mountainside. It was replaced by an inscrutability that made Anne's eyes film over.

She turned away.

Through the grimy windscreen glass, Charlotte watched as Anne stumbled forwards, catching the heel of a shoe on the pavement kerb, and then, steadying herself, started walking towards the main road, the bag of shopping still in one hand. The clothes still lay on the street, left behind; a trail of unwanted emptiness. The sleeves of a tattered tweed jacket pointed brokenly outwards, the angles unnatural and hollowed-out.

In the car, there was a wordless moment of total suspension. Neither of them moved. Charlotte watched her mother walk all the way to the end of the street, her shoulders hunched against the wind, her steps unnaturally hurried, the shopping bag swinging against her legs. She watched her reach the junction with the main road and then hesitate briefly before turning left and not looking back. Charlotte was so shocked, so confused by everything that had just happened within a few brief moments, that it took her longer than it should have done to open the car door. She fiddled with the handle, her hands fumbling over the lock. Charles, seeing what she was doing, tried to stop her.

'Charlotte, wait –'

But she was out of the car, out on to the street and she was running, running, running, her school shoes making a slapping sound against the tarmac, her skirt whipping against her legs. Running somewhere, anywhere and nowhere all at once. Running away. Away from here. Away from them. Running away, into the safety of nothing.

Normally she hated running. She dreaded the approach of the annual school sports day because a well-meaning teacher would always force her to take part and Charlotte would dutifully run as fast as she could, knowing before she had reached the finish line that it would never be fast enough and knowing, without looking, that her mother would be attempting to hide her slight disappointment with an upbeat sort of resignation. But that day, she ran and ran and ran and she did not feel the usual suffocating lack of breath or the sharp ache of a stitch. She ran because it felt good to be doing something – anything – that did not require her to think. As she ran, her mind emptied itself; the thoughts pushed out of her skull by the sheer mindlessness of her speed, the force of the wind hitting her cheeks.

She could feel the soles of her feet become numb and the tender flesh on her ankles begin to tingle with rawness. For several minutes, Charlotte did not recognise the landscape and it did not cross her mind that she had no idea where she was going. But then, after a while, her surroundings shifted into focus: there was the wall that circled Kew Gardens, there was the small off-licence where the girl behind the till knew Charles by name, there was the Esso petrol station where two main roads met and there, just a few yards away, was the entrance to Carlton Avenue.

She had ended up at home even though it was the last place she wanted to be. Perhaps, she thought miserably, there would never be anywhere else to go. There would be no escape from Charles and Anne and the weird tangle of their lives together.

She bent over, resting her hands just below her knees, letting the breaths come in scratchy bursts. She noticed that dark wet droplets were landing irregularly on the grey slabs of the pavement and she wondered whether it was raining but then she realised it was

184

coming from her and that she was crying. Charlotte pulled the sleeve of her school jumper over her hand and wiped the tears and snot off her face, leaving a slimy trail on the misshapen navy-blue wool.

But oddly, although she was crying, she did not feel especially sad. Somewhere inside, she was inexplicably calm. It was as if the worst had happened and, because of this, she had nothing left to fear. She felt strangely adult for the first time in her life. She decided then that she would not let this upset her because she did not want them to see how much they had hurt her. By masking it, by dealing with it on her own terms, Charlotte could be in control.

After a while, her breathing became more regular and she noticed that the tears had stopped. Her mind felt curiously anaesthetised and the sensation was not altogether unpleasant. For so long, her head had been so crowded with incomprehensible thoughts that it was a relief to have had the balloon of it punctured, the pressurised air released from within.

She walked the last few yards to the front door of her house and she registered the brass knocker and the letterbox slot, its metal dulled by years of weather, and she noticed the roots of the horse chestnut tree pressing up through the patio stones, warping them out of shape like scales along a dinosaur spine. She checked it all off a mental inventory so that the house seemed at once familiar and yet simultaneously detached from her sense of self.

She knew that what she had to do was to take the spare key from underneath the doormat, put it in the lock and open the door. She knew she had to walk back inside and carry on. She would not weep like a child, she would not cry like someone who needed comfort: she would become inviolable. She would take a deep breath and she would protect herself and she would grow into someone who was better than them both. In that moment, she convinced herself that she did not need them. She would be their daughter, still, but they would never know her, not really. They would never understand the deep, dark hole inside. The hatred hidden beneath the folds of her heart would give her the strength she needed. The darkened varnish would obscure the truth of what lay beneath.

She did not know then that this would prove so difficult, that in spite of it all, she would continue to crave her parents' love, to court their admiration, to live her whole life in the hope of seeing them smile. She was still only a child.

Charlotte turned the key in the door and found it was already unlocked. She walked in and saw her mother sitting at the kitchen table at the end of the hallway, her head in her hands, and in that second, she knew that Anne had seen everything and that she, Charlotte, could not forgive her.

Anne's head jerked up at the sound of the door shutting. 'Charlotte?' she called, her voice clear and level and impenetrably normal.

'I'm going upstairs,' said Charlotte tonelessly. She went straight to the bathroom and locked the door behind her and she put a plug in the bath and turned on the taps and watched the water steam up the mirrored cabinet above the basin. She held her hand underneath the fluid heat until it was almost too much to bear and her skin started to scald. It did not hurt as much as she thought it would and she felt powerful because of it.

Years later, she would ask herself why he had done it in such a public place. After months of careful discretion, of deliberately not going too far, of touching with quick fingers and watching in stolen glimpses, why had he risked it? Did he think he was too powerful to be caught? Or was it that he had been unable to stop himself, that his customary control had abandoned him? Did he want to be found out, to push Anne to a point of no return? Or was it, in the end, that he did not believe what he was doing was so very wrong after all? Was it, sickeningly, his form of love?

For a week, Charles disappeared. His absence was never alluded to. Charlotte and Anne carried on their daily routine with such punctilious precision that both of them began to feel cushioned by the appearance of normality. It was a strangely peaceful time. The threat of Charles – the constant cloud of slight unease and tense anticipation – had been lifted and Anne was so grateful not to have to speak about what had happened that Charlotte found she was allowed to do whatever she wanted. She could stay up late watching unsuitable television and decide not to go to school the next day and she could eat too many salt-and-vinegar crisps before supper and Anne would let her, would be too nervous around her to refuse. It felt good to have her mother being so atypically indulgent and it gave Charlotte a sense of achievement, a fragile belief that she had dealt with everything in a sufficiently dispassionate, grown-up fashion. Part of her hoped that Anne was impressed by her daughter's maturity. Another part of her knew that, without even trying, Charlotte was now the dominant partner in the mother–daughter relationship. It was a knowledge that simultaneously scared and thrilled her: she liked the feeling of power it gave her but she also wanted to be looked after. She wanted her mother to say something, to be the one who spoke about it first.

Yet Anne never confronted what had happened. She never once spoke of it. The closest she came to it was when, a few days after the incident, she walked into Charlotte's bedroom to say goodnight. Sitting at the edge of the bed, Anne seemed jittery and uncertain of whether to touch her daughter or not.

'Do you want to know what I do when something bad happens?' she whispered into the darkness.

Charlotte nodded, her eyes closed as if she were trying to sleep.

'I think about it in my head and then, in my mind, I take a big rubber and rub it all out. And then I get a paintbrush and I paint over it in red so that I don't have to look at it any more.'

There was a pause.

'Are you all right, darling?' asked Anne, tentatively reaching out to stroke a tendril of hair off Charlotte's cheek. She nodded, wordlessly.

'You know you can always . . .' Anne broke off. 'You can always talk to someone if you want to. I mean, someone not to do with the family. A stranger. A counsellor or something. If you think you'd like to.'

Charlotte turned away from her to face the wall. After a few seconds, Anne stood up and walked out, shutting the bedroom door softly behind her.

For years afterwards, Charlotte would wonder why Anne had chosen not to confront the truth. Was it that she loved Charles too much to believe it of him or was it that she knew the depth of his brutal power but did not want to acknowledge it? Was it that Anne had been so shocked by her own behaviour that she needed to convince herself it had never happened? Or did she genuinely think that she was doing what was best; that by not talking, the nastiness of it would somehow dissolve in Charlotte's mind and be forgotten?

Perhaps it was simply easier for Anne to rub it all out and paint over it in red brushstrokes.

Easier to turn away and never mention it again in all the weeks and months and years that followed except in the most oblique terms.

Easier to carry on pretending. Because, after all, isn't that what they were all doing already?

When Charles came back, the shared deceit continued. He appeared without warning while they were having supper one evening. He was tanned and his hair was more blond than usual and he was wearing a white linen suit and had a rucksack on his back.

Charlotte did not look up from her plate of spaghetti. She waited, alert to the slightest alteration in atmosphere, to see how her parents would behave before committing herself to a reaction.

'You're back,' said Anne with unnatural brightness.

So that's what we're going to do, thought Charlotte, we're going to carry on as if nothing has happened, and although she was contemptuous of her mother's weakness, she also felt she could breathe more easily for knowing it.

'Yes,' said Charles and he slid the rucksack straps off his shoulders and unzipped it, removing a badly wrapped package from inside. He put it on the table next to Charlotte's plate without explanation.

'I'm going to have a shower and then some supper would be nice.' He smiled an uneven smile. Anne nodded her head quickly. 'Yes, there's some pasta left over.'

'Good. A home-cooked meal is just what I need.'

He walked out of the kitchen and the sound of his heavy footsteps taking the stairs two at the time thudded through the ceiling.

Neither of them spoke until they could hear the shower being turned on and then Charlotte realised she had been holding her breath. She exhaled gently, hoping not to draw attention to herself.

'Well, aren't you going to open it?' said Anne, motioning towards the package in front of her.

Charlotte put down a forkful of spaghetti and swallowed, feeling a lump of something uncertain squeeze down her throat. Her mouth was dry. She pulled the present towards her and saw that it had been hastily wrapped in old newspaper pages. The writing was in a language she did not understand but she thought it might be Spanish or Italian.

Although she was usually careful about opening gifts, wishing to savour every delectable second of surprise, this time Charlotte tore open the loose folds, ripping off the Sellotape so that her fingertips became dusted with black. She was surprised how excited she felt and then she wondered whether it was anger that was making her heart pump so ferociously against her rib cage. The last sheet of newspaper fell away and lay crumpled on the table.

Inside was a straw donkey, with a red sombrero perched jauntily on top of its ears. The donkey stared at Charlotte with baleful glass-buttoned eyes. She looked at it for a few seconds and then she stood up, cleared away her plate, and walked wordlessly out of the kitchen.

Later, when she went to her room, she noticed that someone had moved the donkey and put it on the low bookshelf that faced her bed. The donkey stood there looking at her from beneath its red hat and she saw that its polished eyes mirrored her every movement. She felt uneasy lying beneath the duvet, aware of her own reflection shining out of the two blank spheres of the donkey's expressionless gaze.

Anne

THE HOTEL WAS A nondescript building in West Kensington, its peeling white walls pockmarked with exhaust fume soot. There were tiled steps leading up to the front door and a blue-and-white-striped awning over the porch. The bay window had a laminated 'Rooms Available' sign propped up against the glass.

Anne checked the number against the folded piece of paper in her hand. Reassured that this was indeed the correct address, she walked inside. The hallway carpet was a swirling mass of red and gold. There was no one at reception so Anne had to press the bell. She waited for several seconds, her fingers playing nervously with the strap of her handbag. After a while, she heard the shuffling of footsteps and a large grey-haired man wearing slippers and an unbuttoned white shirt appeared from behind a set of frosted windows. He looked Anne up and down with a perceptible leer on his face. His mouth was open just wide enough that she could make out his swollen red tongue and a row of yellowed teeth sticking out irregularly from his lower gum.

'Yes?' he said, his voice choked with phlegm. He cleared his throat. 'Can I help you?'

'Yes, the name's Cockburn.'

The man took a pair of half-moon spectacles out of his shirt pocket and laboriously started to check each page of the guest register, running a dirty finger down the handwritten columns.

'Mr Cockburn?' He smirked. Anne felt her face flush.

'Yes, that's right.'

'He's up there already.' The man slid the key across the counter but did not remove his hand, so that Anne was forced to graze against him as she reached to pick it up. His flesh was puckered and clammy to the touch. 'Two flights of stairs,' he said, looking her steadily up and down. 'First on your right.'

'Thank you,' said Anne, her voice shaky. She started towards the stairs before she could change her mind.

The assignation with Marcus Cockburn had been quite deliberately arranged a few days after Charles had returned from his mysterious sojourn, bringing back that ridiculous straw donkey for Charlotte. She had bumped into Marcus while doing the weekly supermarket shop in Richmond, finding comfort in the undemanding blandness of routine after the hideously surreal tinge of the preceding weeks. He was carrying a basket in one hand that had been overloaded with contents and looked too heavy to be easily manageable, so that he was walking with a half-limping gait and appeared even more pathetic than normal. She had hoped to scurry past him without alerting his attention, but he spotted her by the bread shelves and half-walked, half-jogged to her side like a man desperate to catch a bus and yet too embarrassed to sprint.

'Anne,' he said, and then she had to turn and smile politely. 'Fancy meeting you here.'

'Yes,' she replied, 'fancy.'

'I've just popped in for a few things. Antonia's having some of her tennis club round for dinner.'

'How is Antonia?' asked Anne, and she noticed that the casualness of the question caused Marcus to wince.

'Oh, fine, fine, you know.' He was sweating slightly across his top lip. 'Fine,' he said again for no reason. There was a pause. 'Are you hurrying back for something, Anne, or can I tempt you to a quick drink?'

And although she knew that she should have refused, Anne found herself agreeing. For the first time, she realised that she wanted Marcus's undivided attention. She craved his uncomplicated adulation because it required no effort from her, no exertion of emotion. She knew, even then, where it would end.

In the pub, he had stared at her fixedly while she downed two double gin and tonics in quick succession. The jukebox was playing something thumping and heavy with the twang of guitar. After a while, Anne realised she recognised it from a jeans advert on television featuring a stupidly handsome man undressing in a launderette. The pub was too noisy to make out the words but she snatched bits of the chorus, which seemed to be about someone deciding whether to stay or go. She smiled to herself, just drunk enough to believe that the lyrics seemed especially pertinent to her situation. As she drummed her fingers gently against the table, Marcus moved his face closer to hers so that she could see the thin bloodshot lines criss-crossing against the whites of his eyes.

'Anne,' he said, his hand trembling as he placed it over hers. 'If ever you need someone to turn to . . .' Marcus let the thought cloud the air between them. 'You must know that I've always been –' he searched for the right word, 'extremely fond of you.' He started to stroke her hand so softly that his fingers felt like limp lettuce against her skin. 'Oh Anne,' he said, looking at her imploringly with shiny eyes. He sighed deeply and shook his head, turning away as if to hide the extremity of his feeling.

Anne looked at him. There was something melodramatic and insincere about his posturing: he was a man obsessed with the idea of being in love, a perpetual romantic who believes he is destined for a grand passion, without being aware of his own limitations. She felt that the only reason he had chosen her to be the recipient of his unfocused attentions was because she was safely attached to someone else. Marcus could indulge his whimsical bursts of ardour and then return to an undemanding wife who counted herself lucky to be with him. He was, if anything, strengthened by the realisation that their supposed love affair could never be because it dovetailed with his storybook ideals of doomed love, pitched against the odds.

She believed there was a small part of Marcus that genuinely thought, despite all indications to the contrary, that Anne loved him. He told himself that it would simply cost her too much to admit how she felt.

In fact, Anne, giddy-headed from too much alcohol, felt nothing but faint revulsion for him, for his hypocrisy, for his unthinking betrayal of his stupid wife, for his hang-dog stare and his misplaced belief in his own poetic heroism. And yet she also felt an over-whelming need to be reassured of her own sexual attractiveness, to be desired by someone who did not threaten her.

Ever since that awful morning when she had stumbled across Charles and Charlotte in the car on her way back from collecting a donation of clothes for the Red Cross shop, Anne had been seek-ing revenge. Revenge against Charles, yes, but most of all revenge against herself for being so weak, so gutless, so hopelessly in thrall to a monster of a man. She was sickened by her inaction and crip-pled by her guilt, but she could not face up to it. She could not bear to look at Charlotte's thin, pale face, at her silent, accusing eyes across the breakfast table. She had done what she thought was best: to carry on as if nothing had happened, to ensure the daily routine was as normal as possible, to wipe clean the surfaces of their consciousness and to make them all believe in it. And so, gradually, she blotted everything out. If she had not seen it, she reasoned, it need not exist.

But the pretence was thin and the varnish of it was cracking. She found that she wanted to do something to wound herself, that would give her a physical pain to match up to the emotional turmoil. And so she had arranged to meet Marcus one weekday lunchtime: a seedy rendezvous in a grubby little hotel with a proprietor who sold rooms by the hour. She told herself that this was all she was worth. Curiously, this knowledge made her feel better.

Room 235 smelled of stale cigarette smoke and the mustiness of rising damp. There was a television mounted in one corner and a bobbled pink bedspread edged with tired-looking frills. Marcus was sitting in a foam-filled armchair by the window, reading a newspaper, when she walked in. He stood up hastily and the news-paper fell to the floor with a whispering crinkle. He did not say anything, but walked straight across the brown shag-pile carpet and pressed his mouth firmly against Anne's before she had a chance to close the door.

His lips were wet and soft and loose like overstretched elastic. His tongue delved into the back of her throat, a thick eel swimming against the current. Anne found she could not breathe until he pulled back from her and then she saw he had a sickly smile on his face and that his chin was streaked with saliva.

'My darling,' he said, and the words were so incongruous with the setting that Anne wanted to laugh in his face. Instead, she started to undress. She wanted to get this over with as quickly as possible.

'Anne, there's no rush,' said Marcus softly, attempting to stop her from unbuttoning her skirt. 'We've got all afternoon.'

'I haven't,' she said flatly. 'I've got to get back.'

He looked crestfallen but started to unlace his shoes and slid out of his trousers. She noticed he was wearing tight blue briefs, the hems slightly frayed, and that his thin legs were covered in a mat of black hair. Anne stripped down to her bra and pants and Marcus walked up behind her, folding his arms around her stomach and drawing her so tightly towards him that she could feel his erection in the small of her back. His breathing was rapid and panting and she could taste the bitter ammonia smell of his sweat.

She turned to him and started to kiss him with such force that their teeth clashed and she felt the thin skin at the corners of her mouth begin to tear. She could hear him groaning, a sound like the creaking of a tree before it falls. She wanted to block him out completely, but Marcus kept drawing back and looking at her face, placing one hand on each cheek and shaking his head in self-conscious wonderment, as if he could not quite believe she was there.

Anne pulled him towards the bed. He began to kiss her neck and shoulders before moving with a slippery insistence down to her breasts. She could feel the edge of his teeth scratching against her nipples. She noticed that the top of Marcus's scalp was dry and flaky and that spores of dead skin were nestled along his parting. A wave of nausea rose up from her stomach and she shut her eyes, but she found that she could still smell him: a pungent steam of unwashed shirt collars and fried food.

He felt bony and insubstantial against her and his skinny arms were pitted with raised brown moles. He had none of Charles's strength or power and Anne found she was repelled by his constant fondling of her. It was as though he had read a manual and was executing each instruction to the letter, expecting her to moan in grateful surrender, but instead she simply wanted him to take her, as roughly as he could. She wanted it to be swift and emotionless, a vicious transaction that gave them both a physical release and nothing more. She wanted him to be callous towards her, to dominate her, to pin back her arms and force her into submission. She wanted to be punished and for it to hurt.

But Marcus was too soft. When he finally pushed his penis into her, she could barely feel it inside. He slid in and out, in and out and his eyes were half-closed in an approximation of bliss. His groaning got louder and more rhythmic.

'Anne,' he said hopelessly through gritted teeth. 'Oh Anne.'

She gripped on to his back with her fingernails and wound her legs round his buttocks to try and bring him closer, to crush his body against her hip bones, to flatten herself underneath his weight, but however much she tried she couldn't feel anything. After a few seconds, he gasped and rolled off her, the thin stream of his semen trickling out of her on to the bedspread.

Anne got up and went to the bathroom. She wiped between her legs with a towel and washed her hands. She walked back into the bedroom, gathered up her clothes and wordlessly got dressed. Marcus was staring at her, one bent arm resting against his forehead, a light sheen of sweat covering his thick chest hair.

'Will I see you again?'

Anne laughed sharply. 'Of course you will.'

'When?'

She looked at him coldly. 'I'm sure the Trenemans will be having a lunch party soon.'

Marcus flinched but he did not move. 'Why do you stay with him, Anne?' he asked, his voice laced with anger.

'I'm sorry?'

'With Charles,' Marcus said, and she saw that his eyes were narrow and black. 'Everyone knows he's fucked half the street.'

Anne did not react. She ran her hands through her hair, carefully tucking the stray strands behind her ears. She put on her jacket and retrieved her handbag from the floor. She got out her lipstick and unscrewed the top and applied a glossy coat of pale red to her mouth. She smiled, as if to try it out.

'Thank you, Marcus,' she said. She left the room with his eyes still following and closed the door with a soft thud behind her.

PART II

Charlotte

FOR A BRIEF PERIOD in her early twenties, Charlotte had been to see a psychotherapist She was called Roberta Mill and her offices were on the first floor of a nondescript terraced house in Queen's Park, surrounded by off-licences and dingy newsagents. Roberta Mill (Charlotte never referred to her by her first name alone, even in the privacy of her own thoughts) had been recommended by a friend and was an inscrutable woman of indistinct age. She had shoulder-length, rough blonde-brown hair that looked as though it would be brittle to the touch. Her eyes drooped at the corners, as if weighed down by invisible, tiny weights. She wore loose-fitting velvet clothes, capacious skirts and sensible shoes that looked vaguely medical.

Every time that Charlotte went to see her, she found herself increasingly desperate for Roberta Mill to like her, but the therapist seemed impervious to any sort of charm. The most uneasy moment of every session came at the very beginning – Roberta Mill would come downstairs to open the front door; she would say hello and smile, casting her eyes over Charlotte as if evaluating her, and then she would say nothing more for several minutes. They would walk up the staircase in a silence that felt desperately uneasy. Charlotte would try to make conversation – banal, polite comments about the weather or the traffic or something to lift the atmosphere – and Roberta Mill would remain utterly wordless with an enigmatic smile fixed in place.

Inside the small consulting room, Charlotte perched on a two-person Ikea sofa (she recognised it as being from that season's

'Fjord' range) and Roberta Mill seated herself in the single armchair opposite and then she would simply look at her until Charlotte felt like speaking. It took several weeks to get used to but Charlotte came to value Roberta Mill's silence. In a funny sort of way, it made her feel safe, as if she did not need to make the effort to charm, as if she were not being judged on her likeability or her small talk, but was simply being given the space to speak freely about whatever came to mind.

But still, she wanted Roberta Mill to like her. She became obsessed with it. Any insignificant personal detail that the counsellor let slip into the conversation was filed away in Charlotte's memory. Once, when Charlotte had said she wanted to get a cat, Roberta Mill had responded with an approving, 'Cats are very nice animals to have', and Charlotte was thrilled when she realised it was one of the most intimate confessions she had ever made. Charlotte began to depend on Roberta Mill's good opinion in exactly the same way she used to feel about teachers at school. She wanted them to admire her, to praise her cleverness, but also to think she was special: able to pick things up quickly and apply her intelligence well. The unintended consequence of this was that Charlotte was never fully honest in her therapy sessions. The need to remain in control, to prove that she was getting better, was paramount. She never told her exactly what happened with Charles because, bizarrely, she didn't want Roberta Mill to think badly of her father.

After twelve weeks, Roberta Mill said confidently that she thought Charlotte had 'worked very hard' and was, effectively, cured.

Yet there was one exchange that stuck in Charlotte's mind. They had been talking about the usual things – family, work, repressed emotion – and for some reason, Charlotte had mentioned that her eczema was particularly bad at the moment.

'Why do you think that is?' asked Roberta Mill, head slanted to one side, her green-grey eyes searching Charlotte's face for reaction.

'I suppose it's stress-related.'

There was a long silence. Finally, when it was clear Charlotte was not going to say anything more, Roberta Mill asked, 'When did you first get eczema?'

'When I was about eleven or twelve, I think.'

'And what was happening in your life around that time?'

Charlotte thought back, and suddenly, her mind was crowded with memories of the car, her father, the tick-tick-tick of the indicator, the Lego-brick houses, the science test she was going to be late for, the sight of her mother through the windscreen, the clothes scattered across the road, and then the running, running, running without knowing where she was going. She gulped and felt the wet tingle of tears push against the back of her eyes. She had never before made the obvious connection between her eczema and everything that had been going on. Something about this made her incredibly sad.

'There was some stuff with my parents,' Charlotte said, clearing her throat. 'They weren't getting on all that well and I felt . . . I felt like an intruder. I never felt at home for some reason. We never spoke about things, but . . .' She collected herself, aware of her own embarrassment at talking so melodramatically about something so seemingly trivial. 'It wasn't that bad.'

'Finish what you were going to say,' said Roberta Mill gently. 'Finish that thought.'

'We never talked. I was so worried all the time, worried that I was doing something wrong or that they were unhappy or that they would divorce – although that might have been a good thing, I guess. I just remember this overwhelming feeling of . . .' Charlotte searched for the right word. 'Well, tension I think is the best way of describing it.'

Roberta Mill shifted in her seat, uncrossing her legs and leaning forward slightly. She clasped her hands on her lap. 'It sounds to me as if you were a child desperate to express yourself, to say how you felt, and yet without the opportunity to do so.'

Charlotte nodded. The therapist sat back in her chair, letting the thought drift, and smiled warmly, waiting calmly for any response. Charlotte felt tears start to trickle down her cheeks and wiped them away with the back of her hand until Roberta Mill offered her a box of tissues, leaning across to put it on the arm of the sofa. 'What would you say now to your parents that you couldn't say then?'

It surprised Charlotte to realise she already knew the answer. 'I'd ask my mother why she didn't care enough to protect me.'

Charlotte twisted a piece of tissue until it became a thin, white string that she could wind through the fingers of one hand. She thought about the admission she had just made and knew that it was the single most truthful thing she had ever voiced to Roberta Mill. Yet the honesty of those few words did not leave her feeling the relief she half-expected would come with confession. Instead, she felt terror.

Later, Charlotte would wonder whether she was so used to keeping secrets that the secrets themselves had become part of her character. Was she frightened that by revealing them, she would no longer be herself? Or perhaps, more truthfully, was she worried that she would no longer have an excuse? That actually, she was rather a boring person when separated from the darkness within her. Was there part of her that enjoyed the tortured pose, the hints of hidden mysteries, the oh-so-artistic tendency towards depression? Had she made things worse than they actually were because she needed something to blame for all that she disliked about herself?

What if, once the secret was exposed, Roberta Mill thought it was mundane or pedestrian, not enough of a reason for someone to need therapy at all? What if she laughed at her? It was somehow more important that Roberta Mill liked her, rather than being allowed to know Charlotte as she really was. Because Charlotte as she really was might not have been enough.

'Charlotte?' Roberta Mill said, inflecting her voice with gentle persistence. 'Why do you think you would ask your mother that?'

Charlotte looked up at her blankly. 'I don't know,' she replied, and although this was a lie, it made her feel safe because even if she was not in control of what had been done to her, she was, at least, in control of what she revealed about herself. And that, more than anything else, gave her some sort of power.

Charlotte

ANNE HAD NOT COME to the hospital. When the nurse walked back into the room where they had taken her to calm down, Charlotte could see immediately from her baffled, semi-embarrassed expression that Anne would not be collecting her. The nurse stammered out a brief summary of the phone call, clearly ill at ease and not sure what to make of the inexplicable situation she found herself in. Charlotte almost felt sorry for her. She nodded her head once and then took a final sip of tea from the mug they had given her. It was chipped on the handle and emblazoned with the words 'World's Best Boss' in jaunty, brightly coloured letters.

The nurse was saying something else now, her lips moving, her eyebrows raised in concern but Charlotte couldn't hear what it was. She smiled, with what she hoped was a fair approximation of sanity, gathered her bag and coat and stood up.

'Thank you for being so kind,' she said to the nurse, who looked momentarily dumbfounded to have been halted in mid-flow.

'That's all right.' She hesitated. 'There was no real harm done but if . . . if you ever want to speak to someone . . .' The nurse let the thought trail. Charlotte nodded once more, as kindly as she could, and then walked outside into the linty grey evening light.

She forgot that she had her car here and instead started to make her way down the road towards the Tube station. She noticed her hand was aching, a dull, sore sense of half-removed pain, and she couldn't work out why until she remembered what had happened: she had hit her father. She had waited all these years for her revenge and this was all it had come to: slapping and screaming at him as he lay half-dead in a hospital bed. She felt like laughing, a bundled-up sense of mirth pushed against the back of her throat. How ridiculous she was.

She walked into a newsagent's, an old-fashioned bell ringing out as she opened the door.

'A packet of Lucky Strike Light, please. And a lighter.'

The wrinkle-skinned proprietor looked at her lugubriously, his brown eyes peeking out from behind a blue plastic dispenser of lottery scratch-cards. Wordlessly, he turned around, took the cigarette packet from the well-stocked shelves behind him and slid the blue-and-silver packet across the counter.

'What colour?' he asked.

'I'm sorry?'

'What colour lighter?'

'Oh, I don't mind. You choose.'

He selected one in a bright pink transparent plastic and gave it to her. He smiled briefly, pushing up the folds of flesh under his eyes like a Bassett hound.

'Pretty colour for a pretty lady,' he said. '£7.20.'

'Thank you,' said Charlotte, handing him the money.

She went outside and lit up, taking long, languid drags that made her slightly light-headed. Charlotte had never officially smoked but, occasionally, she craved the burnt caramel tang of a Lucky Strike. It was a brand that appealed to her for its romanticised connections with American GIs and 1940s forces sweethearts. She liked the taste of the tobacco, acrid against her tongue, and the fug of reliable numbness that now pulsated pleasurably through her body.

She took out her mobile and called Gabriel. He answered on the third ring.

'Hi, sweetie, how was it?'

'Gabriel, I need to talk to you.'

She could hear him breathe out heavily on the other end of the line.

'Sounds ominous.'

'It's not, it's not. I just . . . there are things I need to explain to you. Things I should have told you from the beginning.'

She took a drag of her cigarette.

'Charlotte, are you smoking?' he said, in a tone of bemusement. She knew that Gabriel quite liked her secret smoking habit; that he couldn't help but find it illicit and sexy in spite of himself. The knowledge that he should disapprove somehow heightened its appeal.

'Yes.'

He chuckled. 'Well it must be bad. I hope you're not going to tell me you feel like a man trapped in a woman's body or something.'

She laughed lightly. 'No, I promise it's nothing like that.'

'OK, well, come back to mine, then. I'll cook you dinner.'

'OK.'

'Charlotte?'

'Yes?'

'I love you. Don't forget that.'

'I won't.'

So she had told him everything: about her father, her mother, the cocoon of unspoken tension and gauzy half-truths that had wrapped themselves around their family. She had never spoken to another person so honestly before and it left her feeling both relieved and vulnerable, exposed like the tender, pinkish flesh of a newborn kitten.

Gabriel said almost nothing throughout, simply clasping her hand in his across the kitchen table as she let it all stream from her. Even when she got to the hardest bits – the episodes where her father had touched her; that day in the car; her mother's refusal to acknowledge what had happened; the evening in Piccadilly when it all came rushing back – he did not respond other than to squeeze her hand more tightly.

Charlotte was oddly grateful for this affectionate reticence. She did not want him to be angry because it would have made her feel like a failure for not having been angry enough herself, as if there were something wrong with her for accepting such ugliness without confrontation. Nor did she want him to condemn Charles outright, because, in spite of it all, there existed in her a residual grain of loyalty towards her father. She was the one who had been hurt by him, who had chosen, in the years that followed, to push it to one side as best she could, and she did not want her feelings appropriated, moulded into someone else's notion of what was right, of what they would have done in the same situation. All she wanted was someone she loved to listen. She wanted him to believe her and then to carry on loving her with the full knowledge of who she was. She wanted him to look deep into the darkest parts of her, to squeeze into the twisted corners of all she had become, and not to flinch, but to understand and be tender.

It took her two hours to tell her story, sometimes crying, sometimes clenched-up and furious inside, sometimes simply emotionless from the exhaustion of carrying it all, an over-full pool of murky water that for years had threatened to spill over and break its banks, the mulchiness flooding into her without warning.

Gabriel asked only one question. At the very end, when he was sure Charlotte had stopped speaking and when he had walked over to the other side of the table to crouch down and take her in his arms, he said, with such cautious gentleness that he was almost inaudible: 'Do you think you should talk to your mother?'

'Perhaps,' said Charlotte, and she thought back to Roberta Mill, but she knew she would feel too scared of what might be revealed to try.

'It's none of my business, of course,' he continued carefully, stroking her hair as he spoke, 'but maybe there is a little bit of you that can't forgive your mother because she's easier to blame. You're scared of your father but what scares you most is that he might not love you. You take what you can get from him. But with Anne, you don't have those qualms.' He paused. Charlotte said nothing. 'You know she loves you,' Gabriel said, 'and perhaps that means you can hate her more easily because there won't be the same sort of repercussion. She'll always love you.' He cleared his throat. 'Even if she failed you horribly.'

She did not reply but the silence had its own peculiar weight. She knew that this silence would be the closest she could get to an admission of truth. Gabriel knew it too and he did not press her. Instead, he stood up and drew Charlotte's head to him so that her cheek lay flat against the tautness of his stomach. He stroked her hair softly. She could smell the fabric softener scent of disinfected lavender on his shirt and, beneath it, the nutty mustiness of his sweat. She was overcome by a desire to touch him, to feel his solidity against her. She slid a hand underneath his shirt and let it rest on the familiar jut of his hip bone.

'You're safe now,' he said after a few minutes. 'I'm going to look after you for the rest of your life.'

The comfort of this was so intense, so all-encompassing, that Charlotte's breath caught in her throat. She tried to say something back, to thank him, to tell this man that – improbably, despite all the anxieties and the obstacles and the tangled mess he had made of his past – she loved him. But she couldn't. Perhaps she didn't need to; perhaps he already knew.

They went to bed after that and he held her all night. Even when she woke, restless and shifting, in the half-light of early morning, he found a way of wrapping his arms around her again without ever quite waking up. She slept a long time, a dreamless, black velvet sleep, and when she finally opened her eyes, she checked her watch and saw it was almost midday and that Gabriel was no longer beside her.

For a moment, she thought it was still the weekend, and then rapidly the realisation dawned that it was Monday and she should be in work.

'Shit.' She scrambled out of bed and was on her way to the en-suite shower when the bedroom door opened.

'So you're awake.'

'Gabriel?'

He laughed. 'Don't worry. I called your work and said you were sick. They were very understanding. Here –'

He handed her a large mug of coffee. Steam rose from the hot blackness and dampened her face.

'Thanks,' said Charlotte, still bewildered by the sudden transition from sleep to wakefulness.

'You've got sheet creases on your face,' said Gabriel, smiling. 'How are you feeling?'

'Fine,' she said, automatically, taking the mug back to bed with her and piling up the pillows against the cast-iron frame so that she could sit upright.

Gabriel followed her back into bed and lay beside her, leaning his head against his arm and looking directly at her. He touched her waist lightly.

'You don't have to be fine, you know.'

Charlotte didn't respond. Gabriel sighed.

'I want you to know how touched I am that you confided in me last night,' he said after a long stretch of silence. 'I know how much effort that took. And I want you to know that I will never disappoint the faith you showed in me. What you've been through – well, it makes me so upset to think of you going through all of that as a child. It's more than anyone should have to cope with.'

Charlotte looked at him and smiled. He always sounded unnecessarily formal when he was nervous. 'It's OK,' she said. 'None of it is your fault. I love you. I wanted you to know why I might be a bit bonkers sometimes.'

'You're not bonkers,' he said with utter seriousness. 'You're the finest woman I've ever met. It's the people around you who are bonkers. Christ.'

He started to chew on his fingernails, a horizontal crinkle appearing across his forehead as he thought. 'Do you think,' he started uncertainly, and then changed his mind. 'Forget it, it's none of my business.'

'No, what is it?'

'Tell me to shut up if I don't know what I'm talking about.'

'I promise,' she smiled. 'I've never had a problem telling you when you're speaking rubbish.' She took a sip of her coffee and the bitterness felt good in her mouth. She swallowed and could feel the hot liquid slide down her throat.

Gabriel cleared his throat. 'I feel sorry for your mother,' he said quietly. 'What she did was awful – indefensible, even – but it sounds like your father bullied you both and made you act in odd ways and she was just too scared to resist.'

'Mmm,' said Charlotte, but she felt her stomach lurch to one side. Gabriel took her hand and kissed her fingertips.

'Do you know how much I love you?'

'Yes.'

'I'm saying this because I love you. I'm saying this because it's clear to me that Anne loves you. She loves you so much she can barely live with herself, with the guilt of what she's done, and that makes her angry and clipped and bitter and someone who finds fault with everything around her.'

'So why did she just ignore it?' said Charlotte, and the effort of voicing the question that had haunted her for so many years made her shiver. She stared at the ceiling, her eyes tracing a crack in the plaster so that she did not have to look at him. She did not want to have to admit her own vulnerability. She was tired of crying. 'Who would do that to their child?'

'I don't know, my darling. But perhaps she thought that was what you wanted.' He fell into a brief silence. 'Like I said, I haven't got a clue what I'm talking about.'

'Maybe you're right,' said Charlotte, because it was easier than saying anything else. She wanted to change the subject. 'You know,' she said quickly. 'I feel so much better having told you.'

And it was true: she felt a calmness, a sense of sureness about herself that she had never before possessed. Although barely twenty-four hours had passed since her visit to the hospital, she felt her perspective had shifted dramatically. It seemed risible to her now that she had ever questioned her relationship with Gabriel when it offered her such unconditional love. It seemed, all at once, as though the answer to the past was not the past itself, but rather the future that she would build on her own terms. The future that was hers and Gabriel's. Her parents had chosen their lives. Now, perhaps, she could choose hers.

It was such an obvious conclusion that she laughed – at her own blinkered stupidity, at her good fortune, at the joy of having this man in bed beside her.

'What?' he said.

'Nothing.'

She put her coffee mug on the floor and then leaned over to kiss him.

Anne

ANNE STARTED THE MORNING full of good intentions. She woke at 6.30, the muffled sunlight casting lemon-yellow shapes across her white duvet. From beyond the fabric blind, patterned with faint blue pastoral scenes, she could tell it was going to be a clear, warm day and this filled her with a cautious feeling of hopefulness.

As she got up, Anne found that she had unconsciously flung one arm outwards in her sleep, on to Charles's side of the bed, and this troubled her. For weeks, she had kept faithfully to her edge of the mattress. This subtle but indelible encroachment of his space seemed somehow symbolic. She still had not made a decision about the conversation with Dr Lewis.

She swatted the thought away as she took off her nightdress and started thinking about all the things she would get done: she would finish painting the study; she would clear out the kitchen cupboards; she would start eating more healthily in a bid to lose a few pounds; she would take the car in for its MOT; she would talk to Charlotte.

The last of these duties loomed large and grey over everything else, giving her a feeling of almost perpetual unease and a shrinking sense of guilt that spread over her like liquid wax. Occasionally, she found she had forgotten all about it while doing some menial task like weeding the garden. Anne would be kneeling down on the slim padded green cushion, digging into the beds with a rusty trowel, and then suddenly remember there was something she should be feeling bad about. What was it? Oh yes, that was it:

she had to make amends to her only child for being an emotional
failure as a mother.

But by the time she had made herself breakfast – a slice of whole-
meal toast with low-fat butter – and got the rollers and brushes
out to do a second coat of emulsion on the study walls, Anne
found herself overcome with an uncharacteristic lassitude. She sat
on the sofa in the drawing room in her paint-spattered old jeans
and one of Charles's work shirts that had a frayed collar and an
un-repaired hole under the armpit. It all seemed a bit pointless. She
could feel a mild depression settle round her shoulders; a weighed-
down sensation of slowness and self-pity. It gave her vision a
glittering, uncomfortable clarity, like the start of a migraine.

Before the depression had a chance to take hold, Anne grabbed
the car keys and drove to a nearby organic deli with the intention
of stocking up on delicious, nutrient-packed provisions to kick-
start her new healthier lifestyle. She almost never bought food
there because of the shop's overriding smugness. Each time she
went in, she found herself muttering under her breath at the deliberately homely writing on the blackboards, advertising fair-trade
quinoa grains at some outrageously high price and the free samples
of blueberry smoothie sourced from an ecologically sustainable
farmer in Suffolk.

This time was no different. Almost as soon as she got through
the door, a cheery-faced sales assistant in a canvas brown apron
offered her a cocktail stick pierced through a tiny sliver of purple
broccoli.

'No thanks,' said Anne, unsmiling. 'I like my broccoli green.'

The sales assistant laughed ingratiatingly. Anne walked on up
the aisle, pulling behind her a shopping basket that had to be
tugged like a trolley rather than carried in the normal manner. She
wanted some fresh tomatoes and feta cheese to make a salad for
lunch, but when she got to the cheese fridge, a pregnant woman
with a dual buggy was standing in front, making it impossible to
reach past. The woman was wearing a long, floating cardigan that
looked expensive and sheepskin-lined boots that fitted snugly over
her jeans. Her face bore an expression of worn privilege and self-
satisfaction. 'Millie, don't do that,' she drawled to one of the two

blonde-haired toddlers in the buggy, who was poking the frosted edge of the lower shelf with her chubby finger.

Anne waited patiently, expecting the woman to realise she was there and move apologetically to one side. Instead, the woman spent several minutes trying to remember what cheese it was she wanted, rubbing her protruding belly absent-mindedly as she did so, and talking to her children in half-hearted tones. Anne felt herself seethe inwardly.

It was never like this when Charlotte was little, she thought. People simply had babies and then got on with it. They didn't indulge them. They didn't worry about pelvic floor exercises and yogic breathing and the possibilities of giving birth in paddling pools. They didn't expect any special treatment and they didn't spoil their children with excess attention and organic food and computer games designed to simulate tennis matches. They didn't dress them in Oxfam-approved cotton and drive them around in safety seats strapped into the back of 4X4s with one of those nauseating yellow triangles suckered on to the back windscreen announcing the fact that there was a 'Baby on Board'. And they didn't expect everyone else to tiptoe around them, oozing gratitude for their astonishing ability to procreate.

They would have moved to let someone else get to a supermarket shelf.

The anger flickered dangerously in the pit of her stomach. She could feel herself about to give into it and had the overwhelming urge to lash out, to slap this woman in the face. But her rage dissipated almost as soon as she acknowledged it. She stepped back, impotent. Anne dropped her basket on the floor and walked out of the shop. The woman with the buggy turned round lazily, her glazed bovine eyes momentarily startled.

As Anne strode hurriedly towards the car, she found herself thinking about the mother in the shop. She wondered if that was where she had gone wrong with Charlotte. Was it that she had never paid her enough attention? Was she too concerned with Charles, too in love with him still, too obsessed with keeping his emotions on an even keel, too desperate to grab hold of the wayward threads that were un-spooling in front of her? Was that why it had happened?

Was protecting the appearance of her marriage more important to her than helping her only child?

Anne had never told Charlotte that she loved her but that was not because she didn't: it was that she hadn't wanted her to be spoilt. The obviousness of her love seemed so self-evident that it would have been decadent to voice it. And now it was too late: Anne felt too much to be able to express it, to be able to cut through the decades of pent-up silence. She regretted not having told her earlier. She regretted it all.

The mildness of the day surprised her as she got into the driver's seat. She felt herself break out into a sweat, the heat prickling uncomfortably down her back and gathering in a moistness at the nub of her backbone.

And then, she found herself internally voicing the unmentionable thought that she had stifled for years; a thought that cowered in the corners of her mind like the shadow of a coiled animal waiting to spring. Was it that she craved her husband's love more than her daughter's? Had she spent the last three decades desperately chasing the impossible, desperately attempting to make a man incapable of human warmth return her embittered love? Was that what her life had amounted to?

She already knew, in those slivered moments where she chose to acknowledge the truth, that Charles had never loved her, not really. But as she turned the key in the ignition, she realised with a shudder of hopelessness that Charlotte would never to be able to love her enough. Not now. Not given the things she had done. The things she had never said.

Instead of heading back home, Anne found herself driving into town, speeding down the Cromwell Road, surrounded by the thundering roar of lorries and grimy white vans. She turned right after the 24-hour Tesco, a giant edifice of fibreglass and concrete, filled with airless strip-lighting. Inside, she could make out the mini people pushing shopping trolleys who looked as if they never left the building but simply kept walking round and round on an endless loop, lulled by the oblivion of battered groceries and the dead-eyed swiping of checkout attendants.

She pulled up outside a brick building set back from a large roundabout, its windows covered with a greenish reflective sheen. She walked into the reception area. A red-haired girl of improbable lushness smiled at her, her glossy lips splitting like a nectarine segment sliced away from its stone.

'Can I help you?'

'Yes, I'm here to see Charlotte Redfern,' said Anne. 'She works at Finch & Bartlebury.'

'Of course. And your name is?'

'I'm her mother.'

The receptionist laughed tightly. 'Oh, right. I'll call through now. Take a seat,' and she gestured gracefully at a series of brown leather cubes scattered around a glass table strewn with magazines.

Anne perched herself on top of one of the cubes, feeling acutely the lack of back support. Smartly dressed men in pressed shirts and women in spindly heels walked past her, each one an embodiment of youthful glamour and blow-dried style. They looked like extras in an advertisement for shaving cream or shampoo. Anne was embarrassed to realise that she was still wearing her ragged old painting clothes. She tried to cross her legs as elegantly as she could, but it was difficult to keep her balance on the cube and she felt uncomfortably out of place, as if she were a domestic tabby cat trying to fit in with a sleek tribe of jungle panthers.

She began to think it had been a bad idea coming here. She had worked herself up into a lather about nothing. She should pull herself together, take a few deep breaths, walk up to the receptionist and say that she had changed her mind, that she would come back later, then she could drive home without upsetting the soothingly predictable pattern of the day. She could deal with this all some other time. After all, they had dealt with worse things in the past by accepting them wordlessly and moving on in the spirit of shared compromise, hadn't they? Sometimes, she told herself firmly, silence was the best way to cope.

Anne was just about to stand up and apologise to the redhead when she saw Charlotte walking out of the lift across the lobby. She felt her heart thud as she recognised her daughter: tall, lovely and yet still ineffably Charlotte, with her wavy hair, the harassed crinkle between her eyes and the rapid walk that indicated she was late, again. And yet, something had changed. There was, thought Anne, a self-possession about her daughter that she had not seen before, a sense of inner certainty. Perhaps it was simply seeing her in a professional context for the first time, but she looked both utterly the same and yet entirely different. She seemed – Anne searched for the right word – she seemed somehow calm, sure of where she was going.

The difference between this Charlotte and the Charlotte of a few weeks before was striking. It was not until this moment, in the lobby of this anonymous office building, that Anne realised how anxious Charlotte had been for months up to this point, how her shoulders had always been tense when she saw her, how her eyes had appeared strained, as if searching for something on a faraway horizon that she would never quite reach. Anne found herself blinking back tears. Why had she not noticed the muscled tautness of her daughter's unhappiness before now? How had she not known that Charlotte could be this poised? What had changed? Her daughter looked, for the first time, not just pretty but beautiful.

'Hi, Mum,'

'Hello, Charlotte.' Anne found she could not say anything else but just stood there, in her paint-spattered clothes with her greying hair tied back roughly with an elastic band and minimal make-up on her face, staring at her radiant daughter in total wonderment. How had she produced this fabulous creature? Charlotte was staring at her, her mouth set in a thin, unsmiling line.

'This is a surprise. What are you doing here?'

'I thought . . .' Anne had no idea what to say. 'I thought I could take you for lunch. If you're not busy.'

'Mum, it's only 11.30.'

'An early lunch, then. Or a coffee.' Charlotte turned her head towards the big clock behind reception and checked it against her watch. She was wearing a silky pale peach-coloured top, the short sleeves lightly puffed at the shoulder like the wisp of a meringue. Anne noticed that the eczema on her arms had cleared up.

'OK,' said Charlotte. 'But I've got to be back by 12.15.'

Anne saw that she was still not smiling and this gave her face an unnaturally surly appearance, as if she were concentrating hard on not giving anything away. Anne knew that look well: it was exactly what she had been like when doing her homework or when she was upset about something but not saying what it was. Anne had always thought the best thing to do when faced with Charlotte's episodes of pensive cloudiness was to give her space until it passed. Perhaps, Anne thought now, she had been wrong. Perhaps this distance had been misinterpreted as callousness.

She reached out without thinking and placed the palm of her hand against the gentle curve of Charlotte's cheek. It was warm to the touch, soft beneath the tips of her fingers. Charlotte looked momentarily shocked and then turned her face away, embarrassed.

'There's a café round the corner we can go to,' she said, as if nothing had happened, and then she started to walk towards the door. Anne followed her, half-running to keep up with her long stride. She was unsure of what Charlotte was thinking and felt unsettled, almost panicked, about this unfamiliar uncertainty.

The café was old-fashioned, with cracked formica-topped tables and a blackboard advertising cups of tea for 40p. Almost all of the tables were occupied by large men in high-visibility bibs eating fry-ups and leafing through copies of the *Sun*. A few of them seemed to be speaking in Polish, their conversation peppered with guttural laughs and rolled Rs. The front window was fogging up with condensation. Behind the counter, a rotund middle-aged man and woman in matching aprons were taking orders.

'Yes, love?' said the woman as Charlotte approached to order.

'Mum, what do you want?'

'Oh, um,' Anne felt herself begin to tip over into a slight panic. She felt foolish.

'Mum?' Charlotte was looking at her impatiently.

'Do they do herbal tea?'

Charlotte rolled her eyes. 'No.'

'I'll just have a normal tea, then, thanks. Milk, one sugar.'

'The sugar's on the table,' said Charlotte dismissively, waving towards the chrome-topped shakers filled with yellowing grains.

'So it is.'

Gingerly, Anne picked her way through the burly men and the clattering chairs until she found a small table in the corner. She slid on to a chair, carefully ensuring that her handbag strap was looped around one of the legs to prevent any theft. She twisted her hands on her lap as she waited, not wanting to touch any of the sticky-looking surfaces and not quite knowing what she should say. She felt her heart flutter nervously as Charlotte came across, carefully balancing two steaming mugs of tea.

'Here you go.' Charlotte passed her the tea, still unsmiling.

'Thank you.' Anne took a sip and burned the roof of her mouth with the scalding liquid. There was a protracted silence.

'What are you doing here, Mum?'

Anne coughed lightly. 'We haven't spoken since . . .'

'Since I came round on Wednesday.'

'Yes, exactly and I suppose I wanted . . .' she trailed off and let the sentence hang incompletely between them. She stared into her mug and brought it up to her lips so that she could see the shadowy contours of her hairline reflected in the murky brown as she drank the tea. Charlotte was looking at her coolly, her arms crossed. For a few seconds, Anne did not know what the dull ache was in her chest and then she realised she was frightened and that this sensation was slicked with a wet coating of sadness.

'I suppose . . .' Anne began softly, and the words choked out of her so that it felt as though someone were pressing down on her windpipe. She focused on her mug of tea, refusing to meet Charlotte's gaze. 'I wanted to say sorry.'

There was a long silence. Anne chewed her lip, determined to stop herself from crying. She wanted to say so much more but the air seemed to have hissed out of her lungs like a leaking tyre and she could not find the strength she needed to continue. She poured more sugar into her tea. The grains made a soothing sound as they slid gloopily into the liquid. Finally, she lifted her head and looked at her daughter. She was terrified that she would be met by anger or judgement or – worse – contempt, but instead Charlotte was gazing at her levelly and her eyes were softened by something approaching kindness.

'I'm sorry,' she said again, this time more loudly, although her mouth was dry. Anne's face was clammy. She took a thin paper napkin from the table dispenser and patted her cheeks with it. The napkin felt strangely plastic and unyielding on her flesh. When she moved it away, she noticed that a streak of leftover foundation had made an orangey smear across the white.

Still Charlotte said nothing, and her silence seemed to contain both an accusation and an opportunity for penitence.

Anne thought back to that day, she thought back through the confusion of months and years, she thought back through the hints and implications, the never-quite-mentioned awfulness of it, she thought of Charles and how much she had loved him, how stupidly she had been unable to stop even when she believed he was a monster. She thought how much she had been able to forgive, she thought of the shock, the terrible, numbing, nauseating shock of that single moment in time.

She thought of turning and walking down the road, away from the car, away from the tears of her child and the strange, warped power of her husband, and she felt sickened by what she had done. She felt guilt; intense, painful, undiluted guilt, a guilt that bored into the heart of her like a drill pushing through a tender piece of earth, twisting into the depths of the soil towards a dark, viscous trickle of oil.

She was scared. Scared of what Charlotte thought of her and scared, most of all, of what she had done. She was scared of admitting her own awful liability in case it revolted her; in case she could no longer live with herself, with the knowledge of her own culpability. She was scared of how thoroughly she had convinced herself that she had done the right thing, of how she had been able to live for all these years by constructing a pretence so convincing that it became a substitute for her own feelings. She was scared at what she had become: a hollowed-out space filled with disillusionment.

She knew that she had turned into a person who could be bitter and mean and devoid of emotion. She could be cruel. But she also knew that it had all been the consequence of wanting to defend herself, of wanting to defend her family – such as it was – and, most of all, of wanting to protect her daughter by ensuring she never made the same mistakes. Charlotte would never waste herself on a brutal man; she would never define her life around the vortex of someone else's power.

It had all been done for love. All of it.

How could she express all this here, in this café, with these Polish builders, surrounded by the lingering smell of frying grease?

'Go on,' said Charlotte, and her daughter stretched her arm out across the table and took Anne's hand in her own. Anne felt the tears begin to stream down her cheeks.

'I'm sorry for not helping you,' she said, gulping for air in between quiet sobs, and she couldn't remember the last time she had cried so much, so visibly and so uncontrollably. 'I'm so so sorry, Charlotte. I did what I thought was best and I know how pathetic that sounds, how awful you must have felt when I walked away from the car that time but . . .' She broke off. 'You see, I don't think I can be a very good person. I'm certainly not a natural mother. I thought I would be, I thought having a baby would make me complete and happy. I thought it would take away all the other stuff, that it would bring me and Charles closer together. It's such a cliché, I know. But there you are. That was what I thought.'

'And it didn't happen like that?'

'No,' said Anne, wiping her nose. 'But I loved you so very much, Charlotte, from the day you were born. You must believe that.' She looked at her daughter desperately.

'I do,' Charlotte said softly. 'I do.'

'It's just . . . he was impossible to live with. I lost myself. I lost my strength, my own sense of what was normal. I couldn't do anything right so I chose not to do anything at all, and I know you bore the brunt of it but I was frightened and I was helpless because I didn't want him to leave and I can't explain it. I can't explain why I still love him.'

'You don't have to,' said Charlotte calmly. 'He has a power over us. He always will. We want to be loved by him to the exclusion of everything else.' She paused. 'Or at least, we did.'

Anne looked up.

'What do you mean?'

'I mean, he's no longer a threat to us. He can't do anything. He can't show us love or remove it. I don't miss him any more. It took me a long time but I don't. I have Gabriel.'

219

'Really?' asked Anne, as if she couldn't quite believe it. 'I hadn't realised how strongly you felt about him.'

'I know. You made that perfectly clear.'

Anne lifted Charlotte's hand up to her face and pressed it against her damp cheek, inhaling the faint scent of her perfume: figs and summer blossom and the headiness of wild thyme. 'But only because I was worried about you. Only because I didn't want the same thing to happen that had happened to me.'

Charlotte took her hand away, but gently so that it didn't feel like a rejection. She crossed her arms on the table and dropped her eyes so that they focused on the grubby linoleum floor pattern.

'You know,' she said finally. 'You should have spoken to me about it. About that day, I mean.'

Anne bit her lower lip so hard that she began to taste the metallic tang of blood in her mouth. She noticed that she had stopped crying and she dabbed underneath her eyes with the tips of her fingers.

'I should have done,' she said after a few seconds' pause, her voice steady. 'I suppose I didn't for purely selfish reasons. I wanted to pretend it hadn't happened. I wanted to move on and ignore it and I thought we all could.'

'But weren't you worried about me?' said Charlotte, her voice breaking. 'Didn't you think I could have been . . . harmed?'

'No.' The bald admission surprised them both. 'I knew he wouldn't take things further than a certain point,' said Anne. 'He was too clever. And he loved you too much. That was part of the problem, you see. Between him and me, I mean.'

Anne let the thought expand to fill the space between them. 'And he was better after that,' she continued. 'He mellowed. He became more considerate. He had fewer dalliances. He never did anything like that again to you, did he?'

'No.'

'I told him that if he did I'd leave him and take you with me. He couldn't bear the thought of it.'

'Of losing you?'

'No,' said Anne, looking straight into her daughter's clear blue eyes. 'Of losing you.'

Charles

H E FELT LIKE CRYING. There was a shadow he couldn't quite
make out, a black velvet swirl, unfurling like an explosive
inkiness in a glass of water. He was trying to reach for it with his
hands but he found he couldn't move his arms. It was the most
beautiful blackness. It seemed to be teasing him, dipping and rising
before his eyes, coming close to him, almost close enough to feel,
and then slipping away in a smooth, ever-shifting calligraphy.

If only he could just reach out and touch it . . . if only he had the
strength to reach out and hold its softness in his hands and feel its
precious warmth against him, feel the liquid blackness of it dripping through his fingers like slow-moving silt.

He wanted to cover himself in the blackness. If only he could get
to it, lose himself in it, he knew it would make him better. He knew
it was the answer to some question he no longer remembered.

He stretched forward and strained with all his might but still
his arms would not move and the mesmerising shape gradually
receded out of his line of vision, losing focus and solidity and dissi-
pating into a thousand night-coloured granules.

He felt hopeless then, as if he were about to cry because he had
lost all hope of holding it close to him. But he found he could not
cry, even though he felt the tears welling up inside. He could hear
the sound of his sadness and it was a jangling minor chord, like a
string-tuning crescendo of orchestral dissonance.

But then the black shape suddenly re-emerged and he was so
joyful it was hard to remember what the sadness felt like and he
thought how strange it was to be experiencing this battering of

emotion, see-sawing from one extreme to the next when he usually exerted such control over what he felt. The black shape came closer and closer to him, transforming from a nebulous coalescence of dots into a more solid form with four legs and a wagging tail and two triangular ears like envelope flaps and all at once he knew that it was his dog Sooty. It was Sooty!

The relief of certain knowledge was intense and it swept over him so that he found he could move his arms and he could clasp the dog to his chest and bury his head in its fur, that smelled of cow parsley and river water dried by the sun.

And then his mother was calling him in for tea and he could hear her voice, shrill and tuneless, but not the formation of her words. The dog was bounding off in front of him across the fields, its paws cantering across muddy divots, its pink tongue lolling as it panted, a thin patina of sweat covering its coat, which glistened in the early evening light. He was running after the dog, attempting to catch up with Sooty's receding black shape, and he realised that he no longer felt the unadulterated happiness that had swept over him seconds before. His chest was constricting, like a pool of molten metal that had cooled too rapidly. The crushing weight of it was becoming unbearable as it pushed down on him.

His legs were slowing down even though he was willing them to keep running, but they weren't responding to his brain. He felt a dreadful panic then. He wanted to stop moving altogether, to go back into the gentle nothingness of his daily normality, but his legs wouldn't let him. Instead he was trudging forward with painful slowness and when he looked down he saw his Wellington boots were filled with rocks and heavy mud that spilled out with each step he took and yet never emptied no matter how far he walked.

After several hours, he seemed to get to where he was meant to be, which was a doorway but with no house around it: a simple frame opening into blankness. His mother was still calling him. He pushed the door open and he saw her facing him, a blue-striped apron tied neatly around her waist. Her hands were behind her back. Her blonde hair was set in careful curls. Her face was expertly made-up and her plump red lips were stretched in an awful smile, her eyes bulging as they always did when she was angry. She was much, much taller than him and he felt intimidated by her size. He tried to cower down, to make himself as small as possible, as invisible as he could, but her face was contorted with string-veined rage and he knew there was no escape.

'Your bloody dog has traipsed dirt all over my clean kitchen floor,' she started saying, and she was speaking softly, which was always a bad sign, softly but with an undercurrent of unnatural brightness. He could see the pulse at the corner of her head throbbing, beating out a code of disappointment.

She took two steps towards him, two giant steps that covered the whole of the kitchen floor, and then he saw why her hands had been concealed behind her back when he walked in, because she was holding a heavy-bottomed saucepan in one of them, her fingers gripping the handle so tightly that her fingernails had turned white-pink. Quickly, too quickly for him to raise his arms to protect himself, she brought the saucepan down, hitting him across one side of his head with a clattering thud that sent him crumpled to the ground. The pain was so blinding, so acute, that he wanted to scream but he found that no sound came.

His mother was shouting at him but he could no longer see her face, so that his entire sensory perception was taken up with the sound of her words. 'You filthy little bastard,' she screamed. 'How dare you. I cook and I clean and I do it all and for what? For a stupid, ungrateful boy like you to ruin it all.'

She hit him again with the saucepan but this time it seemed almost perfunctory, as if the strength had gone out of her, as if the thrill of it had lessened. He felt the coolness of the saucepan's rim against his hairline and then he fell back into a sort of wakeful numbness and he went very, very still for what seemed like hours, during which his mind was blank. After a while, he heard his mother walking away, her step incongruously dainty against the floor tiles.

He opened his eyes and saw nothing and he realised he was safe again and cocooned by the strange fluid of incomprehension. A few seconds later, the blackness appeared from the corner of his eyes, looping in and out of his vision like the tantalising twirl of a gymnast's ribbon.

He did not know where he was or what he was doing or how long he had been here. He simply knew that he had to stretch out and get hold of that black shape. He had to touch it, to grasp it, to keep it next to him. He tried to grab its edges but they dissolved in front of him and re-appeared somewhere else. His arms would not move. He could not get at it. The black shape kept swooping and slipping out of his reach.

He felt like crying.

Janet

JANET HAD BEEN PREPARING the dinner for days. She would be queuing in the post office to buy airmail stamps and the thought of what kind of napkins to buy would rise, unbidden, to the surface of her mind. Or she would be doing her usual thirty lengths in the local pool only to find that she had lost count because she was thinking about whether serving cold soup as a starter would be too pedestrian.

Almost as soon as she had issued that impromptu invitation to Charlotte on the pavement outside Anne's house, she had felt herself engulfed by a wave of pleasure, tinged with incipient panic. Janet hadn't meant to ask Charlotte over and she certainly hadn't expected a positive response, assuming, as she tended to do, that bright young people probably had far better things to do than charitably keep her company.

But Charlotte had looked so upset, so bereft standing there on her own, struggling to get the key into the lock of her car door, that Janet couldn't help herself. She had seemed so alone, like a child fumbling with the edges of the adult world, trying to pin down its confusions and contradictions, and something plucked at Janet deep inside so that, before she knew it, she had asked Charlotte to dinner and Charlotte had accepted. And not just Charlotte, but Gabriel too, a man whom she had never met and whose presence was bound to make her a nervous wreck, given how unaccustomed she had become to male company in the eight years since Nigel's death from a cruelly aggressive form of colon cancer.

Janet and Nigel had never had children. They had tried, of course, but there was some problem and, curiously, neither of them had felt the need to pursue it. If it happened now, Janet thought, they probably would have gone through endless rounds of futile IVF treatment, but in those days, there hadn't been the option. She had grieved for her lack of children but, at the same time, Janet was of the belief that if things weren't meant to happen then it was best not to tamper too much with the natural imperative. They had talked about adoption briefly but she could tell that Nigel, a kind, mild-mannered man in all other matters, was horrified at the thought of having to bring up someone else's child. And, in the end, she came to the conclusion that their life together was enough: it was a gentle, contented existence of mutual respect and affection, underpinned by a deep, deep love that neither of them ever felt the need to vocalise.

When he died, Janet had been shocked by her reaction, by how viscerally she felt his loss. She did not leave the house for two weeks. She could not sleep but spent the nights pacing through the corridors, as if perpetual movement could banish the unutterable emptiness and chase her grief away. She did not wash or get dressed and she picked at food that gradually spoilt and went stale and had to be thrown away and then, when there was nothing left to eat, she drank her way through the spirit bottle dregs that had accumulated over the years in various cupboards. She had tried, half-heartedly, to kill herself with a kitchen knife but she discovered she was a coward and could not go through with it.

And then, at the end of a fortnight, Janet had been hungry. It was the first purely physical feeling she had experienced for some time and she felt grateful for the uncomplicatedness of an urge that required her simply to act rather than think.

So she had got dressed and gone shopping and since then she had been proud of the fact that she had never once relapsed. She had dipped a toe into the darkness and it was enough. Her optimism returned. She regained the equilibrium of good-natured friendliness. To the outside world, Janet became Janet again. It was only in her loneliest moments that she allowed herself to walk to the brink of the crevasse, to peer into the cold, sharp oblivion beyond the fringes of her consciousness. And then, scared by her own ugliness, she would pull back quickly. No one else would ever know. No one suspected that Janet's banal, likeable appearance contained within it such twisted shadows.

She had recognised this same darkness in Anne the first time she met her at the annual carol concert, an event that never failed to cheer Janet up with its air of bonhomie and festive celebration. Anne had seemed disconnected from what was going on around her, a translucent vapour in a roomful of brightly coloured solids. Janet felt for her immediately without quite understanding why. It was only afterwards, as she got to know Charles, that it began to make sense.

Janet had never liked him, although she could see, objectively, why so many women found him charming. But there was something about Charles that invited her mistrust. He seemed slippery and, at the same time, there was a blankness to him that she found disturbing. Janet felt she was unable to pin his personality down to any one characteristic. He was a strong man, aware of his own power and undoubtedly charismatic. Yet his personality seemed to shift shape according to its surroundings; he seemed to reflect what you wanted to see rather than reveal himself in any substantial way.

Janet knew that Charles found her perplexing: one of the few women he was unable to win over and control. She presented a sort of challenge to him and, as such, he had always gone out of his way to try and please her, to flatter her into submission, to cajole her into the sort of unquestioning admiration he was used to. But she had never been convinced, partly because she hated what he had done to Anne – stamping out her small sparks of joy and leaving bitterness to fester in its ashes – and partly because she could occasionally glimpse the ragged edges of a nastiness he tried so hard to conceal. It was only ever a tiny moment – his mouth would twitch in suppressed anger when Anne clattered a plate too loudly, or his eyes, after twinkling with some joke he had just made, would seem to drain away, voiding themselves of emotion. It was the sort of thing that was easy to overlook but Janet was a shrewd observer of people. She knew that her own unremarkable appearance and quiet nature gave her the privilege of watching without being noticed.

'Janet. Always so quiet and always so watchful,' Charles had said to her once when they ran into each other at the Trenemans'. Janet had met Giles Treneman at one of the Salvation Army jumble sales. He was red-faced and cheery from the exertion of unpacking various boxes and clumsily re-arranging the contents on the fold-out table in front of him. Janet felt for Giles instantly: he seemed like a small, lost boy who needed looking after. It was only much later that she discovered he was Anne's neighbour of more than thirty years. He started inviting Janet to small social gatherings arranged by his plump and kindly second wife, Peggy.

'His first wife died,' Anne told her. 'Cancer.'

'Oh,' said Janet, taken aback by the brisk way in which this information was relayed. 'What was she like?'

Anne looked at her levelly. 'I never particularly took to her,' she replied, her voice emotionless. 'Peggy is much nicer.'

On this occasion, it was a summer lunch party and everyone was slightly sozzled and over-tired after too much food. Janet had gone into the drawing room after the meal to look at two small water-colour landscapes by an artist that she thought she recognised. As she was peering at the pastel brushtrokes, trying to make out a signature, she felt Charles loom up behind her, his bulk displacing the air around her so that it seemed to drop in temperature.

'I just wanted to take a closer look at these,' she said, looking him straight in the eye. For some reason, she had never been intimidated by Charles. She suspected this was because she had no need of his attention and therefore could not be bullied by him.

He smiled, one side of his mouth curling upwards. He stood so close to her that she could feel his breath against her cheek. It smelled of the bubbled sourness of champagne.

'I know you don't like me,' he said, out of nowhere, his voice perfectly level.

Janet, taken aback, did not know what to do. She started to fidget with her wine glass. 'Of course I like you, Charles,' she blurted out, feeling herself go red in the face.

'I know you don't,' he repeated. 'But that's all right, Janet, because, you know what?'

She shook her head. He grinned, took a swig from his glass and snorted loudly with laughter. The mood changed. He seemed to be moving too quickly, his pale blue eyes suddenly manic and unfocused. Janet started to feel frightened and then told herself not to be so silly – all the other guests were in the next-door room. He wouldn't do anything to her here, would he? 'Because, Janet,' he pronounced her name with cutting precision. 'I'm not sure I like me either.'

She made a move then, attempted to get away from him, but he had blocked her into the corner of the room so that she could feel the frame of one of the paintings prodding into her back. Charles was much taller than she was, but he stooped forward so that his face was inches away from hers. His skin was almost completely smooth and colourless except for two deep wrinkles gouged out thickly in between his eyes.

'But the thing is, Janet, that you don't count,' he said, and the self-conscious care with which he spoke his consonants made her realise that he was drunk. Very, very drunk. Janet had never seen him drunk before, in spite of his prodigious capacity for alcohol. He was someone who appeared incapable of losing control. Everything he did was exactly intended. Charles chose his targets with great care; he never misfired.

'As a person, I mean,' he continued. 'You're one of those people who will never make a difference.' He waved his hand around, gesturing towards an invisible dust mote. 'The planet is untroubled by your presence on it.'

It was the only time that Charles had managed to get to her. He saw it immediately, a chink of weakness.

'You think that being nice is the most important thing you can be.' His voice dropped to a slurring whisper. 'You're wrong, Janet. You're wrong. Niceness gets punished. Innocence is there to be broken in. It's better to be on the other side.'

She cleared her throat before she spoke, determined to regain composure. 'The other side?' she asked, not quite looking at his face.

He laughed. 'Yes, Janet. It's better to be nasty.' Abruptly, he turned his back to her and left the room. Janet shivered and drew her cardigan closed across her chest.

As Charles walked away, she noticed a long blonde hair stuck on the back of his navy blue jacket. The hair ran all the way from his neckline down to a spot between his shoulder blades where it ended in an elegant curlicue. She wondered, for a moment, whose it could have been.

That had been the last time Janet spoke to him. Within weeks, he was lying in a hospital bed and she was not, if truth be told, entirely sorry about it. The exchange with Charles lodged in her mind. It became more important to her than ever to be a true friend to Anne, to offer wordless support against the tumult of conflicting emotions she must be experiencing. Although Anne had never told Janet anything about her marriage and although their conversations were mostly limited to mundane observations and occasional misunderstandings, Janet could sense that both Charlotte and Anne were struggling with something that linked them inextricably while pushing them further apart. They were two women whose growth had been stunted by the same man, whose confidence and sense of self had been warped by being planted in his shadow. But Janet could never have broached the topic with Anne directly.

She knew that the image Anne projected of herself was extremely important to her and that Anne needed to feel in control of their friendship in a way that she had never managed to stay in control of her marriage. Janet didn't mind this. She felt she could put up with Anne's obvious slights and unsubtle displays of irritation because she knew they were not intended for her, but for Charles. They might sometimes be hurtful, but never for long, and she was also capable of great acts of kindness. But the crux of it was that whenever Janet looked at Anne, she saw someone as lonely as she was and she wanted, more than anything, to help.

And that's how the dinner party came about. As soon as Charlotte said yes, Janet knew that Anne would be unable to resist the excuse to see her daughter. She thought it would be good for them all to get out of their own houses, away from the hospital, and relax in each other's company. They had been existing in a state of suspended tension ever since Charles had been knocked off his bike, and that was almost two months ago. The strain between Anne and Charlotte was palpable, even to an outsider like Janet, and she worried that Anne would end up pushing her daughter too far, especially because of her supercilious attitude towards Gabriel, who, by all accounts, sounded like a perfectly nice young chap. Divorce was so much more common now than it had been in their day, thought Janet. It didn't mean that someone's character was profoundly flawed. It simply meant that marriage was more disposable; that there was an easier way out. Couples no longer felt bound to stay together for the sake of it and Janet believed that, broadly, this was a good thing. It was so easy to make a mistake when you were in your twenties and unsure of the gaps that lay between what you wanted and what other people expected of you. She had been lucky with Nigel. They had both just known.

In the end, after an endless leafing through recipe books, she decided against the soup. Instead, she made a roast chicken with all the trimmings: parsnips, potatoes, bread sauce and lemon thyme stuffing. She got dressed in loose brown trousers and a beige knee-length cardigan. Although she looked like the sort of woman who didn't bother much with clothes, she was actually very particular about the quality. Janet liked maximum coverage to conceal her almost spherical body shape and had next to no interest in fashion, but she favoured items that lasted – cashmere and fine knits – and spent far more on clothes than anyone else might expect her to.

As the salty aroma of crisping skin started to fill the kitchen, Janet heard the doorbell ring. It was 8.15 p.m. They were on time.

Janet; Anne; Charlotte

WHEN SHE OPENED THE front door, she saw all three of them huddled together in an unlikely triptych underneath the porch awning. They stood side by side and yet not touching, and Janet noticed that Gabriel's hand hovered protectively against Charlotte's lower back, as if guiding her forwards.

Janet beamed. 'Hello, hello, come in.' She bustled around nervously, her gaze focusing on the mid-point between her guests' feet and knees so that she did not have to make eye contact. She abhorred being the centre of attention. 'Come on through. It shouldn't be too much longer.'

'It smells delicious, Janet,' said Charlotte as she took off her coat and hung it over the banister. She was wearing a blue jersey wraparound dress and high heels. Janet had never seen her looking so smart: she supposed Charlotte had come straight from work. 'Can I do anything to help?'

'Not at all. It's all under control. Now, you must be Gabriel.' Janet extended her hand to shake his and noticed that he had long, elegant fingers like a piano player.

'I am. It's so nice of you to invite me,' he said, smiling. 'Thank you.'

'Nonsense,' she said, making a swatting motion and immediately feeling her face flush. Janet stole a quick glance at him as he made his way through to the drawing room. She liked his face – open and sincere – and the way that he always checked to see where Charlotte was or whether she needed anything. He held the door open for Anne, she noted. He seemed very kind, the sort of man who attracted attention without ever demanding it; a comfortable person to be around.

She went into the kitchen to make the drinks and, after a few seconds, she heard Anne's footsteps behind her.

'Let me do something, Janet.' The way Anne spoke it sounded less an offer of help than a command, so Janet frantically searched her mind for a suitable task to keep her occupied. Anne always had this effect on her – she made Janet feel nervous and not quite impressive enough. She did not want Anne examining her kitchen and her cooking methods because it would set her on edge and she would fumble and do something silly with the gravy, but she was either too polite or too intimidated to say so.

'Now, let's see. Oh yes, it would be great if you could get some ice cubes from the freezer, Anne, thank you.'

She looked at her friend as she opened the fridge door. Anne had lost weight in recent weeks, so that her natural slenderness had become more pronounced and her collarbone now jutted out from beneath a silver-grey blouse. Janet had always been envious of Anne's figure, the smoothness of her flesh and the casual ease with which she still moved. She was the type of woman whose beauty was accentuated by her wrinkles, as if the faintest imperfection simply served to highlight the flawlessness of the whole. In comparison, Janet felt like a red-cheeked blob of un-sophistication.

A sigh escaped before she could stop it. Janet was mortified. She scrabbled around, desperate for something to say to mask her discomfort. She twisted her hands together and felt the reassuring nub of her knuckles.

'How are things, Anne?'

It was just the sort of open-ended and essentially meaningless question that Anne usually hated, but today she seemed to be in a more expansive mood than normal.

'Things are . . .' Anne paused with the ice tray in mid-air. 'Things are good, actually.' Anne seemed startled by her own admission. She let it drift, unelaborated, and began extracting the ice cubes, pressing each one out by bending the edges of the Tupperware tray towards her.

'Oh,' said Janet, taken aback by Anne's atypical good cheer. 'That's nice to hear.' Then she stopped speaking quite deliberately to allow the space for Anne to fill. She opened the oven to baste the chicken with its own juices and, then, Anne spoke.

'Actually, Charlotte and I had a little talk the other day.'

Janet looked up and found that her glasses had fogged up from the heat. 'Oh blast,' she muttered, taking them off and wiping them on her cardigan. When she slid them on again, the kitchen returned to its clear-edged clarity and she noticed that Anne was smiling, the edges of her lips twitching uncertainly.

'That's wonderful,' Janet said, because she could see immediately how important their 'little talk' must have been. It was the first time she had seen Anne look so relaxed in ages. The faded wrinkles that ran the length of her forehead like stretched washing lines seemed to have lifted, so that her face no longer looked as though it were in the grip of a perpetual frown. She wondered what they had talked about and then she realised that the content didn't really matter: it was the fact that it had happened at all that seemed important.

Janet mulled over what to do next. She didn't want to say something stupid or thoughtless that would cause the frown to return and yet she wanted to reach out to her friend, to touch her arm gently and let her know how pleased she was for her. But theirs had never been an especially physical friendship and she felt awkward at the thought of it.

The silence was broken by Anne. 'We cleared the air,' she said. 'There were things I needed to apologise for,' she added more quietly. 'Things I should have said before now, but ...' Anne shrugged her shoulders. She stared into space for a few seconds, a forlorn expression creeping in at the corners of her eyes, and then she seemed to shake herself out of it. 'But I didn't and now I'm glad I have.'

She smiled briskly at Janet. 'Oh goodness, this ice is melting.'

'Don't worry about that, Anne.' Janet started to walk towards her and then changed her mind so that instead she simply jiggled slightly on the spot. 'I'll open the wine,' she said, to cover her indecision. She started humming softly to herself. It was an infuriating habit she had, a sort of nervous tic that she couldn't control.

And then, just as Janet was beginning to feel she should say something without knowing what, Anne did something entirely unexpected. She walked across to Janet and hugged her for a few brief seconds. The hug was so out of the blue that Janet didn't have time to put down the corkscrew and found that she was holding it awkwardly so as to avoid jabbing Anne in the back with it. The two of them stood clasping each other for a few seconds, neither of them accustomed to the warm physical proximity of it. Then Anne drew away, patting Janet on the back as she did so, their eyes not meeting.

Wordlessly, they each went back to their practical tasks at opposite corners of the kitchen. The air was thick with unspoken conclusions.

After a few moments, an ice cube thudded on to the worktop as Anne pressed it out too rapidly and it skidded across the floor, leaving a slug-like shimmer across the linoleum. Anne bent over to pick it up but it kept slipping away from her as she tried to grab hold of it. 'Oh come on,' said Anne impatiently. Janet glanced at her and saw that the frown had re-appeared, a thin, dissatisfied crinkle just beneath her hairline. There was, she noticed, a stiffness to Anne's movements, a slight slowness as she bent down, an almost audible creak of the joints, a jarring of vertebrae clicking and unfolding into place.

She saw that Anne was growing older, and that she was now so accustomed to the inevitability of disappointment that she would probably never fundamentally change. But she saw something new too: she saw a glimmer of hopefulness, a smoky wisp of fragile optimism. Janet felt an overwhelming affection for her friend, for her brave attempt to change what she had become for the sake of her daughter. And even though Anne would never manage it completely, Janet knew that she would spend the rest of her life trying and that, perhaps, was enough.

Janet's eyes filled with tears. She had to pretend the cork was stuck in the wine bottle so that Anne would not notice.

The roast chicken was an unqualified success. Janet was surprised how well it all went, how easy it was for the conversation to flow.

She had been worried that it might be stilted, given the recent distance between Anne and Charlotte and the appearance of Gabriel at the dinner table. But, in fact, it was Gabriel's presence that made the evening go so pleasantly. He was polite and witty company, never once seeking to dominate the proceedings but able to step in when the silence lasted a beat too long.

'I must say, Janet, that this is one of the best roast chickens I've ever eaten,' he said, pushing his knife and fork together on his plate.

'You always say that,' Charlotte joked, prodding him affectionately in the ribs. 'It's like the Olympics: the last one is always the best ever.'

Gabriel rolled his eyes. 'I don't always say it.' He paused. 'And if I do, it's only because I genuinely mean it.'

Everyone laughed. Anne, sitting on the other side of the table next to Janet, tried not to but couldn't. She was being charmed in spite of herself.

'Are you a good cook, Charlotte?' asked Janet. 'Young people these days seem to be able to do so many things.'

Charlotte smiled, and her pale pearl earrings glinted in the candlelight. She pushed a wayward strand of hair away from her face. 'I'm flattered that you think I still qualify as a young person.'

'Nonsense, Charlotte,' said Anne. 'You're only thirty.'

'You're virtually foetal in comparison to the rest of us,' said Gabriel.

'Speak for yourself,' Anne replied, adopting a mildly flirtatious tone that Janet had never heard before. She was clearly enjoying herself.

'I'm an all right cook, I suppose,' said Charlotte, twisting the stem of her wine glass so that the crystal cast a cone of light across the tablecloth. She pushed her finger towards the shadowy outline of it, stopping just before she got to the central brightness as if afraid it would scald her.

'You're a great cook,' said Gabriel. 'Although there was that time that you baked an entire sea bass without taking out its innards.'

'Yes, there was that time. Thank you for reminding me.'

'It was very thrifty of her,' Gabriel continued, addressing his remarks to Anne. 'In these times of economic hardship, we should all be doing the same thing. A few dead sprats could feed a family of four for a week. Waste not want not, I say.'

Anne giggled. Janet looked at her, astonished. Anne had actually giggled. She glanced up to see if anyone was ready for a second helping and caught Charlotte winking at her. Janet smiled, feeling the warmth of a shared joke settle around her like a thick blanket. She felt, for the first time in ages, so thoroughly included. She felt part of something. She wanted this evening to go on for ever.

Charlotte leaned across the table to top up Janet's glass. She brushed her fingers across the back of Janet's hand and when Janet looked up, Charlotte was smiling and her lips were moving and after a moment, Janet realised she was mouthing 'Thank you'.

They all tried to help her clear the table but Janet insisted they leave it. There was nothing worse, she thought, than going to someone's house for dinner and then being roped into the endless tidying up, dragged into the uncomfortable jostling in a stranger's kitchen as guests tried to compete with each other to show how much they were doing.

'Honestly, please don't bother,' she said as she caught Gabriel stacking plates, wiping them clean of chicken bones and stray bits of stuffing. 'You don't know where anything goes in any case.' Gabriel looked at her sceptically. 'It would be more work for me in the end,' she persisted.

'OK, well at least tell me where the tea and coffee things are and I can make myself a bit useful.' He picked up his tower of crockery. 'And as I'm going to the kitchen anyway I'll take these with me. But don't worry. I promise not to lift a finger.'

Janet smiled and followed Charlotte and Anne through to the drawing room. The evening air had cooled so she knelt down by the open fireplace and started building up a framework of logs and crumpled balls of newsprint, just as Nigel had taught her. It lit easily, the flames catching on the paper and spluttering into life at the edges of the wood bark. A sulphuric warmth filled the room and Janet felt her cheeks get pleasantly hot. For a while, nobody spoke. From the kitchen came the sounds of coffee percolating and the gentle clatter of teacups and saucers being assembled. It was a contented sort of silence.

Anne was sitting on the armchair nearest the fire, her face softened by the burnished light. She was resting her head on one of the wingbacks, a glass of wine still in one hand. There was a small, but noticeable smile on her lips. Each time she took a sip, she closed her eyes as if to savour the moment as much as she could, wringing the present dry of every liquid atom. She looked happy.

'That was impressive,' said Charlotte and it seemed they had been silent for so long that her words sounded strange. Janet blinked. Anne turned to look at her.

'The fire, I mean,' said Charlotte, her eyes darting between them. 'Were you two half asleep?'

'Absolutely not,' said Anne stiffly, pushing herself upright on the chair and smoothing down her skirt.

'You were, Mum! I caught you.'

'I wasn't,' insisted Anne, but her mouth was curling up at the corners.

'Is it past your bedtime?' asked Charlotte, her voice full of faux-concern. 'Have we kept you up too late?'

'Stop being so cheeky.'

'Yes, Charlotte, you should respect your elders,' said Janet, emboldened by the light-hearted atmosphere.

'Janet!' Charlotte shrieked. 'I can't believe you're telling me off!' Anne smiled and then the three of them were laughing and they almost didn't hear the tinny sound of a mobile phone ringing.

'Whose is that?' Anne asked. 'I thought I switched mine off.'

'It's mine,' said Charlotte, checking her watch. 'I'll let it ring out.'

'You could have put it on silent,' Anne said, a note of criticism in her voice.

'I normally do. I forgot.'

Charlotte's smile slid from her face. Her mouth set in a firm line of irritation. The room seemed to shrink with tension. Why did Anne have to do it? Janet wondered. She couldn't help herself. Janet glanced at the fire and jiggled it about a bit with the poker for no reason other than to occupy herself. It was extraordinary, she thought, how quickly a squall of mutual misunderstanding could brew up between these two. She hoped Gabriel would come back into the room soon.

'What's taking so long with the coffee?' said Charlotte, as if reading her thoughts. She fiddled with one of her earrings. No one spoke. And then the phone rang again. Anne tutted, just loud enough to be heard.

'I'm sorry, Janet. I'd better get it.' Charlotte went into the hall-way and rummaged about in her bag. The phone was flashing a frigid blue light, but it was dark and her fingers grappled to find it underneath the tissue packets and dog-eared business cards.

'Hello?'

'Miss Redfern?'

'Yes, that's me.'

'It's Evan Lewis here. From London Bridge Hospital.'

Janet

J ANET KNEW INSTANTLY THAT there was something wrong when Charlotte walked back into the room. Her face was pale and slack, her mouth hanging slightly open as if she had been interrupted in the middle of saying something. She was still holding the phone.

Gabriel was pouring tea. He put the pot down on the tray as soon as he saw her face.

'What's wrong?' he asked but something stopped him from going to her.

Janet held her breath, waiting for someone to speak, and then she heard a noise and she couldn't make out what it was until she turned to look at Anne and realised that it was coming from her. Anne was bent over in the armchair, her arms crossed over her stomach, the hands clutching at her sides, her fingers scratching into her flesh like pecking birds. She was rocking forwards and emitting a low, moaning sound that was a scream and a cry all at once. The glass of wine had tipped over. A clotted red stain spread slowly across the carpet, inching darkly forwards.

'It's Dad,' said Charlotte and her voice sounded detached and dry and as though it wasn't her own.

Charlotte

CHARLOTTE SHUT HER EYES tightly, pushing the lids down, screwing the darkness up inside her like a crumpled piece of paper, and then, after a few seconds, she opened them again and the room was still there and Janet was still looking at her with concern and Gabriel was still just about to walk over and take her in his arms and her mother was still bent into herself, still crying, still grieving for something that had never been. And then she knew what she had to do. She walked across the room and knelt down by the armchair and put her arms round her mother.

Charlotte drew Anne close to her chest and she could feel her mother's juddering sobs and her scratchy gulps for air; she could feel Anne's shoulders shaking and the shattered vibrations of her crying. 'It's OK, Mum, it's all right,' she said, stroking Anne's grey-brown hair and feeling its brittleness. 'It's over.' Then: 'He's dead.'

She felt her mother's hands pressing against her back and she felt Anne's fingers bunching up the fabric of her dress and then she felt her mother gripping hold of her with a ferocity that lay somewhere between relief and love. She felt it and she held her mother tight and she did not cry and, in the midst of it all, she found that she was thinking back to the strange straw donkey that her father had once given her, its black glass eyes staring at her, unblinking through the darkness of night. She did not cry.

Epilogue

THE AIR SMELLED OF hot earth and lavender. It was late afternoon and the mottled yellow light was about to tip over into the gentle violet of dusk, the change in colour seeping through the sky, leaving a litmus trail of pink. Later, the pale moon would bleed through, its circumference becoming gradually sharper until it was hanging above them, a bright coin pressed against the darkness.

The lawn was parched from a long, dry summer. Flakes of creosote hung off the garden fence like the shreds of a discarded reptilian skin. The plants had just been watered and droplets were still glinting from the leaves of an overgrown rhododendron.

At the bottom of the garden, a small child sat contentedly among the clay geranium pots, her chubby legs protruding from under her dress, and her feet bare. She wore a pale pink hat embroidered with daisies and her fair hair was wildly curly. She was picking blades of grass with her fingers and her attention was almost entirely occupied with this task. Occasionally, when she found a particularly long stem, she would giggle to herself and put it carefully into the lap of her dress for safe keeping.

Sitting at the table with a chilled glass of wine, Anne looked at the child, carefully observing each of her movements and smiling at the intent precision with which she carried out her task. The child was oblivious to the rest of the world, absorbed in her own microcosm, fascinated by the smallest things.

Anne took off her sunglasses. She had not noticed it getting dark and her eyes took a moment to adjust to the new, softer light. The child stood up unsteadily, scattering grass as she moved. Anne looked at her. The child turned and caught her eye, smiling, so that Anne could just make out the tiny glimmer of her two bottom teeth, small and precise like a doll's. The child started to walk shakily towards her, a stumbling sort of movement that seemed to make her legs whir with the effort of keeping upright, her hands clenched into tiny, round fists.

Anne put down her wine glass and crouched forward, arms outstretched in encouragement. 'Gracie! Are you coming to say hello to me?'

Gracie stopped for a moment, startled by the sudden noise, and then she grinned and tried to walk even faster, her feet stamping noiselessly on the lawn, her pink tongue poked out in concentration. 'Come here, darling,' said Anne, scooping her up as she reached the chair.

Gracie installed herself on her grandmother's lap, turning her head so that it rested against Anne's chest. She started to suck her thumb and Anne noticed that the back of her hand was stained with grass. Anne took off the child's bonnet and placed it carefully on the patio table. She felt the warmth of Gracie against her, the sweet burnt-toast and honey smell of her hair, and she brushed down the tight blonde curls at the nape of her neck.

'She looks so like Charlotte, doesn't she?' said Janet, who was sitting at the opposite end of the table grappling with the pages of a Sunday newspaper supplement. Anne wished she would read a magazine instead – the constant sound of crinkling and re-folding was unnecessarily intrusive. And then she checked herself. It was a new technique she had: she was trying to let trivial irritations skim over the surface of her consciousness and, instead of focusing on someone's negative qualities, she was attempting to remember all the good things about them. It wasn't as easy as it sounded. She had read about the technique in a book that she was ashamed of having bought. It was one of those self-help-type things with a vividly coloured cover and a rhetorical question as a title. Anne had picked it up without thinking while in a queue at Waterstone's and found herself oddly comforted by its curious blend of advice and hopefulness.

'Yes.' She smiled at Janet. 'Yes, she does.'

She could feel Gracie's head get heavier and she knew, without looking, that her eyelids would be stuttering shut. It was almost her bedtime, but Anne did not want to surrender her just yet. She drew Gracie into her more tightly, placing a protective hand gently against the side of her face so that she could feel the extraordinary softness of her granddaughter's skin.

It had been almost three years since Charles had died. Anne shivered involuntarily at the thought. It felt far longer than that and yet simultaneously seemed so recent. Sometimes, she woke up in the mornings and forgot that he was gone. She could still feel his presence oozing through the house, even though she had finally got around to redecorating the study and then, in unspoken sequence, she had painted all the other rooms as well. She had thrown out the overstuffed sofa and replaced it with a square, beige minimalist affair that Charles would have hated. She had wanted to get rid of the Aga too but Charlotte protested so vociferously that eventually she changed her mind.

She was closer to her daughter now, and although Anne knew she would never quite have the depth of her love reciprocated, this realisation gave her a profound sense of calm and the calmness was edged with tentative joy. Gabriel had helped. He was a relaxing person to be around – chatty, funny and, most surprisingly, utterly sincere – and he was good for Charlotte. The pregnancy had been an accident and Anne had not been sure, at first, whether it was a good idea. She had old-fashioned notions about bringing up children out of wedlock but then Gracie arrived and she fell in love with her so instantly, so overwhelmingly, that she found herself utterly powerless to be anything other than happy.

They had cremated Charles. Both Anne and Charlotte had agreed, without ever explicitly saying so, that neither of them wanted a physical memorial to remember him by. Anne did not like the thought of visiting a grave, of being judged by its silence or reminded of her failures, and so the two of them had scattered his ashes in the river by Kew Bridge. Neither of them had known whether it was the sort of thing you had to get permission for in advance, so there was a slightly hysterical edge to the proceedings as they took turns surreptitiously throwing fistfuls of grey powder into the murky currents of the Thames. They had laughed and then felt guilty for laughing and that had made them laugh even more. After it was done they went for double whiskies at a nearby pub and they hadn't said anything but they hadn't needed to either and this was the necessary difference.

For a while after casting him off into the Thames, Anne had felt lost without Charles. It was not so much that she was grieving for him, because she felt that she had done that already in the weeks before he died. It was more that she didn't know how to act in the midst of this unasked-for emptiness. She wanted to feel relieved, to embrace her new-found freedom, to begin afresh a life that she had put in neutral, but she found that without Charles she had no anchor. She could no longer define herself in opposition to something. At its most basic, she no longer had an excuse.

Part of her, the buried part that lay misshapen underground, still missed him. She despised herself for this weakness, for the abiding strength of her love despite the battering it had taken, and she tried for a long time to ignore it. She would find herself staring into space in the supermarket, bewildered by the amount of choice on the shelves around her and incapable of making the simplest decision about what she wanted for supper.

Then Janet had suggested a holiday and Anne, to her surprise, had said yes. They spent three weeks in a hire car driving around Italy, winding down Tuscan roads bordered by olive groves and walking through hilltop towns with open marketplaces and red-bricked bell-towers that looked as if they would crumble to the touch. They had eaten fresh pasta and they had drunk Chianti and Janet had arranged everything so that Anne did not have to think. By the end of it, Anne was renewed. Nothing had been said, but it felt as though Charles's shadow had finally lifted. She was grateful to Janet for that. More grateful than she could ever express.

'Penny for them,' said Janet, and Anne looked across at her friend. Janet's nose was pink with sunburn and her bifocals were speckled with dirt. Her lipstick had faded and bled slightly into the puckered lines around her mouth.

'Do you know, I was just thinking of our Italian jaunt.'

Janet's face suffused with pleasure. 'It was lovely, wasn't it?' Anne nodded, carefully trying not to wake Gracie. 'Perhaps,' said Janet hesitantly, 'we should do it again this year?'

'Yes, Janet.' Anne smiled. 'Yes, we absolutely should.' She could hear Charlotte and Gabriel inside; the murmur of their conversation and the clattering of things being washed up and put away. She could feel the weight of her granddaughter against her chest and the saturating warmth of a day's sunshine on her skin. There was contentment here, in this place, in this garden, in this moment of time. She recognised it and she breathed it in and she felt it trickle down her throat and then she breathed it out and it split into tiny pieces that scattered over her like breeze-blown blades of grass.

'Bedtime,' she said, and Gracie stirred quietly at the sound of her voice. She held her granddaughter tightly in her arms and she walked back into the house.

Acknowledgements

Jessica Woollard of the Marsh Agency, for being a wonderful agent and for thoughtfully arranging to give birth only after the contract had been signed.

Helen Garnons-Williams at Bloomsbury, for her perceptive insights and clever suggestions, all of which I would like to pretend were my own.

Simon Oldfield, for being so supportive from the start.

Edie Reilly and Olivia Laing, for reading the manuscript and being kind enough not to laugh in my face.

My parents, Christine and Tom, and my sister, Catherine, for always being there.

And finally, Kamal Ahmed, for absolutely everything.